# Martin Sloane

a novel by

## Michael Redhill

Anchor Canada

Doubleday Canada hardcover edition published 2001
Anchor Canada paperback edition published 2001

National Library of Canada Cataloguing in Publication Data

Redhill, Michael, 1966-
Martin Sloane
ISBN 0-385-25987-5
I. Title.
PS8585.E3425M37 2001a     C813'.54     C2001-903371-0
PR9199.3.R418M37 2001a

Cover images:
"Ambulance" and "Bride/Groom" © CSA Plastock/Photonica
"Boy w/ Father" and "Horse/Carriage" © copyright 2000 PhotoDisc, Inc.
Cover and text design: Carla Kean
Printed and bound in Canada

Published in Canada by
Anchor Canada, a division of
Random House of Canada Limited

Visit Random House of Canada Limited's website:
www.randomhouse.ca

FRI 10 9 8 7 6 5 4 3 2

*For Anne and Benjamin*

*I have burdened you unduly, my dearest friend, with this long account of an enigmatical condition ordinarily kept to myself.*

— HUGO VON HOFMANNSTHAL,
*THE LORD CHANDOS LETTER*


*Make ready the room where you will live with me,
for I shall have them bury me in the same chest
as you, and lay me at your side, so that my heart
shall be against your heart ...*

— EURIPIDES, *ALCESTIS*

IT WAS A LIE THAT BROUGHT MARTIN SLOANE TO A
picture house on O'Connell Street one night in the fall of
1936. (This was how I began, finding my way into his story, trying its doors.) He was eight, and it was the first time he'd ever
gone anywhere by himself. It was a twenty-minute walk from his
house and by the time he reached O'Connell, night had fallen
and the wide boulevards were blazing with electric light. The
hotel-lined street was busy with horse-taxis, news-hawks, chest-
nut carts; its café storefronts full of customers. Martin imagined that back at home the windows of his house were glowing
orange with safe nighttime light.

He walked toward the cinema, the heavy coins in his pockets enough for the movie and a bag of steamed nuts. No one
noticed him: although only a child, he was simply a part of what
he walked through. A city dweller. Head up, cap clenched in
one hand, he went down the middle of the thoroughfare, on the
grassy strip that separated the two avenues. At that moment he
thought his happiness complete, thought that it must have been
like the happiness of being older, the way he imagined anyone
might have felt, walking to the Grand Central Cinema at six
o'clock at night to see the early show of *The Informer*.

In this he was in league with his father, who the previous
week had walked over the river, in the middle of the workday, to
see the picture. He'd come home red-faced with excitement.

You Irish with your bogeymen, Martin's mother had said.

1

They *must* see it, said his father.

Not these children, Colin. She is too impressionable, and he is too young.

The papers had argued back and forth over the film's merits, some saying it was scandalous and a temptation, others that it told a sore truth. It was the story of an Irishman, the drunkard Gypo Nolan, who'd sold out his friends to the British. Now it was as if the *Mail* and the *Herald* were arguing in the Sloane kitchen over dinner and it soon became a forbidden topic of conversation. But his father had certain conversational gifts. He convinced Martin's mother that her objections were about picture houses in general.

No, Colin, she said, it is about this film.

You mean to say, said his father, that you don't object in *principle* to the viewing of motion pictures?

If they are wholesome, then no.

I don't believe it, Martin's father said, staring at her in disbelief. I thought for certain you were against the pictures in general.

Not at all, said Martin's mother, happy for common ground. Send him to see *O'Shaughnessy's Boy*, down at the Grand Central. It has that nice Mr. Beery in it.

And so, the following Sunday night, Martin's father gave him directions to the Grand Central Cinema, at the bottom of O'Connell beside the river, and there, Martin paid his half-shilling. And, following his father's instructions, he went in to the parlour beside the one showing *O'Shaughnessy's Boy* where people were gathering for the six-o'clock showing of *The Informer*.

When the lights went down, rain began to fall in the street. Martin sat in the darkness, the voices of the actors intermingled with the quiet pattering hiss outside the thin cinema walls, and he was transported by it all, by his illicit visit to the movie hall, by the sensuality of Gypo Nolan's drunken sin. The movie ended in heartbreak, the big man trying to outrun his fate, and when Martin went outside, the city had been transformed into mirrors of light. In the Liffey, the centre of town shone upside down in a cold radiance. He could see the buildings in the slick-ened car windows, on the street, against glistening rainjackets passing along the sidewalks, as if the whole place had sunk under the sea.

Martin's father was waiting in the car with the motor run-ning in front of the cinema. He waved through his window, swiping it with his forearm so he could see out. In the car, his father handed him a towel. So? he asked.

It was good, Martin said.

His father pulled out into the slow-moving traffic. The horses drove down through the streets with their heads lowered. Were you frightened?

No. But I think we shouldn't have lied.

I suppose we could leave the country now, said his father, and he laughed to himself. This was one of the things Martin did not understand about adults, this laugh he sometimes heard. Let's not call it a lie, though, his father said. Let's call it a secret.

Now they were driving up Berkeley Street. His father's favourite sweet shop was here, and as they drove past it they could see the windows were fogged and there were people inside. We could both use a cup of chocolate, his father said. To warm up.

Donnellan's was popular with everyone, and Martin's father kept his face averted from the other customers. He ordered two mugs of chocolate and a fruit bun for them to share, and when he came away from the register, a table was open in the window. They sat, and his father asked Martin to tell him the whole story of the film.

But you've seen it, Martin said. You already know how it goes.

I *have* seen it, said his father. But I want you to tell it me, the way you remember it.

Martin thought back to the beginning of the story and began telling it, and as he told it, it was as if he were seeing the film all over again, except that the Grand Central was in his mind, his mind was the cinema. He told of Gypo Nolan's betrayal of his old friend, turning him in to the British for

3

twenty pounds. The shock of watching the betrayer spend the money on drinks, and fish and chips. The way he teetered back and forth between remorse and pride. Then the trial, the lies Gypo told to cover himself, endangering even a neighbour, and afterwards, the mad run from justice. How it had electrified Martin to watch it, even the horror of Gypo, dying in the church at the feet of his victim's mother. *Frankie, your mother forgives me!* Certainly, in the end, Gypo had regretted his actions, but regret is not enough for the people around you, Martin had thought, people have to see that crime is paid for. In this way, life was not like religion, in which, as far as he understood, sorrow in your heart came first.

That was it, his father said when Martin was finished. He nodded and fingered his chin. That was very good. Now, tell me what it was about.

*About?* Martin thought for a moment, not sure of what to say. It was about not lying.

Stop worrying about that, said his father. If I say something's okay, it's okay. Now what was it *about?*

Martin chewed on a piece of candied peel, rolled the bittersweet scrap around in his mouth. It was about being kind to others, he said.

It was, a little. Something else, though.

He could come up with nothing. He felt his face begin to burn and he tried to think what Theresa, who was quicker of mind than he was, would have said. He knew she would be thinking of what their father might have wanted to hear, and after another moment, Martin said: It was about you shouldn't drink when you're flush.

No, Martin. His father looked disappointed. He tipped back the end of his chocolate and picked his hat off the table. He left a coin.

The two of them walked back to the car in silence, and Martin searched his mind for the hidden meaning of the film, but he was so distracted by the anxiety of disappointing his

4

father that he couldn't think. Finally, driving up past the canal, his father spoke quietly.

Would you say it was about having a home?

A home, said Martin, agreeing gratefully.

Gypo doesn't merely turn in a friend, Martin. He gives up the only thing he belongs to, thinking he will go to America with his blood money. But instead, he remains, and he is lost in the only place he has ever belonged. That is as good as dying.

But he does die.

Yes, said his father, mercifully, he dies.

They turned down to where they lived. For his whole life he had passed these houses, walked over the stones in these streets. Every night, the lights in the distance would appear between these same houses, slanting down alleys. He had never known any other place than this. His father had always said that every star had its place in the sky, every person theirs on Earth. Except you could not take a star out of the sky. People, though, he'd said. People vanish from the places they should be, people go to darkness all the time. Outrunning their fates.

And that had been Gypo Nolan's lot.

Molly was still holding the box called Grand Central in her hands, staring at it as if the movie were playing deep inside it.

How was that? I asked Martin.

Just about perfect. Except the candy store was called Goldman's. She reads me like a book, he said to Molly.

She laughed. I can't see you as a book.

He turned back to me. And the Grand Central had little pinlights stuck into their ceiling, so that when the room went dark, you could see above you a little pretend night sky. He raised his hands above his head and waved his fingers toward the ceiling.

Just like the one you'd see on a clear night over Dublin, I said.

Yes, said Martin. Just as if the roof had been lifted off.

Molly put the box back down on Martin's workbench. She

5

laid it down so gently it didn't make a sound. Did your mother ever discover he'd let you go?

He got away with it, he said. It wasn't the worst thing.

What was?

Martin raised his eyebrows at her, surprised that someone who'd known him only eight hours would ask such a question. Molly leaned against the bench, waiting him out. In the years I'd known her, she'd always been the kind of person who could expect answers to her questions, no matter how brazen. That was her effect on people; resistance was futile. But after a few moments of the two of them pointing their mandarin smiles at each other, she lowered her head and her black hair fell over her eyes.

It's been a great day, she said. But maybe I should let you both go.

Martin moved around her and started collecting the boxes she'd pulled down from his shelves. Maybe Jolene can run you to the bus station, he said.

She watched him slide the artworks back into their cubbyholes — Pond, Linwood Flats, The Swan. Did your father ever see these? she asked.

He pushed Crossing into place. It was a box that put the viewer in the sky over a ship crossing the ocean. A woman's face was painted on the deck, and where the smoke from the stacks washed across the glass front of the box, a man's face seemed to hover. I wish he had, he said.

Well, at least he's in them. It's not a bad place for a person's soul to end up.

No, said Martin, pushing the last box flush against the others. I suppose it's a good place to be.

# Bloomington

# I.

THE SWAN, 1950. 6" X 14" COLLAGE. PAPER, SEQUINS, FOUND
IMAGES. PRIVATE COLLECTION. DEEP IN A FOREST THE SNOW IS
FALLING. BEHIND THE BARE TREES, A SWAN DRIFTS ACROSS A
FROZEN POND.

SOME PEOPLE BELIEVE IN A CONNECTED WORLD IN which every one thing is cognate with every other thing, the bell tolling for you, for me. In this kind of world, orders are revealed within our own order, our beginnings woven with other beginnings, endings with endings. In this way, life is seen to rhyme with itself. For a long time this was my own religion.

But now, if I go all the way back to my own birth, I find only disconnected memories. A dusty shag carpet, a writing pad by a phone, an orange wall. I think I can recall an early dream: bedroom curtains opening on a carousel? Later, my mother in gardening gloves, smelling like soil, or my father undoing her shoes for her when my brother was in her stomach. A bananaseat bicycle, a bumpy road between two towns, jackdaws creaking in the air over gravestones. Some time later, a piano brought down from Syracuse, the one my mother played as a girl.

But this childhood narration doesn't rhyme with anything. Not even with itself, for what could a dusty carpet have to do with gardening gloves, or a piano with gravestones? So many times in thirty-five years, I've known the feeling of that little girl I once was being erased. The girl followed by the young woman who was then given the hook for another, later, woman. I feel only a rough kinship with them, like they are co-conspirators in what has become of me. A lifetime of versions. But the little girl? She's gone. I don't have her. It's only when you're old enough to understand that the past is gone forever that you begin to store your own life, and like most children, at least as I recall, I thought I would be eight forever. Or eight and taller, eight with hips, eight with boyfriends. Never anything but eight.

I probably didn't start keeping track of my own life until I left my childhood home. Then I'd lie awake in my dorm bed testing to see if I could remember how all the doors in the house I no longer lived in opened. Which ones swung easily on their hinges, which had a sticking point you had to tug it through. Which doorknobs were loose, which stiff. The folding closet door in my bedroom that slid open on a track and then came off the track and swung free. I thought to myself, once I'd forgotten the doors of my childhood home, my childhood would truly be over.

Martin Sloane was fifty-four when I started writing to him, fifty-six when we became lovers, now that's the thing that seems shocking, the raw fact of that. Before then, I had a clear vision, so I thought, of the kind of person I would eventually love. It would be someone a little like me. Like me, but with improvements. Someone more open, someone a little smarter, a little stronger emotionally. But someone who'd fit in back at home, should I have ever wanted to return. After meeting Martin, I went down my list. He *seemed* more open, but I couldn't really tell. He *was* smarter, but emotionally stronger? Did I really want that tested? Did I want to *lose* that test?

The problem of what other people would think was more serious (I dreaded the gossip) but in the end it was more easy to deal with. By the time I couldn't live without Martin, it didn't matter what anyone thought.

The first time we met in person his face surprised me. Although he was thirty-five years my senior, his face was smooth, his short mussed hair jet black with only flecks of silver. (I was to have more grey in my hair by the time I turned thirty.) His nose was too big for his face, and his eyes were as dark as his hair. His face made me think of the busts of dead men, the illusion of living eyes made by holes in the stone. So that from one angle, they would seem pitiless, and from another, they'd spring to life.

He'd just walked off the bus in Annandale, where Bard College was. I was waiting with a car I'd gotten from Rent-a-Duck, a rusted-out VW bug with a pipe for a gearshift and a steel plate over a hole in the floor. He was lugging his artworks in a plain old garbage bag, and I rushed over to him and forced him to put the bag down and let me stack the artworks, so they could be carried, tower-like.

Just dump them in the back, he said.

Let me be in charge of them. You're a guest now.

If anything breaks, I'll fix it. We'd gotten to the bug. This is a great little car, he said.

They were out of Jaguars. I put down the boxes gingerly to unlock the trunk. The lid had to be propped up with a stick. Then he began plunking them in, like they were groceries. He put the last one in and took the stick out, and the lid slammed shut. I'd watched him with paralyzed wonder.

You can't treat them like they're permanent. He went around to the passenger side. They'll get ideas. He tried to put the seatbelt on, but the business end of it had been melted into a glob in some previous disaster. This is going to be an adventure, he said happily.

I started down the country road that wound between towns, one side a river, the other a forest.

Can I work the shift? he asked.

What do you mean?

You say *shift*, I change gears.

Do you know how to drive?

No. But when I was just a kid, my dad had a Saloon car and once we drove it from Dublin to Galway and part of the way I sat on his lap and shifted the car. So I have that part down good.

Did you travel a lot with your family?

Just that once. So, you tell me when, all right?

You're not sitting on my lap.

I can do it from over here.

Shift, I said. And so we drove the eight miles back to Bard, me calling the shifts over the labouring engine, and Martin trying to get the gear into the right position, until we were on campus and he jammed it in reverse as I was trying to get him to gear down. I heard something big and metallic drop down and smack the road and the car leap-frogged over it and we both flew out of our seats and hit our heads on the roof. The car came to rest in some grass. We sat there panting as people I knew gathered around.

Well, this is Martin Sloane, I told them, getting out. He's going to have a show at the Blithewood. Martin was still sitting in the passenger seat, looking at his palms, dazed.

My friends helped him out, introduced themselves; some of them knew he was coming, knew how hard I'd worked to get him to town. Then everyone took a box and we all crossed the field to the gallery, the glass fronts catching and reflecting the light at odd angles so the little crowd looked like a broken mirror spreading across the green. Martin glanced back at me and laughed.

You having fun now? I said.

You think we'll see any of those again?

You obviously don't care.

He made an Oliver Hardy face and shrugged, then got in step with me and linked his arm in mine. I like your friends, he said.

I tightened my arm, my heart whacking against my ribs, and I pulled him against my side. I like you.

But I crashed your car.

That you did.


Bard College was close enough to my hometown of Ovid but far enough away that no one from there could walk to it in half a day. The campus was a pastoral green hidden in the woods. Grassy patches, whitewashed buildings, a chapel in the trees. Towering maples clenched in brilliant vermilion down the main drives. The big athletic field with its unmown edges reeking of springtime through the summer and fall.

I'd been assigned one of the smaller dorms at the edge of the playing field, more a cabin than a dorm, with an angled rooftop and a jumble of windows, called Obreshkove House. I was on the second floor, with a window pointing out to the forest, where I sometimes saw deer in the gloaming. Molly Hudson was my suitemate; she'd arrived on the first day of school while I was out registering for classes. She liked me, she later explained, on the evidence of my bookshelf, and alphabetized her own books in with mine, a gesture that touched me.

She was well prepared for college, and determined from the start to run our social lives with ruthless efficiency. I've bought us a little fridge, she announced on the day we met, in case we want to have cocktails with the friends we're going to make. She opened the door to the fridge to reveal four cocktail glasses frosting underneath the ice-element, and beneath them a loaf of bread, a small bottle of mayonnaise, and a single packet of corned beef. For anyone who comes over peckish, she said.

I stood in the doorway, looking suspiciously on her good sheets and her fabric-wrapped clothes hangers. How old are you, Molly?

Nineteen, she said. Today. Just squeaked into the class of '88.

She had no doubt that she was already the centre of a coterie that didn't exist yet. Coming from a grief-darkened house (since the death of my mother, almost ten years earlier, my father had remained in a state of evergreen loss), I suddenly realized that a bright room on the edge of a forest was the perfect coming-out for me — a gradual emergence from sadness into a new life, fronted by one of the daughters of Syracuse. Molly was enrolled in a general arts program, but her father — an important attorney in that city — had made her promise to declare law as her major by the end of her sophomore year. They'd shaken on it, a "gentleperson's agreement," she put it, and one she was to keep.

I stood back in a kind of awe as I watched Molly adapt to the rituals of freshman life. She joined clubs, started petitions, put graffiti forward as an important grassroots expression of discontent. (She reversed this position when she entered an ecofeminist phase for three months in second year, declaring that spraypaint was an ejaculatory rape of the environment.) Naturally, she also began blazing sexual trails, ones I couldn't follow due to an inborn shyness, and a rational bent of mind that was still working over the mechanics of sex. While Molly was mapping sensation, I worried where my eventual caring, expressive, gentle partner would put his knees. A parade of paramours began tramping through our suite as Molly (so I believed) methodically made love to our freshman year in alphabetical order. The sounds of sex — quiet, musical, desperate, or exquisite as they were — became the general music of those rooms. She never seemed to settle on anyone, which I took as a sign of incredible impartiality, but she surprised me late one night with the sound of her weeping. Moments before, I'd heard another of her lovers quietly close the door on his way out. I crept into her room, my housecoat cinched around my waist.

What did he do?

He left, she said.

I went to sit on the end of the bed. The air in her room smelled bearish. They all leave, I said. I thought you didn't like them staying over.

I don't. She was holding a pillow tightly over her belly. But I want them to come back. And with that, she lowered her face into the pillow and started crying again. I waited, bewildered, unaccustomed as I'd always been to giving comfort. I don't think I was a cold person then, only that grief undid me. After a moment, she raised her red-streaked face and gamely smiled. Men like to leave me, she said.

At least they like you. I can't get anyone to look at me.

Looking's the problem, said Molly. They don't care about anything they can't see.

I moved closer, tentative, and put my hand on hers. Then they're really blind, I said.

I suppose that's the moment we became friends, rather than roommates; the moment the future started to get written.

The first-year classes at Bard were like panning in a river: they sifted people into groups, and before long it was easy to see the aggregates forming: the athletics groups, the drama people (with their little moustaches), the ghostly druggies, the frat boys. In the ranks of the English majors, I wasn't sure where I fit in. I was neither welcome nor spurned by my classmates, but this was only because the rigours of reading left little time to develop social graces, and many of us were lonely. Relationships of a kind sprang up when you discovered someone in class held your opinion, although you might only discover this in the form of a well-rehearsed answer to one of the prof's questions in a room of two hundred other English majors. "I liked what you said about *The Faerie Queen*" would be a safe opening gambit, but on the whole, the first-year English students were a rac-coon-eyed, oily-haired group, whose interests (at least through to December) were restricted to epic poems declaiming the rewards of clean living. Without Molly at cocktail ground-zero, I wouldn't have made any friends that first fall.

I took up racquet sports in the hope of meeting people on my own, and learned that panting and sweating was not the way to do it. Then Molly decided to sign us up for sculpture in our second semester. Mrs. Borovin, our teacher, arranged for the class to see a sculpture expo in Toronto that March. I'd never been to Toronto, even though it was only five hours north of Ovid, and I'd hardly even had a sense of it or Canada. The country above us always struck me as storage space, like an attic, so the revelation that there was art there was interesting, although odd. I have no memory of crossing the border in our old school bus, nor of coming into the city. I don't remember the March weather, nor the look of the people, or even what the buildings looked like.

The art was boring. Blotchy clay sculptures of men in motion, or women with breasts so heavy the statues had to be braced to the gallery wall with strips of metal. Mrs. Borovin stood us in front of one dull bronze or miasmic fabric draped over steel mesh after another, and talked the class through the basics of three dimensions. I drifted away, and eventually into the street. There was another gallery beside, smaller, with only a couple of what appeared to be display cases on the walls. I was surprised to find that the cases themselves were the artworks. Wood-framed boxes with glass fronts behind which some antic arrangement of things gave off a feeling of intense nostalgia. I had never felt anything from art (so I realized then): I was more interested in the brush stroke, the way the canvas was stapled to the frame, or the evidence of a pencil line erased. But here, I was distracted toward another place. The boxes contained bereft little worlds — a sand-filled teacup, a broken clay doll. One (it appeared empty) had a little drawer at the bottom with a jewelled handle, which, when you opened it, revealed a handwritten story pasted to the bottom. *For the rest of time,* it said, *it was as if the little place was getting smaller and smaller, although they could still see it, a dot on the horizon.* I closed the drawer and looked again into the space above it, and finally saw, against a backdrop of greyish blue, an almost infinitesimally small pebble with an even smaller pine tree — carved out of the broad base of a single pine needle — standing on it. Another box, embedded right into the wall, featured a front made out of wooden slats, and peering past them, I could see the backs of four birds — two large, two small — in a miniature living room. It took me a moment to realize I was looking down onto them from above, like a god in their ceiling, their smooth brown forms among the furniture a family settling down after supper. Another had a blue curtain drawn shut over the contents, with handles coming out of the top of the box to open them, but I was afraid to touch it.

The one I found hardest to turn from was a box on a pedestal, made of glass on all sides, which was filled with a viscous blue fibre draping down from the top. It was difficult to see what was suspended in the middle of the space, and I had to stand for a while on each of the four sides, collecting the visual information, until it resolved into something identifiable. It was a mermaid. Her body hung limply curved, her hair draped on each side of her face, loosely falling into the depths, and her tail curving on the other. I startled when I realized what it was. It was called "Sleep" and I was overcome with greed. I wanted it like nothing I had ever wanted before. It was like the way a lover hungers for the body of the one desired: I wanted no one else to ever see it again except for me.

I crept over to the man at the desk, palms sweating, heart racing, and I told him I wanted to buy it. He folded his newspaper and looked at me over it.

I don't think you can afford it. How old are you, anyway?

What does that have to do with it?

You can't just go buying artwork like it's candy.

If I can afford it, it doesn't matter why I'm buying it.

Tell me how old you are.

Twenty, I lied.

Well, come back when you're forty, and we'll talk. He returned to his newspaper. I got out my purse and unzipped the billfold. I had ninety dollars. I took the money out and went over to his desk, slapping it down under my palm.

That's all I have. You tell me what I have to do.

I already told you. Not for sale.

I'm leaving a deposit.

Look, honey, you're not even old enough to vote where you come from —

Excuse me, I said, but the voting age is eighteen where *I come from,* and I very much plan on voting in the next election, thank you very much.

Why don't you just take a program and vamoose, he said. I'll sign it for you if it makes you feel any better.

Why? Are you the artist?

No, I'm the gallery owner. It's as close as you'll get. He shoved the money back across the desk.

I took one of the programs, then saw the show's manifest tacked to the wall beside the door and took it down. There were a couple of red dots beside some of the pieces, but "Sleep" was still unsold.

This says "Sleep" is $180. Ninety's enough to hold it, isn't it?

That's a typo. It's $1,800.

I stood in the doorway staring at him, then took the money out again, folded it, and wedged it into a space between the doorjamb and the wall. That's my deposit. I'll come back with the rest. And I'm taking this. I waved the manifest at him as proof.

Daringly, so I thought, I wrote to the artist when I returned to Bard. I told him about my experience looking at his art, plying my adjectives, and I asked him to wrest, if he could, the thing I loved from Mr. Sullivan. I suggested perhaps he needed someone not quite so allergic to money representing his work. But Martin surprised me by writing back and returning my deposit, saying it was he, not Sullivan, who'd asked the gallery not to allow any sales to individuals. He was skittish about private persons owning his work; he wanted to be able to visit it.

This admission lit a fire under me, and I wrote him to say I still wanted "Sleep," and he could come any time and see it. He didn't bend, but he continued to write me, and over the period of a year or so, I gradually forgot about the artwork that had so moved me and began to want to see *him*. So I began to machinate a way for him to come to Bard. I asked him to send some slides of his artworks, and I approached a pliable curator at one of the campus galleries with them, a wraithlike woman named Mrs. Vankoughnet. It was as easy as that.

*Done*, I wrote back to him in October of 1985,

*You're due next April. Now we should talk about where you'll stay. There are a couple little hotels just outside campus, but since you'll probably only come for the opening, why don't you stay in my dorm? Obreshkove's an open easygoing place and you have a nice view of the field and some big metal sculptures. My roommate says she'll probably go visit her parents that*

*weekend, anyway. You'd like Molly, but she's quite a boy magnet. I showed*
*her the slides, by the way, and she likes your work too, so I'm sure she'd jump*
*at the chance of having a great Canadian artist sleep in her bed.*

*Don't take this the wrong way, but I'm single. I just want you to*
*know in case your wife is anxious. What I mean is, I don't want anyone*
*to be uncomfortable with the fact that it's a single college junior setting*
*all this up. Anyway, I think people should be up front. Is this too*
*personal? So far, I should say, you've been very adept at appearing*
*quite personal in your letters but upon rereading them, I can see you've*
*actually told me nothing about yourself. Is there anything to tell?*
*I remember reading Flaubert somewhere saying that you had to be*
*orderly in your life so you could be violently original in your work. If he's*
*right, you must be as interesting as sawmill gravy in person. Still, why*
*don't you tell me the basics? The name of your wife and children, for*
*starters? (If you have any ...)*

*My uncle says I am being a mover and a shaker by getting you down to*
*Bard. Is that how you see it? Are Canadians like the English? If so, I've been*
*pretty pushy in terms of how you guys are.*

*God I really like you. I was just realizing this. Your letters get bet-*
*ter when I reread them. I hope you will let me take you to my favourite*
*cake and tea joint when you get to Bard (although this place is in*
*Rhinebeck — a little hole-in-the-wall of a town near here) and we will*
*talk about all kinds of things. Last time you wrote you said that you*
*thought collage was a nostalgic impulse. I think you're wrong. Can we*
*argue about this? Kurt Schwitters would laugh up his sleeve at you for*
*saying that. His collages are like writing letters. Letters are collages,*
*aren't they? Educations are collages, too. That's why they call it college*
*har har. The café I'm taking you to is called the Blue Chair. They have*
*chocolate chip cookies as thick as your fist. Write me soon.*

After crossing the field in a small army of hands, the boxes made
it safely to the gallery. Mrs. Vankoughnet seemed impressed
with Martin and shook his hand as if he were already important.
She gave him some documents describing the gallery's obliga-
tions to him, and vice versa, but he wasn't interested in them,

and two days later, when it turned out he was to have signed them, they'd vanished.

Bringing Martin to campus gave me a kind of celebrity that had previously been Molly's, and I basked in it. For the rest of the first afternoon, fellow students from the fine arts programs followed us around like trained geese, asking Martin questions in little embarrassed voices. No one knew how famous or unknown he was (the truth was closer to the latter), but the fact of his being from another country made him authentic in the eyes of students who'd grown up in cow-towns all around the state. They formed a semicircle around him, drifting back as we walked through them.

Where do you get your ideas?

I don't think I have ideas, Martin said, and everyone laughed, as if he were joking. I don't, he repeated.

But, said one of the girls, there *are* ideas in your art.

I don't do it on purpose, said Martin.

Are you a surrealist? said a tall printmaker with a shaved head.

No.

Would a surrealist *admit* he was a surrealist?

Yes.

You idiot, said someone else. It was the Dadaists who went around saying they weren't anything.

The little crowd started buzzing. No, said someone else, they admitted they were Dadaists! They all pretended they didn't care about the art world, but they were *soooo* big on making sure everyone spelled "Dada" right.

Go ahead, spell "Dada" wrong for me.

I pulled Martin away from them. Let's have supper somewhere else, I said.

I want one of those cookies you've talked about.

We left the freshmen behind, waving their arms.


I made him wait outside the dorm while I changed, then got into a borrowed car in an agonized-over dress that rode up every time I clutched. Keep your hands off, I said, then pointed to the gearshift to clear up any confusion. I'd borrowed a car from a friend who hadn't witnessed the fate of the other one. Martin sat quietly in the passenger seat, his hands folded over his legs. For the first time since he'd arrived, there was an uncomfortable silence, an appropriate silence for two people who hardly knew each other, and the feeling that I was out of my element briefly took hold. Then I nervously started rambling, shooting in the dark for subject matter that he might want to add his two cents to: the benefits of small schools over large ones; the problems of teenage pregnancy; some thoughts on the differences between Americans and Canadians in which some ideas of the colour of currencies were forwarded, and finally, a short tractate on cows and weather.

Finally he said, I'm not actually Canadian, as you know. I still think of myself as Irish.

You don't sound Irish, though. I mean you don't have an accent.

I was convinced of the importance of not having one when I was growing up in Montreal. But hiding it made me feel all the more Irish. Like a man who gets home from work and puts on a dress.

Huh? I said.

I just mean I wanted to fit in.

Did you speak French?

Seulement un peut.

I've always wanted to.

Funny, he said. That's what they say up there too.

I took the turn for Rhinebeck, and we drove down the town's little main street, with its churches and gas stations. This looks just like where I grew up, I said. A little blot with people living on either side. He looked through his window and nodded. How long ago did you leave Ireland?

Forty-five years, six months, fourteen days, and seven hours, he said, then turned to look at me. I must have been trying to keep a straight, sensitive composure and failing, because he laughed. It was around forty-five years ago. I was eleven, he said.

We went into Bella Notte and the waiter brought us a wine menu without carding me, so we ordered a bottle and toasted each other. The scent of the wine filled my head like a sound, and after a glass, my courage returned.

Let's go back to this no-ideas idea, I said. You really think your work doesn't *mean* anything?

Well, it must mean something, it's just that I don't think about it. I mean, it doesn't matter to me.

But aren't you interested in what people see in it?

No.

I tilted my head at him and narrowed my eyes. Okay, I challenge. What?

It's what you say in Scrabble when you think someone's made up a word. That made him laugh, and he covered his mouth, muffling the sound. It was strange how he seemed at one moment complete-ly open and the next was concealing everything. The laugh had the effect of looking like he'd been caught in a lie and I pointed an accu-satory finger at him. Aha! So you just don't want to talk about it.

Not so, he said. It's just that if I was any good with words, I'd *put* it into words. But I'm not. So the way I feel is the way my work looks, and that's its meaning, or as close as I can express it. And what other people think about it is, again, a step away from what it "means" because they're describing something, and —

You're no good with words.

Yes. He finally exhaled and looked down, smiling, and stared into his soup. He looked fantastic to me, sitting there as real as anything, with his almost-messy hair, his dark blue shirt open at the neck. Sometimes, if he turned just right, I'd see a flash of grey hair within his shirt. I felt like someone who'd sud-denly come into more money than she knew what to do with, except it's not easy to find a place to stash excess feeling. I was also acutely aware that many hours had now passed and I had yet to say the kind of stupid, uninformed thing that was probably inevitable. The wait was killing me. I said, I just want to let you know that I'm setting some kind of record here for not acting like an idiot. And you should probably, you know, make some allowance for me to put my foot in my mouth, or something.

You mean, you haven't yet.

That's right. It's been clear sailing, so far, believe it or not. We laughed. I actually forget what we talked about after that. It disturbs me that I could have lost even five minutes of that first evening, that there is no witness to it. That's the marrow of all our stories: the forgotten moments that could make everything clear to our future selves (who are also busily losing the present). But I do remember that at one point — I see empty plates in front of us — he said, You'll understand what I mean one day.

You mean, when I'm all grown up?

He held up a hand in surrender. No, no, I didn't mean it like that.

Are you actually worried you could offend me?

Well, I don't want to end up sleeping outside.

That could turn out to be good luck for you, I said and turned scarlet, reaching for my wine.

After that, I can see his face, warmed from the heat of the wine, can hear the music filtering through the little room from speakers at the front. The way the room thinned out as the night went on. He was just fine with words. He talked of old packaging and cartoons and how people made early photographs; he talked about automata and magic apparatuses, the old belief of the sphere-within-sphere universe, which was the model of the cosmos that still appealed to him most.

Concentric worlds, he said. Easier to keep track of everything. I pictured those glassy spheres in the palm of his hand, and me in the smallest one at the very centre. Curled up in the warmth generated throughout the celestial realms by his hands.

It was late when I got us back to Obreshkove House, and the roads between towns had been so dark that we were driving through the stars. Martin hadn't seen a sky like that since before he'd moved to Toronto and he opened his window and leaned his head against the bottom of it to watch them.

I carried his bags into Molly's room and left them on the floor. We stood in the space between the two bedrooms. Do you need anything? I asked.

No. I'm fine. He cruised along the bookshelves, stopping and tilting his head here and there. You read a lot of poetry.

You don't?

He searched my face. Why does it feel there's a right answer to that question?

Someone like you would appreciate poetry. It's one of those things that seems to have made it out of the past. You know what I mean?

His face brightened. Did you hear that someone caught a coelacanth in Lake Ontario?

A what?

It's a fish, he said. An extinct fish. Someone caught one and now they're not extinct anymore.

I'm sorry, I said, but I think I fell asleep for the half-hour there when we made the transition from poetry to fish.

You said poetry feels like it shouldn't have survived, and yet it has.

Mmm, I said. Something hidden in the deep.

Yes.

A fossil record.

We stood there smiling at each other. An old language dusted off for use among people again. He turned back to the shelves, browsing the thin collections. Then glanced sidelong at me. Did you want to go to bed?

My stomach flipped. Uh, god, I said, flustered. I leaned forward to try to catch his expression, but he was squinting at something. I don't know, Martin ...

That's fine, it's —

*No, no,* I said. It's just ... I squeezed my eyes shut and clenched my fists. Yes, I said calmly, I do. I took the book he was holding out of his hand, tossing it onto a chair, and drew him away from the shelf. My face was pulsing with heat, a delicious fear flooding my stomach. I smiled at him, filled with anticipation. Come on then, I said.

He just looked at me, smiling vacantly.

I led him into the hall, reaching blindly for the light switch as I passed it, flicking it and dropping the apartment into darkness and then I pushed forward into him, tilting my mouth up toward him, and brushed my lips across his. My heart in my throat as I fumbled for the door to the bedroom. We stood there in the threshhold of it, me pressing my mouth to his, his face cupped in my hand, and feeling him ... what? You can kiss me, I said quietly, but he remained immobile, as if the touch of my mouth had turned him to stone. What's the matter?

It's just ...

*Oh god!* I stepped away from him in horror. You meant did I want to *sleep*. It's *late*, do I want to go to *bed*, I must be *tired*. Oh *fuck!*

Jolene, he said, his voice tight.

Please don't be laughing.

I'm not.

Turn on a light.

No, he said. Just, let's ...

Oh god, oh god, oh god —

We stood there in the dark, the sound of my heart hammering against my shirt the only disturbance. I was certain we could both hear it, like Poe's murderer hearing the heart under the floor. I'd had more than my share of exquisite humiliations before, but never with someone I'd actually liked. I imagined myself hurtling through a window.

I'm a complete idiot, I murmured.

No, no.

It's okay. I knew it was just a matter of time before I said something dumb.

I would never have just come out and asked you like that. I'm not that kind of person.

I know. You're *decent*. I tried to say it like it was an appalling thing to discover about a person, especially at a time like this. I heard him laugh softly.

I don't want you to think that I —

It's okay, Martin. I probably *should* go to bed. Before I accept an erroneous marriage proposal or something.

Now he laughed out loud and surprised me by gathering me into him and holding me. Come on, he said. Why don't we stay up awhile and talk? I don't want you to think —

We'll talk in the morning, I said, pushing away. It's fine. Honest. I felt for the doorknob again, and turned it and slipped into the room. Then stood there on the other side of the door, my face burning, my *hair* burning, and stayed utterly still. It took me a moment longer to realize I hadn't even shut myself up in the right room: Martin's bags were at my feet. *Stupid girl! Stupid stupid girl!* I felt nauseous with embarrassment, knowing I'd have to show my face again, to go to the door beside this one. I could hear he hadn't moved either. *Martin ...* I whispered, *what are you doing?*

I'm standing here.

Uh-huh.

I feel bad.

*You* feel bad.

You just took me by surprise, Jolene. It doesn't mean.... He didn't finish the sentence.

What? What?

He didn't know how to put it. *I would never have just come out and said it like that.* How *would* he have put it? I put my mouth to the door and spoke quietly. Is this a no-good-with-words moment, Martin?

Mm, he said.

I opened the door and stood square in front of him. I don't want to have a fling. That would be disgusting and I don't want people to talk. I already like you a lot.

Me too.

I stood there for a moment more shaking my head. My eyes had adjusted to the dark, and I could see his face in the faint greyness of the apartment, like something being reeled in from the depths. I didn't want to risk a change of venue. I went and lit a candle at Molly's bedside. She was one for candles, said it gave a tinge of intimacy to one-night stands. I hoped it wouldn't be bad luck for me. I sat on her bed, and watched Martin slowly come over in the yellowy glow of the candle's light, his face planes of shadow. He sat beside me and I felt his fingers touch down on mine. We sat there and held hands.

Is this more your speed? I stared out into one of the darkened corners of the room, already tired out.

Yes, thank you. Don't be embarrassed, Jolene.

Me? Embarrassed?

It's nice to know when someone wants to be with you, he said. It stops a person from worrying.

And you were worrying.

I would have. It hadn't occurred to me yet.

Thanks.

I *do* like you, Jolene. I liked you from your letters. I didn't know if it was going to be okay to tell you that.

Martin, my head's exploding.

I wanted to feel a certain way when I came here.

How?

Welcome.

I pulled his hand up to my mouth and kissed it. Thank you, I said. That's a good way to put it. You are. I held his hand against my chest. And I'm glad we finally made it through that door. But I have to tell you, I said, I'm feeling *way* unsexy right now.

That's only because an old fool almost ruined your evening. Not because you're not sexy. He leaned down and kissed me underneath the ear. Okay?

Okay, I said, but I don't think I actually made a sound.


We lay under the covers, drowsing. I pressed my face against his neck and breathed him in. He didn't really have a scent, at least not a scent I expected, the pleasantly sour smell of men, with its

29

salt and flesh. He smelled like rain, like clean laundry. Even after lovemaking he gave off nothing, left no path in the air. I closed my eyes against his cool skin and almost fell asleep, but he began to hum. Turned to me and opened his mouth and began singing quietly in a croaky voice. *When day is done and shadows fall, I dream of you, Da da da da, da da da da, the joys we knew.*

I'm sure that's not how it goes, I said.

He caught the loose end of the song trailing past and started singing louder. *That yearning returning to hold you in my arms, Won't go love, I know love, Without you night has lost its charms!*

I reached up from under the covers and gently pinched his mouth. Most people just smoke, I said. I released his lips. You can tell me what that was, though.

"When Day is Done." The story is, at night, he misses her. We don't know the same songs, do we?

The barbershop quartets don't come to town that often.

He grinned and shut one eye, pained. We'll have to cross-pollinate.

*Really.*


I took him back to the bus station when the weekend was over, and we stood outside in a light drizzle, and were mute. I hadn't told him yet that I'd lost my virginity to him; I felt embarrassed that I had even considered it important, but it seemed the kind of thing you should tell a person. In the end, I didn't know how to put it, and said nothing. (When I did tell him, more than a year later, he was aghast that I hadn't warned him beforehand. What would you have done, I asked him. I don't know, he said, I would have wanted to mark it somehow. You mean an ad in the paper? No, he said, serious. It's just sad when something important goes by and no one notices ...)

The bus pulled in and he took my hands. You haven't asked if there's anyone in my life.

I didn't want to know. Is there?

I'm hopeful.

I smiled and kissed him. I guess I'm sealing my fate, I said.

When I got home, Molly was pulling the sheets off her bed, and we stood staring at each other through her doorway.

Sorry, I said, looking at the bedclothes.

Sorry? I'm having them framed!

⌇

Martin and I spent most of our early weekends meeting in other spots around the state. I taught him to drive. I showed him how my father liked to hold the steering wheel, with his hands at the bottom, the wheel lying in his palms. Driving in a relaxed pose like that induced my father to make a sound I used to find strangely soothing: it was the sound of his ring tapping against the steering wheel. Just an occasional, light *tick*. It was sometimes the only sound on the way home from a dinner somewhere, driving back through Ithaca, or Letchworth, or Albany. A reassuring sound that there was someone awake in the car, watching over you.

Click your ring against the wheel, I said.

Martin looked over at me, confused. Why?

I like the way it sounds.

*Tick*. And again, *tick.*

I thought I'd want to share him with my friends, but we instead retreated to privacy, opening our stories over suppers and walks, incubating an intimacy I began to guard like some-one with knowledge of a diamond trove. He'd gone some time without a woman in his life, a result of having his nose in his work. And also a general confusion about what women his age wanted (he said, as a group, they seemed worried). As a result, he hadn't gone on a date in over a decade, and his last dates were convincing disasters.

On these first weekends, on our travels, we'd stop in little towns, read the grave markers for the revolutionary soldiers. Martin would go into the Woolworths or the dusty little corner stores and come out with his triumphant purchases: a book of cut-out animals, a pack of soap-bubble pipes, a die-cast milkmaid carrying her pails, an old velvet ring box with a stain of tarnish on the inside and no ring. Or else a paper bag filled with lemoncream snacking cakes (which he could live on), a fragrant peach at the bottom for me. He'd make me things from what he found. The milkmaid ended up in the ring box: you lifted the lid to find her lying on a bed of hay, the pails and the iron bar removed, so she lay there, succulent, her arms outstretched as she awaited her lover. The animals from the mobile were pasted on the inside edges of the box: lion, otter, viper, elephant.

Strange assortment of beasts for a barn, I said.

They're code.

I stared at it until I figured it out. Then dragged him to the floor, out of view of the windows. Maybe this was in Albany. Maybe that beautiful inn we found at Allen's Hill. I look back now and that life seems like pins in the map I was making.

We spent the rest of the summer and into the fall living like this. And I'd come back to campus full of the stories of an increasingly exotic life, pulling out a new artwork made for me, or increasingly, as time went on, keeping it to myself. To our friends, Molly and I started to seem like different people, like we'd moved up with the juniors. We stayed in Obreshkove over the summer, and in the fall, with many of our sophomore year moved on to other dorms, or even other universities, we became the grand dames of the house, treated with a kind of distant fear or respect. I'd leave on Friday and she'd have the place to herself for whatever recent conquest was going to take up her weekend. (To her credit, some lasted longer than a weekend, but rarely did they go as long as three or four.) Our Sunday nights were spent decoding our weekends, flopped on the sofa in our gowns, smoking cigarettes and eating the sandwiches no one ever requested. So we'd sit, sometimes with a glass of wine, going over what had been said, what it meant, new revelations, sensual progress. My stories were of going down one road, and hers were of detours. Mine, constancy; hers, change.

Don't you get bored? she'd say, and I'd tell her not at all. In fact, the more time I spent with Martin, the more it seemed as if nothing could be more complicated than being with just one person.

Don't you get tired, I asked her, talking about favourite bands and favourite movies? You don't get much past that, I imagine.

She laughed slyly. I get far past that. It's when they shut up that the fun begins. I'm just playing the field, baby. I'm taste-testing.

But once in a while, that hurt she'd showed the night she cried in her room crept in.

Maybe there's something missing from me that you've got, she said one night. Your guy sticks around for it.

You push yours away, I said. You let them all know you're not serious.

Her eyes went dark. I don't tell them. They just know, Jolene. They sense that *thing* that I don't have.

What is it, then?

If I knew …, she said, and I started trying to move the conversation off the thin ice. I didn't know how to help her. How can you help someone name an absence? The truth was, though, I felt it as well and didn't know what it was, or what to call it. It just made me cautious. So I took care not to harm my friend with my own happiness. This was why I made certain that Martin and I spent our weekends away from the dorm. While at Bard, he and Molly never met, although his gifts to me — found things, little boxes, tokens — filled our house.

I thought what I had with Martin inoculated me against disaster, or at least the kind of unfathomable loneliness Molly seemed to suffer from. Martin had already addressed our age difference, dismissing it, as I had, as an inescapable detail. I'm not giving up a chance at happiness because it looks strange to some people, he'd said, sensibly. (He was not always sensible. It was not the topnote of his personality. If I had to say what was, I'd say it was a quality of attentiveness. Attentiveness and its corollaries of daydreaming, a hatred of disorder, wariness.) Sometimes in the silences between talking, a solemnness would enter between us, and I'd be tempted to ask what was wrong, but I wouldn't. It was part of this vigilance I understood, obscurely, to be how he liked to be in the world. Plus, I didn't want my peace disturbed, and I knew averting my attention from such formless auguries was how to maintain it. I was learning about who he was, bit by bit, taking it in and settling it among the other details until a picture of a man who had overcome sad beginnings emerged. His first ten years had been years of incremental losses; he'd been sick, his mother had moved away, then they'd been forced to leave home and go overseas to keep the family together. Many of the middle years I knew nothing about, thirty or so years in which he might have been married, divorced, been crushed by love, escaped death, considered other lives. That would come later, I thought, I would fill in those spots later.

My own beginnings, meanwhile, surrounded me still, and this disparity between us (I had no missing years) sometimes crept up on me and made me feel that I was falling in love with a pair of book-ends. But I loved him. I loved him, and I knew the edge of happiness in his life was unfamiliar to him, and I wanted to protect it. He would lie in my bed on the last nights of his visits (he came twice a month for long weekends by the beginning of my senior year) and tell me he wished we already had years of shared life behind us. He longed for a common past. So someone else has a copy of it, he said.

An emotional archive with me as curator.

And me as yours.

I like that, I said. And we continued to learn the other like explorers expanding their maps of the known world. I didn't know, at that age, that those kind of maps have no north, no true north.

# II.

JEWELLERY BOX, 1957. 6" X 4" X 4" BOX CONSTRUCTION. WOOD, FOUND OBJECTS, MECHANISM. ALBRIGHT-KNOX MUSEUM. A CHILD'S JEWELLERY BOX, WHEN OPENED, REVEALS A HALF-ALLIGATOR, HALF-BALLERINA TURNING UNDER A PARASOL.

A YEAR AND A HALF LATER, I'D FOUND A GOOD JOB teaching English lit at Indiana University, one of the most beautiful universities in the country. It sat on an expanse of rivers and greens; tall shady chestnuts, poplars, and oaks formed a canopy over the centre of it. Martin and I had settled into what we both quakingly called a relationship. Once in a while we even slept together without making love. We also fought occasionally (like *a real couple*, I caught myself dizzily thinking), mostly over things that one thought was more important than the other. Some aspect of manners or habit; a disagreement of fact, something taken the wrong way. But it was hard to fight with Martin. He had a polarity that bent conflict away from him; he preferred to give in or postpone; he rarely saw a disagreement through to the end. And in this way, I usually prevailed, winning by default. It was an uncomfortable process for me. I wanted to lose. I wanted him to care about something so much that he had to take it away from me, had to convince me to give in. The only area of our lives where this obtained had to do with who visited whom. He always came to Bloomington; I never went to Toronto. I'd bring it up persistently, trying to gnaw away at his reasons, or at least to understand them.

Not this again, he'd say.

I have next Monday and Tuesday off. I'll take a bus on Friday. We'll have three whole days.

No, Jolene.

You have to.

Why do I have to?

Because I'll be very upset if you refuse me.

He'd sit down. Perhaps he'd be eating a slice of pie I'd made. Wearing one of his bulky blue sweaters. (I tend to remember, among other things, his clothing. Maybe simply because I kept a lot of it for a long time.) There's nothing for you to see in Toronto, he'd say. It's a boring place, my apartment is dark and dusty, and I don't see a lot of people.

But you have *some* friends.

Yes. Acquaintances.

And you don't want me to meet them?

How about if I bring a couple of them down and they can meet you here? You can all have a drink together and talk about how lucky I am.

You're not being very nice.

Look, Jolene. I like there being one place in my life where everything is perfect, and that's here. There's you, and this house, and my little workshed that you built for me —

You're welcome.

Yes, thank you, and I like to have it to look forward to. When I know I'm coming down to see you, it makes the days much easier for me.

Then why don't you move here?

Because I'm used to being alone. *Most* of the time. I'm slow this way, Jo. You know that.

I'd usually start crying around here, feeling hopelessly confused. I was so special to him that he had to stay away most of the time and didn't want me to visit him where he lived. Are you ashamed of me? I'd ask.

No, he'd say firmly. I love everything about you. But I don't love everything about me, and I just want to bring you the best parts.

I want them all, though.

This is most of me, Jo. Please try to be happy.

And he'd win. That was the one fight he'd always win.

I hadn't seen Molly since graduation — good intentions come to their usual end, or so I told myself — but we'd kept in contact, sending cards for birthdays and Christmases, talking occasionally by phone. I kept meaning to invite her to Bloomington, but it was hard coordinating our three schedules, and the fact that Martin and I continued to live in separate countries made our long weekends something I was reluctant to share. But now — it was the fall of 1989 — the Bergman, the main gallery on campus, had purchased an artwork from Martin, and it was to be unveiled in a presentation ceremony. It seemed to me I was already sharing him with a crowd for that weekend, and one more wasn't going to make a difference. Molly was elated and within an hour of the invitation she'd called back to say she'd purchased her bus ticket (Molly shared with Martin a terror of flying). She said she had to work the next day if she wanted to finish a case she was preparing; so it was twelve hours together, full stop. We'll make it feel like a week, I said, and when I hung up I felt a thrill of anticipation.

There had been times when we'd been roommates when I felt I'd been holding up an end of a bargain I'd never really signed on to. Outwardly, her sociability made her seem invincible, but privately, I know she burned with worry about herself. I was pressed into duty to keep those fires low, something I only realized after we'd been apart for a while. And yet, without Molly's example, I doubt I would have had the confidence I needed to connect with Martin. I just used some of her skills differently than she used them. It's funny, I've always found that the thing you admire most about someone is often the thing that gives them the most trouble, although in small, learned doses, it works wonders for you.

No one would have believed Molly was a lonely girl, but she was. And I, fairly shy by comparison, was filled up by one person. It turned out to be a deep difference between us, one that made me anxious. It is impossible not to harm someone with your good luck if they lack it themselves. But once I'd gotten out into "the world," I looked back on it and her with some admiration. What I struggled with was external mostly. My mother's death. My father's grief. (That I would have thought these things external points to how aware of myself I was in those days.) Molly fought herself and grew. It was a deeply loveable quality in her, and I did love her. So I was excited, although nervous, to see her again. The nerves passed right away, though: when she came off the bus in her long grey coat, her face just as I remembered it — grey-rimmed glasses framing bright green eyes — my heart leapt up. I ran forward and we collided in a hug.

I pulled her over to where Martin was standing, sheepish and grinning. He offered his hand, and she let go of me to shake it. A mock handshake, like they were businessmen. Then she pulled him to her and she hugged him too. She stepped back and fumbled in her giant shoulder-strap purse and passed us each something still in its bag. I took a light summer dress out of mine. I hope you haven't changed shape too much, she said. Hold it up. I did, and its diaphanous fabric caught in the wind and wrapped itself to me. It'll fit, she said, delighted.

Martin's bag contained an old watch. The face was partly melted, the glass over it bubbled and frozen in a warped pattern. A raised green crust swirled over the metal band. I found it scuba diving, she said. A couple years ago. I thought of you when I saw it. I thought maybe it was the kind of thing you'd like to have. For your work or something.

It's very eerie, he said. It's wonderful.

I thought you'd *love* it. I just kept it hoping one day we'd actually meet! Look, she said, touching the melted glass. It's like it went down on a burning ship and this is the only thing that survived.

He hugged her again. This is very thoughtful of you, he said.

We brought Molly back to the house and the three of us sat outside in the afternoon sun. She kept looking at me and shaking her head, like she couldn't believe it was really me, and we found ourselves laughing excitedly, nervously. Martin went to wheel out a makeshift wetbar, with a bucket of ice and some of what he called cordials. Molly and I tried to remember all the strange cocktails we'd once invented. Four O'Clock Aftershave was one of them: blue curaçao and crème de menthe. Disgusting. Or the one with all the transparent, almost tasteless liquors in them: gin, vodka, and Everclear (more a cleaning fluid than an alcohol). We'd named it Silent Creeping Death. A touch of cassis made it palatable; an eggcup's worth was enough to render a person insensible. We'd employed it in the seduction of various members of the debating team (the score there was Molly 4, Jolene 0 — I had a problem with dosages, which is to say, I kept falling down drunk). The three of us settled for beers and sat in the slow, wavy heat blinking at each other. The willows shaded us a little from the late sun, their huge branches a summery balm. Molly, used to the humidity of New York, found the high blank heat of the Midwest almost unbearable. She sat fanning herself with a hand, her skin glistening.

My god, what do you midwesterners do for relief?

Stay still, I said. Take showers.

I can't imagine getting used to this.

It must have been a steamy twelve hours on the bus, I said.

Thirteen, Molly said. It was a little sticky.

They have lovely air conditioning on airplanes.

She shuddered. It's thirty below up there, and that's just one way it can kill you.

I'm with her, Martin said, and they shook hands. Anyway, you get used to this, he said. It's almost what I grew up with. Well, except that it was cold and it rained all the time.

You never told me he was funny.

Oh, he's funny, I said. Wait till he has a second beer. He juggles too.

We finished our beers, opened more, and talked a little about everything, books and magazines recently read, movies missed, and so on. And then I had a strange thought: what if one of them knows something about the other that they're not supposed to know? I tried to recall all the conversational indiscretions I'd made in speaking with one or the other at various times. What did Molly know that she oughtn't? Martin? I was suddenly paralyzed with the thought of whatever that thing *was*, being introduced innocently into the conversation and the ballooning silence afterwards.

Molly asked him, Do you live down here now?

Oh geez, he said, no.

I turned to him with my eyes narrowed. Whaddyou mean, 'oh geez no'? I said. Tell me again what would be wrong with living down here, Martin.

Molly glanced back and forth between us, mouth pursed. I should change the subject.

Nooo ... I think he should tell us what he means.

I live in two places, he explained to Molly. In Toronto, I'm alone and I do my work. Down here, I'm with Jolene.

And you do your work, I said. I pointed to a ramshackle building at the back of the lot.

And yes, he said, I work here too. In fact, I work in both places and I love Jolene in both places, but it's only in one that we're together.

That's sweet, said Molly.

But I'm banned from Toronto, I said.

You're not banned.

He's always telling me what I wouldn't like about Toronto. His apartment has no bathtub. The city is cold.

In the winter, you mean?

No, said Martin. Well, yes, but what I mean is the people aren't as friendly up there.

I wouldn't be going to accept the key to the city.

He stared hard at me. His expression said, Any reason why you're doing this right *now?*

Just because, I said out loud.

Fine, he said. I come here because I love getting away from

a place I hate being in to one I love being in. And it isn't true the other way around: you love Bloomington, you'd hate Toronto, and there's nothing to do up there. So I come here. I go to all the *trouble* of coming here.

I *want* to come to Toronto.

Fine, he said, raising his arms a little off the armrests. You'll come, then.

I pulled my head back a little, astonished. When? I turned to Molly. You're my witness.

I don't think I better get —

Whenever you want, said Martin.

I jumped up and made him shake hands. You heard him, Molly. He said *whenever*. You heard him, right? I leaned down to him. Remember, you just said *whenever*.

I heard him, said Molly, draining her drink. I'll be back in a second. She got up and went back into the house. We watched her go in through the sliding door. She'd seemed a little put off.

Are you even *drinking?* Martin asked me.

I sat down on his lap. A little.

She doesn't need to see this nonsense. You're making her uncomfortable.

She can take it, I said. She's Molly. Water off a goose.

A duck.

A duck, you're right.

Well, quit it. She came a long way to see you and you're behaving very spoiled.

Can I really come?

Sure, Jo. I don't want to fight about it anymore.

No! Don't give in! Tell me I can come because you *want* me to come.

I do. I want you to come.

Yayyy!

But if you come, no complaining about how dull it is.

If I'm bad, maybe you'll have to spank me.

Shush, he said. Molly was coming back out and she was in a

smallish yellow bikini. We both stared for a moment, gobsmacked, before making a show of getting out of our chair and gathering things up, as if we'd fallen behind in an agenda only she recalled.

Let's find somewhere to go swimming, she said. Okay? It's too hot.

Sure, sure, I said. I'd forgotten how beautiful she was, gorgeous sleek black hair, and her long, generous body. I picked the beer cans out of the grass as she stood between us, towel folded over her arm.

So that's your workspace, huh? she said to Martin. Will you show me later?

Actually, I said, Martin doesn't let anyone in there. Not even me.

Okay.

She gets to come in once in a while just to keep the peace, Martin said, but it's really a mess. He leaned in toward her and laid his hand on a bare shoulder. It's nothing personal, he said.

Molly smiled at him. No offence taken.

He stood there, touching her, a circuit or two blown. When you're finished fondling my oldest friend, I said, why don't we go for a swim.

They both laughed and Molly stepped away from him. A swim, he said. Good idea. And you're coming to the opening tonight, aren't you?

That's why I'm here! Molly said. *By invitation only!*

Then you'll see a few of the new things then.

Excellent. He began walking into the house.

I watched him vanish through the door. I'm *sorry*, I said when he was out of earshot. We're being obnoxious.

Nonsense, said Molly. It's great to see you guys.

Well, we've got a lot of catching up to do, I said.

Martin reappeared with my bathing suit and a couple more towels.

You know what I was just thinking, Molly said to him. I was thinking about this one thing you made Jo. I'd love to see it

44

again. I don't remember exactly what it was ... a hornet's nest, or a honeycomb, she said. And there was one little hole, that if you looked in it, you could see in the middle a tiny doll wearing a crown. I always wondered how you did that, how it got it in there.

I don't remember that, I said.

Well, I cut the nest open, said Martin. Along a line of cells so the cut would be invisible. And I hollowed it out a little and built a platform inside out of balsa, pinned the little queen there, and then I closed it up. And that was it. Pushed little pin-holes through certain cells so the doll would be lit right, and hollowed one out to look down.

The hornet's nest? He nodded at me. The hornet's nest. I *know* that piece, Martin.

Okay.

I stared at him a moment. I'm not going to get it.

I didn't suggest you do.

I can't fucking believe this, I said, and I ran into the house and went into my closet. I never threw anything out that he gave me; the artworks I kept safe, or put on display, but the mounds of detritus that he also gave me — little love tokens, things I thought maybe one day he'd ask after — remained in storage. In a minute, I'd found the nest and ran back out with it, and turned it in my hands, looking for a peephole.

You're lying, I said.

That's the one, said Molly. I saw light coming out of it one day when I passed the shelf everything was on. I convinced her to put all those things you made in a common room so every-one could enjoy them.

I don't believe this. I couldn't find any so-called peephole. You *are* lying, I said. Martin took it from me and held it out at arm's length. Then turned it slowly one way at eye level until, suddenly, a gold light burst from one of the cells. He passed it back to me. I looked into the glowing hole, and sitting in a nimbus of pale afternoon sunlight was the thing I'd never seen.

A tiny doll the size of a thumb, papery wings on her back, sitting alone with a crown on her head in the middle of the hive. I stared at her, rapt. Finally, I passed it to Molly and looked over at him, my mouth open in disbelief. How is it possible ... you must have thought I *hated* it.

I knew you hadn't found her.

I would *never* have found her.

Yes, you would have. There was going to be a day when somehow she'd have been revealed to you.

I forgot you had wings! Molly said. She lowered the nest, her eyes shining. Martin took it back from her and started walking to the shed with it.

I might clean it up a bit though, he said.

Oh! said Molly, following him. Can I peek?

*Molly!*

Sure, he said. You can peek. He unlocked the door and leaned in to put the honeycomb on a shelf for later. Molly stood back, peering over his shoulder.

Looks all jumbly in there, she said.

It's a pigsty, he said. That's the real reason I don't let a soul inside. He closed the door and came back across the lawn toward me. He was trying to contain a stupid grin.

Look at you, I said. You're so proud of yourself.

Took you three years.

Were you *ever* going to tell me?

These things come together for their own good reasons, he said. I don't want to push them.

Push them! What else is in those boxes in my closet? They're sitting in the *dark* covered in *dust*.

They'll let themselves be seen when it's time, he said, and raised his chin at me.

I'm coming to Toronto *next week*. I need to keep a closer eye on you, mister.

Molly was still standing in the grass, watching us expressionlessly, her towel over her belly. So ... swimming? she said.

46

We loaded some beers and a watermelon into my car and headed down 28 to a gravel road that led to the quarry pits. It was now late in the day, and the sun had baked into the stone — a weft of hot air rose from the road. Molly dropped her hand out the window, sighing.

You should be careful you don't burn, I said.

You know me, she said, batting her eyelashes. I just smoulder.

Most of the locals had stopped going to the quarries in September, so we had them to ourselves, and I directed Martin to the smallest one, farthest away from the rest. He pulled over and Molly got out and quickly laid out a towel on the flat rock that led to the edge of the quarry. I started changing behind a tree. Martin sat by Molly with a cap over his eyes and peered down into the glassy water, more than forty feet below.

Which of us hasn't seen you naked? Molly called to me.

She does this at home too, Martin said. Runs outside and changes in the trees.

I could see them, fragments of skin and colour, through the branches and the leaves. I'm not changing in front of you both, I said. You know, the two of you seeing each other seeing me naked.

He wouldn't care if we both skinny-dipped. She turned to him. I'm assuming.

There's no sunblock.

Sunblock wasn't actually the topic.

He shielded his eyes from the sun and looked at her. I'm another generation, he said. I'm not with-it enough to look at a naked woman I don't know that well and act nonchalant. He paused a moment. Not to say I wouldn't mind *stumbling* upon such a scene.

Molly laughed. I came out in my one-piece and hauled her up to standing. You're not coming in? she asked as I pulled her toward the edge.

He doesn't do water, I said.

We stood and looked down. Long-ago industry had carved out these pits and left them to fill with water. It was like looking through a window onto one of the summer skies of your childhood. I was a bit buzzed from the beers and the sun, or I would never have considered jumping. Molly took my hand and we counted to three and leapt. We gulped air, a delicious moment of death, and then the cold, cold plunge. I came up gasping and blinking, the water so cold, so piercing. I could feel it leaching the sun from me, the baked-in heat of the day dissolving.

This smallest quarry had been nicknamed the Elephant Graveyard because there were two Volkswagen bugs at the bottom, one green, one blue. People had spread a story about a nighttime drag race and a dark burst over the edge. The green one was closer to the other side: the winner. No one believed it, but it was hard not to conjure the bodies of two boys in their cars below us, their hair moving back and forth in the water like ferns. The tingle of picturing a hand on your ankle. The two bugs were unreachable without airtanks, and no one, as far as I knew, had ever gone down there. The cars swayed in the distant light like treetops.

Molly was groaning with happiness, floating on her back. This place is incredible. If you want to swim in New York, you join a health club, or risk herpes from the public pools.

Yuck.

We both floated on our backs and looked up. The yellow walls rose at perfect right angles to the water. Martin looked tiny at the very top. The bickering was very cute, she said.

I don't get a lot of opportunity to see him squirm.

Or me.

Right.

She swept her arms back and forth through the water slowly. Mmm, she said. This is perfect.

Isn't it.

So you're happy, aren't you?

I am. Yes. We drifted a little, the sky unblemished to all horizons. What about you? I said. You keep getting cut off with the Martin and Jolene show.

Oh, you know. It's the same old story. Men like to conquer me and I let them, but I scare the shit out of them. Too smart, too beautiful.

I'm supposed to say that part.

There might be someone, I don't know. He keeps kissing me on the cheek.

That's gallant.

It's just as well. This is the good part, you know? Nothing's gone wrong yet.

Since when do you have such a bad attitude? I said, but before she could answer, I pushed off her with my feet and arced over backwards under the water. The bugs glowed in their dead light below me.

— unlucky, she was saying when I came up.

Huh?

It doesn't matter. She gave a strong slow pull underwater and drifted away a little, then swung her arm back and forth through the air. Wave, Jo. He's waving.

I looked up to the top of the stone wall, where shafts of sunlight were pouring down, and waved to him.

I didn't upset you this afternoon, did I? she said.

No, I said, although I'd been deeply embarrassed. How did you know about it, though? How did you remember?

I just remembered it from the house. It was one of my favourite things.

I didn't know you even looked at them.

I did.

I tilted my head into the sun, squinted at her. Do you want it? I said.

He made it for you, Jo. You can't just give it away.

I know, but I've kind of lost my privileges, I'd think. We'll ask him afterwards.

No, don't, she said quickly. It's not meant for me.

I nodded, treading water. Okay. She tipped her head back and rewet her hair, then submerged and swam toward the far wall, a lithe shadow under the surface.

≈

That evening, we all dressed in good clothes and went to the Bergman ceremony. Martin was in his "openings" suit: I'd only seen him in it once before, in Washington, and more frightening than making him look his age, it made him look like a respectable man his age, which made us look especially suspect as a pair. Of the three of us, Molly was the one who seemed distracted: she fiddled with her glass and was uncharacteristically wordless after being introduced to various functionaries and friends.

We circulated in the crowd, nodding at the right times in conversations, nibbling the appetizers that went around. The small glass tables throughout the reception hall were littered with cellophane-wrapped toothpicks and empty champagne flutes. Martin had mentioned earlier that he was hoping for something subdued and tasteful. Is coconut shrimp and tamarind sauce with Tattinger's lowbrow enough for you, my love?

Don't rub it in, okay?

Two men in tails blew cornets to announce the ceremony was about to begin and everyone filed through a pair of doors to one of the larger galleries, where a hundred or so seats had been set up. Up at the front, Clark Johannson, the curator, was waiting for people to settle. He was a big Swede, with hands like paddles and long legs. You could always see him walking across campus, bright in his yellow ties and chinos, towering over those beside him. He'd come up to Martin and me a month earlier at a rally down by the student union. Some students had built a shantytown there to protest apartheid, and the field below the road had become the centre of the university's social life during that spring. Johannson had recognized Martin from a show at Tufts two years earlier.

Now he was coming to the podium, slick and glinting in a shark-coloured shirt and a black tie, and he steadied himself with his flipper-like hands. He leaned down into the microphone. Today we're celebrating the acquisition of a marvellous new work of art from the Canadian artist Martin Sloane.

Not Canadian, Martin said out of the side of his mouth.

There was applause. I joined in, but he took one of my hands in his. Don't applaud, he said.

Why?

You don't throw confetti at your own wedding.

A little bit about the artist, Johannson said. Born in Dublin, raised in that city, as well as Galway, Montreal, and Toronto. Divides his time between Toronto and our little town. The winner of the prestigious Carrick Foundation Prize for a body of work in 1975, and he's had some major shows since then, at the National Museum of American Art, the Menil in Houston, the Tufts University Art Gallery, and of course the group show at Castelli, a very popular show in 1983. But his work is hard to come by! Very few galleries have anything in their permanent collections, and what the public gets to see generally goes home with the artist. Mr. Sloane's reputation has grown via a peculiar kind of absence on the art scene. Very clever, Mr. Sloane!

Laughter. A weak smile from Martin.

But today, we unveil *three* boxes, albeit a single work, but three pieces which will take pride of place in our contemporary galleries.

Someone at the back dimmed the lights and Johannson said, I give you Going Under, and I leaned forward with the crowd. In the darkness of the room, we could now see three squares of faint light glowing behind a sheet. An invisible hand drew the sheet back and revealed three boxes on a dais, barely lit from within, as if their surfaces were giving off the last of a light they'd somehow stored. They were breathtaking in the darkness and immediately a silence that was like intimacy came over the crowd. When our eyes adjusted, the box at the left revealed only a miniature buoy floating against a background of inky darkness. The middle box was empty but for (so Martin claimed) eighty-five layers of warped, cracked, bubbling blue paint and varnish on the back wall. The third showed a rotting galleon hidden amongst a copse of weed and thickly laid twigs. Martin's handwritten instructions for installation indicated the effect was to be of muted moonlight. And so they seemed to float in the air at the front of the auditorium, phosphorescent pale, like drowned rooms.

The applause started and grew louder. The lights came on slowly, so that the boxes faded a little, their magic retreating. People at the front turned to face us and Martin stood up beside me, stiff, uncomfortable. I applauded and Molly stood up to kiss Martin on the cheek, and then he leaned down and kissed me, and everyone just stood there clapping. Molly sat back down and I watched Martin taking it in, and after a few moments of smiling, his face tired and he dropped it, and then the three of us remained there, waiting for it all to end.

Back at the house, we tossed our coats over the back of the brown couch and Martin went straight to the back door, murmuring, Back in a minute. Molly turned to me, surprised, but I'd learned to smile inwardly at these abrupt withdrawals. It was one of the things we fought about, but I'd learned to stash my frustration with this behaviour in the Unchosen Battles part of my mind. Sometimes he told me what was on his mind at these times, or he just didn't; I learned to live with this spectacle of concealment. I always imagined that from it emerged the things that I loved, the general peace of the rest of our lives together, his art, his self. I waved off Molly's expression of confusion and said, He'll be just a second. She shrugged and joined me in the kitchen. It was dusk now, that light that presses distances together and makes the world look like a charcoal drawing. I poured us both some of the sherry Molly had brought — we were already a bit drunk, but a little more wasn't going to hurt. The light in Martin's shed blinked on, and we could see his shadow behind the high smoky window. A misty fog coming off the river was drifting through the yard and the light from the window hung in it like something solid.

Trouble in Paradise? Molly said.

No ... it's just. This is actually normal.

Normal.

Well, I'm used to it, I said.

She looked back out toward the shed. It's funny what we can get used to.

It's not a big deal. I put my hand on hers. Don't be insulted. It gives us a few minutes to catch up, see? I led her into the front room and we sat on the couch. It really has been a long time, I said. Molly sipped from her sherry, distracted.

You know, she said, looking over the tops of her glasses at me. I haven't seen you in about two years, but I haven't seen him in five.

Well, you never —

Exactly. I didn't wait five years to meet Martin only to have him go have a sulk on me.

He'll be back in two secs, I said, but she'd already gotten up.

I have my ways, she said, smiling sweetly, and she put her drink down with a faint clink on the glass table in front of us. Before I could say anything, she went out where Martin had gone out just minutes before and started crossing the grass. I rushed to the door and stood on the verge, watching her stride across the now-dark lawn toward the faint yellow light at the back of the property. I was trying to get past the stunned feeling so I could find the thing to say that would stop her in her tracks, but before I could manage it, she reached the door and simply opened it. Then went in and closed it behind her. I stood frozen to the spot, feeling the bite of the cool misted air, my mouth stuck open.

Shortly, across the small expanse separating me from the shed, I heard soft voices. Calm, quiet voices, floating in the air between there and here. Never mind frog-marching her out of there, he was actually talking to her. He didn't *mind* that she had invaded that silence I had always, so assiduously, honoured. This was a different silence than my father's, and maybe I had

53

misread it. I stood in the doorway separating me from these two people I loved and it felt like my heart would just stop beating.

My father's silence had sunk my childhood house in impenetrable gloom; it was a silence I disturbed at my peril, not because my father was prone to violent reactions of any sort but because if roused, he was capable of starting off on terrifying tangents. He might ask if I thought the couches in the house ought to be recovered, or if there were any churches I wished to join (and it seemed to him the more the better, saturated, as he must have thought I was, with my mother's inclination to sin). So I left him to stew, and stew he did, until he died of it. Standing there in my adult home, I wondered if the outcome of our unhappy life in Ovid would have been any different if I had charged into my father's room and made him speak to me. What if I had forced that connection on him, that same angry reaching-out that Molly was forcing on Martin now? Was I capable of that? And was it courage or selfishness? With my father, I'll never know if I could have saved him from his grief. It may be simple why. I may have lacked — I may still lack — the humanity.

I put on a pleasant face and began crossing the lawn. I came at an angle that closed off the light from the single window, and then gently wheeled in toward it so that it burst gold in my eyes like the light in the honeycomb had. I called out to them as I approached, anxious that I sounded as though I was going to catch them in something, although I couldn't imagine what (she may have been beautiful, but Martin's fidelity was something I never questioned). As I came round toward the door, it opened and Martin stepped out.

I was just about to come and get you, he said. I saw Molly behind him stepping out into the dark beside the door. Martin put his hands on my shoulders and kissed me. Rescue me, he said quietly.

I was just thinking you might need some help.

He took my hand and reached for Molly's. She brought one hand out from behind her back to take his, and smiled childishly. Does this mean we're not done yet? she said.

It's an evening of firsts, he said. Let's see how many people we can get in this thing. He led us both back inside.

Entering the shed with them made me anxious because of my own misdemeanors. It wasn't true that I wasn't allowed in Martin's workplace (I'd said that to take the sting out of the potential insult to Molly); I'd been in there with him many times. But when he was out of town, it was assumed I would not go in there by myself. However, with as long as two weeks at a time between visits, I went in frequently, and being able to be among the things that he loved made the wait bearable. I even told myself that he probably knew I did this, since the keys were so obviously accessible, and he'd never actually *told* me not to go in. I'd started small, opening the door and just standing in the verge, like I was now. And then, later, actually entering. And finally, in recent months, sitting and doing as I pleased, opening drawers, taking things out, turning both finished and unfinished things over in my hands, even opening them and touching the objects inside. I'd cracked the rim of a clay bowl in one of them, and knowing Martin had a box full of them — bought in New York City a number of years back for next to nothing — I removed the broken bowl and glued down a fresh one in its place. Each time I left the shed, I left it exactly as I'd entered it, and went back into the house with a queer mix of guilt and satiation. As if there were something in the sin itself that was needed, as well as the pleasure of being there, alone, as it were, with him.

Well? What's been the subject of conversation? I probably have a few things to add to it, whatever it is.

Just life, said Molly, turning. She smiled at me.

Art, said Martin.

Yes, we were talking about *art*, Molly said mockingly.

Really?

Molly was just telling me she's a fan.

Well we all know that, I said, and I smiled.

Stranger things had happened somewhere, I was sure, but not here. Molly walked past both of us to where floor-to-ceiling shelves on either side of the door were stacked with finished artworks. It was the least-safe place in the world to keep such things, I'd told Martin numerous times. But for him they were not "artworks" the way the world thought of them; they were references and guides and records of something that was always in progress, that he constantly referred to. It made no sense to him to keep them "safe."

The shed wasn't much bigger than four outhouses set up in a square, but he'd made the most of the space. There was a single old typesetter's stool that could wheel across the smooth tin floor. Opposite the door was a deep shelf taking up the whole wall, at lap level, which served as his workspace. A variety of things in different stages of completion rested on it. Above the shelf, dark cubbyholes labelled with Dymo tape labels — dowels, 3 inch–8 inch, rings and balls, glass, lenses (although it said lemses), hinges, dowels, 1 inch–3 inch, screws, nails — the latter two of which were in bottles.

Each of the other two walls had a library catalogue drawer against it. These were labelled alphabetically and contained small objects and pictures from everywhere — from postcards to magazines and comic books to stamps to advertising and photographs. Even graphic police and morgue images, none of which had found a home in his work yet but suggested a bewildering openness to unforeseen change. The pictures, and the little toys and bits of fabric and pieces of broken things, were organized by genus and contained in #3 envelopes with holes punched out of the bottoms so they would fit on the pipe slides in the bottoms of the drawers. Upon opening the drawers for the first time, I had the impression of entire worlds labelled and laid out in white rows. The levels of organization stunned, and even frightened, me. If Martin wanted a picture of a leopard frog, for example, there were perhaps a half-dozen to choose from. He'd have them in a single envelope behind a card that said "Amphibians, Freshwater," which was in a set of six drawers labelled "Non-mammalian," which was in a section five rows wide called "Animals," which was itself in the cabinet labelled "Sentient" on the left side of the shed, which he had designated "Natural." It faced the other cabinet, with its own complex taxonomies, which was labelled "Man-made."

Above the drawers, now directly behind where I was standing, there were cubbyholes on both sides, the ones on the right containing manufactured things of every variety — dollheads, coins, cans, apothecary bottles, tintype photographs, the clay bowls, and so on. The left held things mainly found on walks — driftwood, birds' nests, dead insects, moss, bark, hay, stones, sand in bottles, quartz. The contents of the shed had been collected everywhere, but gradually Martin had been bringing down what he had in Toronto as well, and now the two workplaces each contained about half of what he had, as far as I understood it. Around us, on the walls and on the desk in front of us, was the complicated jumble of all the things that got drawn down into his work.

Martin must have told Molly she could look at whatever she wanted, because she was taking things off their shelves, plucking them like she was finding coins in the street. Soon, she had more than a dozen of them out, and they faced us, their glass fronts reflecting us and the night behind. Many, of course, I had seen and knew well, not just because I'd looked at them in here but because Martin had kept them in the house from time to time (he said it helped to see them out of the corner of his eye), and many of them had been on public display. There was Linwood Flats and The Curtain, Sunken and Universe. Voluptuaries (the first thing Martin ever made specifically for me, it was full of butterflies hidden behind twigs), Childhood Game, and Downstairs.

Molly whistled low and then sat down in Martin's chair and looked at the boxes, and they looked like a row of front windows in houses, arrayed there. Let's turn off the light, she said, and Martin did, and when our eyes adjusted, the moon was throwing the shadows of things onto the backs of the boxes. Molly was breathing them in and I looked back at Martin and he was leaning against a shelf on the back wall and watching Molly with a look of Sunday-morning pleasure on his face. Then he closed his eyes, and his face went to stillness. I realized I could relax, I was here with permission, and I stepped up with Molly and breathed them in too. Pine resin and cold iron and moss. In Childhood Game, a crank on the side moved a row of colourful animal faces along a track, like the targets in a shooting gallery. A plate of smoked glass below revealed the underside of the game, family photos pasted onto the targets. (Two separate chains made it look like the animal heads, sinking out of sight, transformed into real people upside down — I'd opened the back of this box with a screwdriver and marvelled at its construction, at the fact that, somehow, Martin would know how to make something like this.) Molly had one hand on her chest and her fingertips over her mouth. They really are beautiful, she said.

They're just a few things I want to keep. He was in silhouette now, the moon against his back.

What's this one? Molly asked. She was kneeling by a low shelf where she'd pulled a box made of glass on all sides out of its place. The front and back panels held an object encrusted with dirt. Through one side, you could see a rusted latch. Through the other, a page from an old Bible, lit up with illuminations. I'd seen it once or twice before. Martin had described it as unfinished — he hadn't even given it a title. But now he took it from Molly and told her it was called The Good Book of Mysteries.

You'll like this story, he said to her. It's based on something my father told me when I was little.

Is it? I said.

Yes, said Martin. This story is for *Molly* though.

Alright.

It was called the Clonmacnoise Bible, he continued, the one my father told me about. It was supposed to be the most beautiful illuminated manuscript ever discovered. It was named for the ancient monastery on the shores of the Shannon where they discovered it. When they found the Bible, buried in the foundation of a nine-hundred-year-old church, it was in a rotted box, and its pages were open to two ancient illuminations, the most beautiful things ever seen. But the rest of the pages in both halves had partially decomposed from water leaking into the box through the ground, not to mention the discharges of all the bodies buried at varying depths in the church floor and in the yards, and then the pages had also petrified from centuries of pressure on the collapsed box. So what they decided to do was, they kept the second half at Clonmacnoise and sent the first half to Trinity in Dublin to be studied. And so began a succession of terrible luck. A curse, in fact.

Really, I said.

Martin shot me a look. The first man who tried to pry the pages apart was the most renowned archaeologist of the time, and after a week of trying to separate one page from another with nearly microscopic wires, he gave up in despair and hanged himself from the corner of a bookcase in the library. The second man, a chemist, tried to find a solvent that would separate the pages without destroying the illuminations, and although he was able to get the very edges of the pages to come apart, he could not see any of the illuminations, and gave up as well. He didn't despair about his failure, but his wife took their three children back to their grandmother's in Belfast, appalled that he would tamper with a religious artifact, and so come in for the wrath of God. This man spent the rest of his days alone and bereft.

Bereft, Molly said.

Finally, said Martin, a group of scientists decided that the best way to separate the pages of the first half of the Clonmacnoise Bible would be to immerse it in oil — since the pages were on an animal skin of some sort and wouldn't be damaged — and allow the oil to soak in, and then subject the book to a long, slow drying process that would likely separate the newly supple pages.

Uh-huh, I said suspiciously. And?

Well, they had the Bible in a kiln with a glass door, and they had it on a low burn. After a number of days, they could see that the Bible's pages were easing apart. When they could almost see the surfaces of the pages, with those bright colours and the long-lost illustrations, they turned the kiln off and let everything cool, and then they opened the door after another day and got ready with the bottles of champagne.

Molly's face was pale. What happened?

It fell to ash the instant they touched it.

Jesus Christ, I said.

So now the other half at Clonmacnoise is in a glass case and if anyone tries to discover the rest of its treasures, they'll lose that little bit they do have.

Molly stood bolt upright. And why is that story for me? she said. Why for me? It means don't try to figure things out?

I looked back and forth between them, lost in the sudden updraft of emotion.

No, said Martin quietly. My father told it to me because something bad had happened to me, and I said that there was no reason for anything, that the world made no sense. My father was a religious man and this upset him.

So what, you were just a kid.

He said to me, just because you can't understand why this is happening to you doesn't mean there isn't a reason. It's just hidden from you, and you have to be able to appreciate life knowing you aren't entitled to know all the answers.

He advised you not to think about your life? Molly said.

No. He was telling me to show some respect for both the beautiful as well as the darker mysteries, that's all. He wanted me to understand that if something refuses to reveal itself to you, prying it apart could ruin something that was precious the way it was.

Including this bad thing that happened to you?

Well, it made me who I am, so I guess there was something good in it. If I think I'm leading a life worth leading.

And are you? Molly said.

I looked from her to him and back, not sure at all what had set this in motion. I leaned forward and gently took the fragile artwork from Martin's hands. A prize in every box, I said. I slipped the Good Book of Mysteries back into place and drew out another box, one whose name I knew. This one has a happy ending, I said. Grand Central.

Molly looked over at it and smiled softly. That's pretty.

*And* I know this one, I said, clearing my throat nervously. It's about a cinema.

A little while later, Molly looked at her watch and announced she had half an hour to make her bus. She went into the house to grab her bag. My god, I said to him, as we crossed the lawn behind her, what was that about?

I'm not sure. He sounded tired.

But what did she *say* to you? Molly reappeared in the doorway. You'll tell me after.

She put her arms around me. It did me a world of good to get away for a day, she said. Her voice contained no hint of her previous distress. Thank you.

Okay, I said, a little lost. I wondered if she had quickly checked through her bag and seen what I'd left there for her. I could see no hint of what she was feeling under what she appeared to be feeling. Calm and collected.

We'll talk, she said. I'll call you. She turned to Martin. Thanks, she said.

He reached forward and hugged her. She slung her little bag over her shoulder, carelessly enough that I knew she hadn't opened it and looked inside, and kissed us both. I just stood there and watched her walk toward the road.

Wait, I said, snapping out of it, we'll drive you.

No, I'll walk, she said. I don't get lost.

But your bus is going to leave.

I'll be fine, she said, and she waved to us both and turned down toward where the main road led to the station.

Martin went back into the shed to tidy up, and I stood in the doorway, watching him, waiting. Well, are you going to tell me what the *hell* that was all about?

He shrugged. Maybe she's unhappy, he said.

She's unhappy? Stop the presses. She seemed miserable all day. Is that what she wanted to say to you? He continued meticulously to shelve his things. Martin?

He walked past me in the threshold and snapped the light off. I stepped back so he could close the door. Then he turned to me sharply in the doorframe. I don't mind if you come in here when I'm gone, he said. But if you break something, tell me so I can fix it.

Oh ..., I said.

We stepped out of the verge and he clicked the lock shut. I'm not angry.

Okay.

But you can't just replace a broken thing with an unbroken thing like you're changing a lightbulb.

I'm sorry, I said, and I linked my arm in his, but he surprised me by slipping his out.

Just have a little more respect, okay? He continued across the grass to the house, and I followed him, knowing (in the way we tend to know things that are, if fact, just the way we've chosen to see the world) that there was no point in trying to make it right. At least not today, a day that had gotten away from me. I went in behind him and shut the kitchen door. It seemed to me that there were two darknesses that night, the one outside and the one in the house, and there was no difference, as if the door were a plate of glass dropped into the sea at night. I pulled the lock up. I had the image of that book of holy secrets, heavy with earth and rain and dust.

⁓

When I was a little girl, my parents had kept a layer of their wedding cake in the chest freezer downstairs. It was the top tier of a white cake with silver icing, the bride and groom wrapped in wax paper and tucked down beside it. All throughout my childhood, I'd go downstairs and scoop out some of the frozen cake from the underside with a teaspoon and eat it in perfect secrecy in the dark of the coldroom. It was furred with ice, but if I warmed the little hunks of cake in my mouth, the slightly sour taste of marzipan thawed out of it, and it was delicious. When I went down there, I'd have to fight the contradictory feelings of curiosity and shame. I was taking something from my mother that she obviously cared so much about. But there are certain feelings that you can't fight, and the urge to be connected to certain people is one of them. When I sat in the coldroom, dissolving the cake in my mouth, I would become my mother. I'd absorb her into my body, and I believed I knew what it felt like to be her. To be pregnant with my brother, to sleep beside my father, to hold *me* to her chest. I could not resist these small tastes.

The plastic bride and groom that she'd saved accurately showed the height difference between my parents, my mother being the taller. My father had always claimed he was tall for a Greek, that at five foot nine (he'd rounded up from seven and a half inches) he towered over his contemporaries. One of his few recurring jokes — he wasn't known for his sense of humour — was that he was the starting forward of the best basketball team in Greece, the Lesbos Rockets. My mother would revert to a stone face whenever this joke was told, and then look from him to us, as if such a thing could corrupt us.

The bride on the cake resembled my mother in more than height. It had her long, graceful features, her slender piano-playing hands (a regret of hers, that her piano remained in Albany in her mother's house), her Modigliani neck, her long black hair. Of course, in all of this she was much like Molly, who had the same New England roots, that British rose beauty sustained through generations of tennis-playing, book-reading, buttermilk-biscuit-baking decendants of the pilgrim ships. My father always said that he'd married the American Constitution, my mother that she was the bride of Orpheus (my father had a beautiful singing voice, and my mother obviously didn't know that much about Greek myth, although she got the ending right). My brother, Dale, won the genetic lottery and got my mother's delicate features. I got a mix — mermaid on top, milkmaid on the bottom. Surf 'n' turf, as Molly used to call me. But by college, I'd come to like my odd dimensions and never took offence at Molly's nicknames. I grew into them. I had a reputation for being sensual, which suited me. My body is the only constant in my life.

Meanwhile, the plastic groom looked nothing like my father. When Dale and I recently returned to the house in Ovid and I emptied the freezer, I unwrapped the bride and groom to look at them one more time. My mother was still sharply white, her features clear and colourful. But my father, who I realized had been taken from a different bride-and-groom set (where, certainly, the bride had been the standard diminutive), was made from lesser material. His features had faded, and the freezer had strangely melted the plastic a little. He seemed an unhappy homunculus with a vague face and a ruined tuxedo.

≫

The dark cast itself over the rooftops, that Midwest darkness with its starblown sky, and at the edge of it all, in our own bed, I slept with Martin. He smelled of bathsalts, his skin radiating heat. We'd sat and washed the day off in the claw-footed tub, drifting in conversation, pulling ourselves back into a twosome alone in our house.

He fell asleep almost right away, but I lay awake, parsing the day. Its warp and weft, a day of long moments. Finally, I slept and the moon crossed the sky. Feeling the bed move, I woke and saw Martin sitting by the edge, his hands braced against the side.

You all right?

Gotta go, he said.

Don't leave the seat up. I drifted back off. I slept. The bed moved and I opened my eyes on his back again. He was motionless.

Listen, he said.

What? I blinked and then I realized that even though he was silhouetted in the window, I could also see the windowframe and even the trees outside, as if he were translucent. Then pinholes of light began to burn through him, like he was a piece of film melting in a projector, and my heart began pounding in my throat. I lurched up, shouting his name and pushing myself back against the headboard. And then he was not there.

I climbed down from the bed and went out into the house where the lights were still off. I had the feeling in my body of an overlong afternoon nap, the chemical fuzz, the sense of wrongness.

I called to him quietly without answer.

I flicked the outside light on and saw the shed beyond, tinny grey. There were no tell-tale cracks of light along its edges. I opened the sliding door and, hunched over in the cold air, called for him, then called a little louder, trying not to wake our neighbours, and the sound of my hoarse voice moving out into the utterly still night startled me. I heard movement down in the ravine and then two dogs flashed black in front of the glowing water. After that, nothing. I stared out at the sickly dark of near-morning, that greyish light that I'd always thought of as the light of the back of the moon, the light hidden from us on Earth, the beaded sweat on my arms meeting the cold wet air. I went back into the bedroom and sat up against the wall, staring at the empty spot in the bed, and I began to drift off again, picturing him in a coat over his pyjamas, walking to the all-night store for something sweet.

# III.

CROSSING, 1987. 14" X 8" X 6" BOX CONSTRUCTION. WOOD AND GLASS WITH FOUND OBJECTS, PHOTOGRAPHS, ORGANIC MATERIAL. LOOKING DOWN ON A SHIP AS IT CROSSES A ROUGH SEA. THE TOPDECKS FAINTLY REVEAL THE FACE OF A WOMAN ON THEM. SMOKE COMING OUT OF THE FUNNELS SPREADS AGAINST THE TOP GLASS OF THE BOX AND RESOLVES INTO THE FACE OF A MAN.

WHEN I WAS TWENTY-FIVE, THE MAN I LOVED WALKED
out of my home late one night and vanished. No one ever saw
him again. There are no other words for this.

Impressions of that night are burnt into memory.
Something I had said? A look on Molly's face. Embracing her,
holding his hand walking into the house, the moon through
willows. Always this order of memory, returning to it, looking
for the crack in it where light can push through, the one cell
bursting gold with revelation. Later, twined in bed, music drifting past outside on a car radio. A door opening, feet on gravel.
History urging itself into being. At dawn, calling his name from
the doorway. Motionless in the reading chair. Standing at the
window. Later, roaring in the dark, on my knees under the
stars. Wet grass against my cheek, eyes staved open, the river
audible through trees.

※

The roads that framed the university were busy thoroughfares,
full of used-textbook stores, pizza outlets, and, farther out,
the bars and other specialized establishments. Such were the
laws of the state that if you had a restaurant with so much as a
shelf of booze behind a counter, that shelf had to be draped
with a sheet at all times so the alcohol was not visible to minors.
The bars themselves, with their Fort Knoxes of alcohol doubled
in mirrors, were considered true dens of sin, and held an

outcast status in the town, hunched on the periphery of things. Here also were the windowless porno stores and the places you could go to sell your plasma. I was uncomfortable at first going into these places, a sheaf of photos in hand, as my inquiries made Martin guilty after the fact of certain tastes. But how I wanted to hear that he had been through those doors. That he had come to commune with the awesome democracy of pornography, or had thinned his blood in preparation for a journey. Travelling light at the cellular level.

But no one had seen him.

At home, I made an attempt to go about my life. I bought groceries, I bathed, I took the newspaper as usual. I have no doubt that outwardly I seemed fine, and to myself — but for some weight loss and a tendency to get lost in conversations — I seemed as I'd always been. Although I also admit that I was having an unusual effect on time. I found I had the ability to stare the second hand on a clock to stillness. I'd look away and when I looked back, it'd be moving again. Some mornings, after gathering my things for class (my pen, a sheet of foolscap folded in half), I would stand at the window and look out on the yard toward the shed and try to piece together what had happened in my life to bring me to this moment. It would take almost an hour to make my way through this warren of thoughts, and I'd startle to realize I was now late for class, but then I'd look at the clock and see that only four minutes had passed.

In November, a month after Martin's disappearance, a student of mine left the class in the middle of a lecture and returned with another faculty member. This man, whose name and face I can't bring to mind, accompanied me from the class. After that, if I ran into my students, they pretended not to know me. I wandered the campus, flicking my eyes over the scenery … it was not something even the most callous of my students could bring themselves to find funny. I was given a wide berth.

I wasn't sure whether to call Molly or not — my recollection of our day together turned dark the longer I thought of it. Its awkward moments had bled across my memory like a stain. But I longed for the old Molly, the one who had reassured me in our college days, who seemed to be a sister to me, who could read my life and explain what it meant.

When I finally did call, I got her machine. The sound of her voice soothed me. I controlled my own and told her what had happened. He's gone, I said. Without a word. I don't know what I did.

A day passed and she didn't return the message. I called again. Molly, I said, please call me.

I waited, but she never called.

The police came, they took notes, they accepted coffee. I watched them from a window in the house as they dusted for fingerprints in the shed. It came to nothing. From then on, I left the door to the shed unlocked, an invitation not to thieves but to the gods who may have forgotten, in their playfulness, where to return Martin when they were done. By the end of November, I ruled out the gods.

At the beginning of December, when the weather finally broke cold, I unplugged the phone. I rid the house of plants. It also seemed best to take down the prints and drawings, and after that it was a natural transition to packing up the books. As Christmas came and went, the house retreated to a clean and naked state, the air as clear as consommé, pure humming nothingness. I hadn't been into the shed since the night of Molly's visit, only the police had. I went out through a crisp crest of snow, and then found myself standing in front of the unlocked door, uncertain. What if I had misunderstood what had occurred in those two months past? What if I opened the workplace door and found Martin weeping over his workbench, his tiny room the only place where he might find some comfort in losing *me?*

I was frozen with the fear of finding the shed empty and suddenly I was transported back to the night of my mother's funeral, when I stood outside my childhood house with the same feeling of being unable to enter a grief-filled place. People — friends, relatives, neighbours — had been in the house all afternoon. It amazed me that they were able to drink coffee and eat buttered buns until there were none left in the basket when it felt to me that I would never be able to eat again. I listened to people talk about my mother, and although I had always thought she was good, her goodness, filtered through the mourners, seemed unreal. I didn't know yet how death changed the dead, but already it was beginning, and their talk paralyzed me.

I tried to find my father, but I couldn't see him in the room, and I began to troll through the crowd of mourners until I reached the edge and found myself standing alone at the front door. I went outside and stood on the lawn. It was getting close to dusk — I could already see the dog star — and the sky was beginning to go grey over the houses across the road. A stain of pink was spreading at the bottom of the street.

I stood and looked at the house I'd been born in, where my mother had waited — there, at the door — for her new husband to carry her in. That story, along with the one in which they met when she came into his father's restaurant in Ovid, were the two signal fables of their marriage; they told them over and over. *I was so distracted by your mother's beauty that I put too much ice cream in her milkshake and it broke the wings off the mixing arm!* There was the window of the room above the garage where I had been conceived, my own bedroom where I'd spent all of my childhood, reading and drawing and dreaming. The front windows of the living room and the den were lit yellow and people were moving in that light, but they were silent and anonymous to me, and I knew they couldn't see me out there on the grass. I felt like I was visiting my life.

I walked around the side of the house, and there I saw a dim square of light lying in the grass — my father was in his study. I made my way to that window and saw him sitting in a chair at the side of the room, his black hair laid flat against his forehead and his eyes red and still. There was a man standing in front of him, talking, gesturing with his hands, his hat in one of them, which was moving in small circles as he spoke. As my father listened, his face seemed to expand, as if air were being blown into him, and his eyes diminished in their sockets until everything about him looked like it would both explode and collapse at the same time. The man was calmer, and then he just stopped speaking, and both of them were silent. The man brought his other hand up to the brim of his hat and he held it against his belly.

Then the man began to cry. He lowered his head and wept, and my father turned his face from him and pushed his lips together, and splayed his fingers over his mouth. It was the most awful thing I had ever seen. I had no idea what the man had come to say, but I believed that it could only have been that my mother had died again, that she had not survived even the relative safety of death, and they had lost her now for good. The man took a half-step toward my father, but then he turned and briskly left the room. I remained riveted by the image of my father's girl-like grief — his paleness, his damp shining palms, the shrinking in his body — but then I broke from it and quickly went back into the relative safety of the house. My father never came out of his study that night, and eventually, the food gone, the sainting of my mother complete, the guests milled out of the house. I didn't dare go into the study, but it had been a mistake not to go and be with him. I was the only one who may have been able to comfort him in the terror of his betrayal. If I could go back there as I am now I might have been able to comfort him.

I went into the shed. It was cold inside; the tin floor buckled under my feet. Some of the cracks in the walls had widened, and tiny drifts of snow lay on Martin's workbench. I felt, standing there, that I was in the cold ashes of a burnt building, and I quietly turned to leave, then leaned back inside to pick up something, anything, that could be brought into the house to keep me company. I pulled out Linwood Flats and took it out onto the lawn and polished the glass with my sleeve. The bare willows beside the creek swayed in reflection.

It was under a willow tree that my mother had died. Some three or four years after her death, my friend Beverly and I rode our bikes out to the spot where she'd crashed her truck on her way to deliver her strawberries to Cortland. I hadn't told Beverly that was why we were there, and she stood looking out over the fields and ditches, her hands on her hips.

It's a road, she said.

But what else?

A road and a ditch and an orchard. Some sky. A tree. She looked around, scratching the side of her arm. That's all.

To me, any person standing in the shade of that tree should have been able to feel the emanations of death in that place. Beverly knew how my mother had died, but only vaguely, and not that it had happened here, not that my mother had struck this very tree and sat against it, staring out at the fields, already mostly dead. I made us sit under the tree facing the road, pretending I needed shade. In the years since the accident, the tree had grown over its scars. It smelled of green life. Beverly chewed on a blade of sawgrass, her legs splayed out into the yellow fronds. You know a willow means water runs nearby, I said.

Well we're right beside Cayuga.

No, I mean a stream or something, I said. Under the ground. The willow has its roots in it, like someone reaching their hand down through your roof at night.

I took Linwood Flats into the house. I sat with it at the kitchen table. A box of simple construction, it showed the view from a street onto the wall of a red brick house. A wooden dowel topped with a sea sponge cut and painted green stood as a tree beside the house. Martin had painted red flowers all over the sponge. Springtime. The box was a window on a window: beside the treetop, another pane of glass looked in on a child's bedroom. The bedroom was empty, and the door to the closet opened on nothing. A valise stood in the doorway to the hall. You had to stand aslant to the box to see down the hall past the valise: a banister, a hall light (which was operational if you connected a wire from the back of the box to a battery), and then, faintly, the bare knees of a small boy, sitting at the top of the stairs. I knew, from the stories I'd been told, that the boy was listening to his parents in the kitchen below. The future unfolding in exhausted midnight exchanges. If you examined the scene long enough you eventually saw a tiny cigar box sticking out from under the pillow on the boy's bed. It had been Martin's keepsake box as a boy.

I rummaged in the hall drawer until I found the old nine-volt battery, twisted the wires from the back of the box into points and connected them to the terminals. The light in the childhood hallway came faintly to life and flickered. I turned the box in my hands, trying to see the child's face at the top of the stairs. But the light was not strong enough, the battery was old; I remembered it dying once already. After a few more moments (during which I noticed for the first time that the light cast a shadow of someone standing in the hall out of view), the light faltered and then went out with a fizz. The box lay inert in my hands again. A sick child drifting back off to sleep. I lowered my head against it. I had planned on packing the shed, but in the end, I couldn't go back in. I went and padlocked the door. Then put the key in an envelope addressed to Martin care of the On Spec Gallery in Toronto. *I don't mind if you come in here when I'm gone,* he'd said. What did he know about himself at that moment? Had I listened to the right thing? Did I ever hear what people were saying? I slipped the envelope into a mailbox. *I'm gone too.*

In the middle of January, in those dead weeks of winter, I plugged the phone back in. A storm had dumped more than eighty inches of snow on the entire eastern seaboard; the newspapers showed streets with rows of humped drifts, cars beneath run aground. I sat on the cool parquet floor in the front room and dialled Molly.

When she picked up, her voice sounded tired, like she'd worked all night. I listened to her say hello into my silence. There was a long pause. Then she said, I know it's you, Scott.

Scott? I said. She was silent, just breathing. It's me, Molly. Did you get my message?

I got it, she said.

Who's Scott? What's going —

Goodbye, Jolene.

My heart jumped into my mouth. *Hey!* Don't — Molly? I waited in the huge silence. Are you still there?

I told you not to give me that fucking thing.

*What* thing?

The artwork. The honeycomb.

Oh my god, Molly. I don't care about that.

It shows, she said. Maybe Martin knew that about you.

What are you talking about?

No doubt he discovered it was gone, she said. You made me a part of something terrible.

I was reeling, trying to hold together the seam of conversation. Just slow down, Molly. Please. I'm going crazy out here.

What right did you have to give me it? Did he tell you to?

No Molly ... but he would have been thrilled to know you had it. You loved it! I just wanted you to —

What? she said. You just wanted me to have one of your tablescraps?

You took it the wrong way.

How do you think *he's* taken it?

The one thing has nothing to do with the other!

Don't you shout at me. Her voice was a low, threatening rumble.

Molly .... obviously I've done something wrong, I said. I'm *sorry*, I am, I want you to tell me what I can do to make it right. But at this moment, I need to talk to someone, and you're my oldest friend —

I don't think we better.

Molly, please — I said, but I could suddenly hear my voice echoing in space. There was the sound of the disconnect — *tock* — followed by the soft, empty, long hum of the dial tone.

≈

In the last days before I left Bloomington for good, I felt as if the world faded out around me, gentled itself out of existence, as if *it* were leaving *me*. I slept on the floor, like an ascetic, and the sun crept across the wood, warming it and then me. I walked around the campus like I was already a ghost, the swirls of dusty snow blowing up beside the brick walls, the vines bare and black. I saw, one morning, that the shantytown was finally being dismantled; the university, on the grounds that it was too cold to carry on any outdoors experiments in democracy, had decreed the town at an end. Grounds staff pulled the shabby buildings down, protected from the protestors by a ring of hard-looking state guardsmen, their black visors pulled down over their eyes. There was no need for the show of force: the shantytown inhabitants, bleary-eyed from being woken before II a.m., stood apart from the dismantlers, blinking helplessly. In half an hour, the town was gone, and only piles of tie-dyed bags and clothing remained among the scattering of raw earth patches where the interiors had been.

The police as well as the protestors filed back into the denuded space, the former to inspect the belongings of the latter as they were claimed. Most of the evicted — well over a hundred people — milled about with their dew-damp sleeping bags drawn up around them. Some were still passing joints like cups of morning coffee, but it looked like the police were going to let it slide, knowing the protest, without its locus, was shortly going to taper to nothing. A few half-hearted cries of *hell no, we won't go* were heard, but they weren't picked up.

I went around the lip of the hill that formed one edge of the now-dead town and noticed a number of what were recognizably professors standing among the protestors. It was clear from the state of their deshabillé that they had not just arrived. Some boldly stood with their arms around pink-faced freshmen — mostly girls with their lace-edged shirts knotted up around their midriffs. There was no question of how those who had lived here during the fall nights had kept warm at night: three or four of the women were obviously pregnant.

The protestors stood where their buildings had been, around their foodstuffs, their pots and pans, their rucksacks. The dead little fires that had looked like miniature black craters half an hour earlier were flickering to life again, and some of the police moved back up onto the ridge. One of them spoke out of a megaphone, You are in violation of Code 18-91 of the State of Indiana. You are instructed to leave the area at once. Please return to your regular dwellings.

Right of assembly! someone shouted back.

You are trespassing on private property. You are in violation of Code 18-91 of the State of Indiana —

Fuck your code! came another voice, and a shudder of movement went through the place. In the distance, closer to the university gates, I saw a few of the state police move down the incline and take up positions at the back of the crowd. Behind them, a phalanx of cops on horseback appeared where they had been. There was a brief sweep of movement as half a dozen or so people tried to leave at that end and were pushed back — the time for reasonable action was now deemed over. A smoking canister of gas arced over my head and landed in the crowd in front of me. I got muscled aside by the cops descending the hill and the protestors rushing up from below. The river of people opened and closed around my body, and as I stood there, the air became warmer, like I was nestled in them, in their heat, in their longing to live the way they wanted to. The whole place was a buzz of love and destruction.

A couple of days later, my bus pulled out of the station and began driving out on Grover Avenue toward the highway that led north to Indianapolis. It felt as if some tether might pull me through the window and drag me back through the centre of town and campus, and then into the front door of the empty house on Service Road, and then through it to the locked shed where I'd left Martin's works abandoned. But the bus stretched this spirit line thinner and thinner until it seemed to break. I flattened back against the seat and I watched the breakfast places go by, Big Wheel, Denny's, International Waffle House, and the snow still coming down in clumps, floating in front of the restaurant windows filled with Texans or Californians or who-ever else was passing through that place that was, mostly, just a place in-between others. As it was, in the end, to me.

Grover stretched along the remnants of township: the very last restaurants, the few scattered flat-top buildings and busi-nesses, and then the stadium, rising red and immutable beside us. Finally, it was the Church of the Sorrowing Virgin. It slid past on the right, silent and still, the final mediating presence, the last chance for salvation before the highway. I looked out the window on it all, and I had that feeling you can give yourself if you say your own name over and over again until it falls apart in your mouth. And you think: Is this really my name? These bro-ken sounds, this air? Is this really me? Is this place my home?

I had decided on going to Toronto. So I could wait for him there, I thought. But I had already lost hope, and I realized, as the years began to pass there, that I had only chosen to live where I knew I was unwelcome, and so where I truly belonged.

# Dublin

# IV.

GOING UNDER, 1968. 3 @ 14" X 18" X 4" THREE-PART BOX CON-
STRUCTION. WOOD AND GLASS WITH FOUND OBJECTS AND OIL
PAINT. WORKING ELECTRIC LIGHTING. BERGMAN COLLECTION,
INDIANA UNIVERSITY, BLOOMINGTON, INDIANA. LEFT: A SINGLE
BUOY SEEMS TO FLOAT IN MIDAIR AGAINST A DARK BLUE BACK-
GROUND. MIDDLE: THE SEA, REPRESENTED BY LAYERS OF PAINT
AND GESSO, IN MANY SHADES OF BLUE. RIGHT: A SHIP LIES AT
THE BOTTOM OF THE SEA, OBSCURED BY WEED AND CORAL.

ONE WEEKEND IN OUR FIRST WINTER, WHEN MARTIN
and I met up in Rochester, we spent a morning in bed and I made up a game.
The Sunday Times was spread all over the sheets, the grey sky outside the
window making it easy to stay in the room. Here, I said, let's test how well we know
each other.

You don't think we already do?

We have our intuitions, I said. One of us will tell a story, and it has to start
out true, but end up false. And the other person has to figure out where it switched.
He shrugged. You go first, I said.

Okay, he said. I'm nine.

You're always nine in your stories, Martin.

It's 1937. I'm in hospital.

I already know this one.

It's a detail from a larger work.

I laughed and pushed some of the paper off the bed to turn around and watch
him on my back. I propped myself up on some pillows at the end of the bed.

It makes it hard to concentrate, with you all spread out in your glory like that.
Cope.

He grabbed one of the newspaper sections and draped it over me, then pulled
one of my feet into his lap and warmed it in his hands. Like I said, I'm nine, and
I'm in Temple Street. I've been there a couple weeks and I'm scared — a lot of the
children in the ward are still very sick. There's a boy in the bed beside me who's
probably eleven or twelve. He's started growing, he's taller than me. His parents
never come to visit; it's like they've left him there and forgotten him. But when mine
come, they bring toys and books for him too, which he never says thank you for. It

85

*makes me angry, but they seem to understand. I always feel strange, after they leave, when we both open our toys and start putting them together, or start reading books, and I know I have these things because my parents love me and are worried for me, but then what does it mean that they've given him things too?*

*Anyway, one night, long after the lights are out, I'm woken up by the sound of the boy trying to breathe. His chest is rattling and he's gasping for breath. I switch on the lamp beside my bed, and as soon as I see him, I'm horrified by the greyness of his face and I switch it off again. I pull the covers up and turn on my side, but then I think, no, he's almost my brother, this boy. So I turn the lamp on again. There's yellow stuff running down from his mouth. I get out of my bed and crouch on my knees beside him and I wipe his chin. He looks frightened. He says, I can't breathe. I tell him I'll get a nurse, but he grabs hold of my shoulder and asks me not to go. So I don't. And we sit there together. I see all the books and toy soldiers my parents have bought him sitting on the table on the other side of his bed, and I can't help thinking that if he's going to die, I'm going to take those things back, that I think of as my own. But I try to pay attention to the boy. I tell him, You're going to be all right. He nods. Then he coughs more of the yellow liquid, and it's flecked with blood. And it gets worse.*

*Worse how? I grabbed the duvet from the edge of the bed and pulled it around me, cowering.*

*He begins to quake in the bed. His hand is in mine and he's making me tremble. I tell him I have to get the nurse, but he won't let me, and his eyes are rolling in his head and he's breathing only every ten seconds or so, these huge gasping intakes of air that sound like someone forcing him to breathe through a tiny hole. And now I'm crying. I'm crying Don't die! Because I think, if a boy my parents have come to love — because I think it's love — if a boy my parents love can die ... then ...*

*Jesus.*

*And he dies. He dies with his hand in mine. And I draw the sheets back over him, and I get into my bed and I turn away and lie awake for the rest of the night. And no one else has woken.*

He leaned back against the headboard and let go of my foot, which slid down along the inside of his leg. I lay there motionless, staring at him. That's it? Some of that is false?

Yes.

It's the end, isn't it? That no one else woke up.

*No.*

*I sat up and the sheets and the newspaper went flying. But it's all true! I said. You've told me this story before!*

*A boy died in the bed beside me, it's true. But I never woke up. It all happened in the middle of the night. We woke up, all of us in the ward, and a boy had died.*

*I dropped my hands into my lap and stared at him. My god, I said. That's sick. You made all that stuff up about him dying in your arms? All that, that pus and shit?*

*You never said what we could make up. I know that's what happened, though.*

*How?*

*That's how we died. That's what got us, the tubercular ones.*

*I settled back down into the sheets. Don't tell me any more stories about tuberculosis or polio, okay? I feel like I'm in bed with Little Dorrit.*

*Your turn.*

*No. Let's not play again. Let's go out.*

He sat there, watching me. He'd told the story without so much as a shake of the head for that dead boy. Although the boy had really died. Sometimes it felt as if there was a colour inside him that could not be altered. Not by his own tragedies, nor by anyone else's. I wanted to test that, I realized, and I relented and took my turn.

*All right, I said. This is one of my stories. When I was a baby, my mother used to garden a lot. It was the thing she loved most apart from me. She'd put me in a hammock surrounded by pillows and while away the afternoon tending her vegetables and flowers. I think my first memory is of the tops of the maples swaying quietly back and forth across the sky. Then later, when I was five — I guess Dale was a baby then — she decided to start something new. I came home one day from kindergarten and she'd dug up the backyard, turned some peat moss and black earth into it, and she told me she was going to start growing berries. For money.*

*I see where your entrepreneurial streak comes from.*

*She had a friend in Ithaca who'd started her own business. She wasn't much of a fruit-grower at first, but she'd salvage what she got the first couple of summers and make some jams and maybe a pie, but then after about three years, her canes started to take. She'd had problems with bugs and birds, but she'd laid some mesh over the plants, and on a tip, she bought a box of ladybugs for the aphids. That's another of my earliest memories. Watching ladybugs fall from my hand into a patch of leaves.*

*So she started selling her berries at roadside in the late summer, and then she expanded to small groceries in nearby towns. My dad bought her a Ford with a big* flatbed when I was seven and gave her a pair of driving gloves, light green leather driving gloves. And then she got serious. She read books, she went to conferences for fruit-growers. She brought back white bags full of powder that she mixed into the soil. It was fascinating to watch her, my dad and I would stand in the kitchen window watching her empty great big bags of fertilizer into the soil. We'd all try to help her in the garden, Dale mainly tottering down the aisles trying to eat as many berries as he could. I guess that's a couple years later. I'd bring her tall glasses of ice water from the kitchen and lie in her lap between the rows. She'd sing "I Get a Kick Out of You," and I thought it was a song about kicking people. One afternoon, she got into her truck and started out for Cortland, which was thirty miles away. She'd been making that trip a couple times a week by that point. This is 1972 now. She had pints and bushels of raspberries in the back, and she was probably tired from kneeling and picking all morning. Nobody ever figured out what happened exactly. She drove into a tree out on Route 8. She went through the windshield.

Martin's face hardened a little hearing that. It was clear it wasn't the false part of the story, but he hadn't been expecting such a thing in my past.

She went over the hood, I continued matter-of-factly, and a few minutes after that, a local chicken farmer found her and she was sitting up against the tree "like she was in a church pew," he told us later, and she was looking calmly across the road at the orchards. Her sunhat was in her lap, and mayflies were stuck in the berry juice all over the hood of the truck. When there were enough people on the scene to carry her off the hood and bring her across the street to someone else's flatbed, four men crossed the road with her body high above their heads so they could watch for traffic. They took her to Cortland, I said. Where the hospital was. I stopped talking.

Well, I know what part I want to be untrue, he said.

Actually, it's all true, I said quietly. The part I was about to tell you wasn't going to be true, but I decided not to tell it.

He nodded. What was it going to be?

I was going to say that it was just one of those tragic things that doesn't mean anything.

Do you want to tell the real ending?

No.

I must have looked bad because he reached for me and pulled me gently across the bed and gathered me into himself. Later, we got dressed and went out for supper and spoke of other things.

By the fall of 1999, I had been living in an apartment on Havelock Street in Toronto for almost seven years. My backyard looked over a park where mothers gathered every Tuesday to stoke a stone oven that had been built there by the city. They baked bread in the oven and made fresh pizza for their kids, and afterwards they all sang songs together, songs my own mother had sung to me. The women outside my window would have been children when I myself had been a child and now they were mothers.

I'd bounced back and forth from one place to another over the ten years, going from a basement to a flat and finally to a house, as if I were coming out of a long hibernation underground. It would have been a good decade in which to suffer a loss if I'd been able to get into all the healing that everyone was doing. I had co-workers in therapy, neighbours in yoga, and I briefly knew a man who drank his own urine. But keeping busy and the passage of time were the only things that helped. Coming up on ten years since I'd left the country of my birth, strangers no longer automatically lowered their eyes from mine. I did not give off rads of grief. I wore normalcy like a lead shield and sometimes I even smiled at people on the streets (something that Torontonians found stranger than open bereavement). Now I was a respected member of a teachers' union. I bowled and I dated. Sometimes I laughed. And I was a citizen of another country, a citizen in *fact,* having given my motherland the old college try. In 1995 I'd become a Canadian.

The fall, of course, was always the hardest, and from September to mid-October, I was restive. My mother had died at the very end of summer, and the only man I'd ever loved had vanished at the beginning of fall. Perhaps fall to winter wouldn't have been so difficult, but passing over from the heat of summer to the cool comfort of fall brought with it the illusion that not all hope was lost. There were still leaves on the trees, still the sun shone down and warmed the earth. Winter had not yet arrived. But I sensed it in the air long before anyone else would have felt the cold bite.

Did I think of Martin? I must have, but I was not aware of it in the way a person might be if words or images went through their mind. Bits of conversation, or flashes of time spent together. My memory of him was more like a ring I'd worn for many years that I no longer felt on my finger, its tiny weight comprehended in my experience of myself. Sometimes I looked down (as it were) and saw it, and was surprised by it: *Is that still there?* And so it was, it was always there.

And the other person I had lost, Molly — I thought of her from time to time as well. But in the fall of 1999, I actually heard from her. I was thirty-four then, and had long stopped dreaming of ever seeing my oldest friend again, or understanding what had happened between us. She was in Ireland. She'd found Martin's artworks in a gallery there. She would wait for me if I would come. What she was doing in Ireland, she didn't say and I didn't ask. I just got on a plane and flew over. I'd been dating someone, a man named Daniel, but I couldn't explain what I was doing, and so I just went. But I left a note. I knew at least to do that.

⁓

The plane approached the west coast of Ireland, and an older woman beside me leaned over my tray table and peered out through the window. The well-worn green graining every contour of the island, the shadows of clouds slipping over and down the hills. The woman's ear was beside my mouth, like a lover's.

"Has it been a long time?"

She hadn't spoken a word to me the entire flight; now she nodded. She turned her face away a little, so I couldn't see her eyes.

"Maybe nothing's changed," I said.

It was fall in Ireland too, the persistence of green from the air disguised the season. But on the streets, it was cool, and the leaves were shading yellow and orange. At home the city had smelled of willow and rain, of late honeysuckle and patio espressos and there was the sound of cicadas, their anxious longing, a sound I'd never heard before coming to Canada. In Dublin, the air had a cold vein in it, and the sky felt close, like the city was cupped in someone's hand to keep the wind off a match.

I didn't want the taxi to take me right to the hotel — I was nursing jetlag and serious doubts — so I got off at the bottom of the street outside city hall, where college-age kids rolled past on skateboards and mopeds, looking like models from a mail-order catalogue. I had expected sloth and decay, but the rumours (the ones promoted by the in-flight magazine) seemed true: Ireland had caught a second wind. On my way toward Aungier Street, I counted three Internet cafés.

I pulled myself along, the buildings and houses packed one against the other, thin red-brick buildings with businesses below and apartments above, a press of life. On the corner of the next block was Spa House, as Molly had described. I looked over my shoulder for no reason, then back at the hotel, and I saw Molly sitting at a table against the long street-level window. I stopped on the other side. She wore a black sleeveless sweater and a green shawl around her neck. A long denim skirt and brown boots. Her hair, still long, was pulled back off her face, and fixed in a low pony tail so it swelled a little, a dark bloom of hair. She was warming her hands on a mug of something, staring out into the middle distance of the restaurant. There was nothing to do but go in.

She watched me come toward the table, not knowing what was the right face to show. So she watched expressionlessly. I took my coat off and draped it over my arms, a curtain drawn between us.

"Hi."

"Hi." I pulled back the chair across from her, but I couldn't bring myself to sit in it. So I stood, awkward between gestures.

"How was your flight?" she said.

"It was fine, thank you."

"Do you want something to eat? They have tea here, and biscuits, hard little biscuits."

"I'm not hungry," I said. She nodded, folded one hand over the other. She wore a wedding ring. "I don't want anything," I said to a waitress who'd come up quietly behind me, and was waiting with pen ready. Finally, I took my coat and lay it over the back of the chair. Molly's eyes followed me down. We sat facing each other, two feet or so between us. The last time we'd been this close, we were holding each other.

"Have you been here before?" she asked. "To Ireland?"

"No. This is my first time." She nodded and looked down at her hands. "How did you find me?"

"I did a search on the Internet for you. I found you on your faculty and then looked up your number. It wasn't that hard."

"Mm. And how did you find out about the exhibit? What are you doing in Ireland?"

"I'm here on business," she said quietly. "I just came across the gallery. I didn't know what I should do when I saw it. But I thought you had a right to know. Although," she added quickly, "I had no way of being sure you *wanted* to know."

"How did you decide then?"

"Selfishly," she said. She brought her wan gaze around to me again. "I thought maybe it'd be good to see each other again."

"*Really.*" She made a helpless gesture with her hands. "And is it?"

"I don't know yet."

We went up to the hotel room. An uneasy fatigue had taken over and I needed to lie down, to be alone with my thoughts. Molly had reserved only one room and I shuddered when she closed the door behind us. "Look," I said. "I honestly don't know what I'm doing here. I just want to say that. I got on a plane when you called. I couldn't think of what else to do."

"I'm sorry you felt pressured."

"I made my own mind up."

"I know. Whatever you want to do, Jolene, you just do it."

I sat on the bed and took a deep breath. She waited, her hands in her pockets. "Last time we talked," I said, "you hung up on me. Correct?"

"I hung up on you."

"You were angry at me. Which is fine. We were friends, and that kind of thing can happen to friends. But I figured when you were ready —"

"Slow down —"

"I thought we'd eventually work it out. But you never did call again, and I had to decide how I felt about that. Do you know what I mean?"

"I know that we're not friends anymore, Jolene."

"Ok," I said. "Whatever happened happened, am I right? We don't have to talk about it."

"If you don't want to."

She smoothed down her denim skirt and sat in a high-backed chair beside the window. There didn't seem like there was anything else worth saying right now, but she sat there, thinking. I wanted her to leave. "Have you thought of what you're going to say to him?" she asked me.

"No. I haven't gotten to that point in my mind."

"You probably want to think about it."

I nodded curtly. Love provokes all kinds of behaviour and in retrospect it all seems warranted: you have to allow for passions. Friendship promises something, though, and with time I could think of Martin more easily than I could think of Molly. "I'd better sleep for a while," I said.

She got up from the chair. "How do you want to work this afterwards?"

"What do you mean?"

"The gallery. Do you want me to come?"

This surprised me. "Oh. Well, you've been already, haven't you?"

"Yes. The show's down. I don't know if I told you."

"When would you have told me, Molly?"

"We can still find out whatever we need to."

"Fine," I said. "Why don't I go look into it when I get up."

"Okay," she said, her voice a little strained, and she strode for the door. "We'll talk later. When you get back from the gallery."

After she left, I slipped out of my clothes and got in under the cool covers. My stomach was upset and I felt anxious and harried. I got up and locked the door and then got back into bed again. *You're in Dublin,* I said to myself. *You're in Dublin, what the fuck are you doing in fucking Dublin?* I'd come completely unprepared; I'd have called it faith if I thought it was anything but carelessness. But what choice had I had?

I felt the old familiar milling of panic in my gut and I picked up the phone to call Daniel. But it would be 5 a.m. in Toronto. I badly wanted to talk to him, but at this urgent hour, I would have had to explain everything to him. So I put the receiver back on its cradle and lay there feeling exposed under the covers.

Daniel had appeared right around my tenth anniversary in the city, as a result of a fire drill at an evening class I'd been teaching, as good a way as any to meet someone, once you reach the age that the regular congresses (parties, bars, other people's weddings) have thinned out. I'd taken on work where it became available, since the things I specialized in were starting to get unfashionable around the time I showed up in Toronto. The evening class was a hybrid, something some smart person had thought up in one of the admin offices of the community college I taught at. For the first ninety minutes of the class, I came in and talked about literature. Then for the last ninety minutes, after a break, a real writer came in and taught a creative writing class. The two curricula were supposed to be linked, but the writer, a dandy with a cowlick, had his own agenda. I didn't care. I was talking about Euripedes and Donne and Shakespeare and I was cheerful. It was always thrilling to introduce young students to authors I loved, allowing them passage through me to poetry. But then Cowlick would come in, and nod officiously at me, and hand out his weekly wisdom. I usually got one of the students to pass along his circulars to me. The most popular of them was called "Please Don't."

Please don't set anything in a glade. Please don't make the dwarf the villain. Please don't call your main character "the boy." Please don't use the word "undead." Please don't speak of faeries, sprites, elves, nymphs, or anything translucent that speaks from a tree branch. Please don't depict epic struggles with wolves, bears, or whales. Please don't permit your characters to perform any nouns as if they were verbs. Please don't allow the detective to explain it at the end. Please don't use action verbs or texture adjectives in sex scenes. Please don't write sex scenes.

"Good books break rules," I told them. "Don't sweat it." And then we carried on reading. On the evening of the fire alarm, we were on Euripides' *Alcestis,* the story of Admetus, a man so loved by the gods that they aid him in a plan to cheat death. The plan is that one of Admetus' elderly parents will die in his place, but it turns out that even the old want to live, and it is left to Admetus' wife, Alcestis, to die for him. Students always applauded the courage and love shown by Alcestis, and when we were finished talking about her bravery and her sense of duty, I'd come in low with the bomb. "What sort of man would let his wife die for him? What sort of *jerk* wouldleave his children motherless so he could go on giving parties for the gods?"

They'd sit silently in their seats, looking down at their papers.

"It's okay," I said. "But do you see how Euripides fools us? We think he's telling us a story of sacrifice, but he's telling us one of cowardice. That's the mark of genius. To get you to put your faith in the wrong place in order to be shown your own failure of nerve."

We went back to the beginning, with a new understanding of the play, and I handed out the roles. It was a delight to have the old words spoken aloud. But then the alarm went off and everyone began bundling their things up. We went out into the quadrangle, following the stream of students in other classes, and I watched with dismay as most of them simply disappeared through the arch-way and into the street. But when I looked around me, my entire class was still present, looking at me for guidance, the dozen or so of them as sweetly helpless as ducklings. I rounded them up near a spruce in the corner of the quad and we all sat down and took our books out again. The alarm continued, dully, to sound. "Go on then," I told one of the boys. We were at the part where Admetus sends his wife off with poetry and tribute.

"My heart/ shall be against your heart," he read, "and never, even in death/ shall I go from you. You alone were true to me."

"Bullshit!" murmured someone else knowingly, and everyone laughed, in on Euripedes' game now.

"Right," I said, "nice send-off, buddy. He's telling her the consolation prize is that when *he* finally kicks, he'll let himself be buried with her! What a creep." I noticed then a man leaning, shoulder against the wall, about ten feet from us. He wore a brown suede jacket, his long hands hanging out of his coat-sleeves. I continued, "Anyway ... Alcestis goes. She does her husband's bidding. And it is a brave thing, a dutiful thing, to die. But what is the duty, and why is it brave?"

A young woman raised her hand eagerly. "Because if she says no, the children are next."

"Thank you, Alison. The children are next. What an incredible story is under the one we're being told." We'd gotten to the kernel of the play, and I knew they felt what I felt: Euripedes was alive. His mind was alive and we were talking to him. An aura of intimacy had joined us to him. Now, finally, the alarm had stopped and it felt like the air around us expanded to fill the silence. But we'd run out of time anyway. "Too bad," I said. "We'll finish the play next week."

They gathered up their things, murmuring amongst themselves, and they thanked me (to be thanked for teaching!) as they filed out under the archway. I slung my handbag over my shoulder. The man was still standing against the wall. "You a fan of the classics?" I asked him.

"Not really," he said. He pushed off the wall and strolled down the little incline toward me. "Unless you mean Otis Redding."

"He's a little after Euripedes," I said, and began walking toward the street. The man walked beside me. It was an easy thing. Without so much as introducing ourselves, there was an agreement that we would walk now for a little while together. I slowed my step. "You teach here?" I asked him.

"Yeah. A photography course."

"Which one?"

" 'Someday My Prints Will Come.' You know it?"

I laughed. "That's clever. Did you make that up?"

"No, it's true. I teach here. Although the course is called 'Taking Pictures Is a Snap.'" He smiled, enjoying himself, and walked with his hands in his jacket pockets now. He was a little younger than me, maybe not yet thirty, with warm eyes and a handsome, square face. His hair was messy, in a studied kind of way (I imagined him mussing it until it was right). "I know you," he said.

"Really? Where from?"

"U of T. I took your Milton and Donne courses."

I skipped ahead a step and walked backwards, trying to see if I remembered him. "You look a little familiar," I said.

"Daniel Silver. It was a few years ago."

"It would have to be. I haven't taught there since 1996. What kind of mark did you get?"

"I passed."

"Mm." I fell back in step with him, squinting up at him. The streetlamps were coming on."How tall are you, Daniel?" His face creased a little at that. "Careful how you answer."

"Five eleven."

"Were you going to ask me out for a drink? Talk about how you could have improved your mark?"

"I got an A. Must have been one of your weaker moments."

"This is probably another one."

❧

I slept for two hours and woke with my nerves jangling, a bolt of fear as I took in the room and remembered where I was. Molly had been back while I slept: there was a sandwich on the desk and a business card for the Hofstaeder Gallery on Dawson Street lying on top of the *Dublin A-Z*. I got dressed and went down to the lobby, looking desultorily for Molly in the lounge, but she wasn't there. I went out into the street, devouring the sandwich as I walked toward Dawson. I carried a vague memory of some of the streets I was walking in, and as I passed down York toward St. Stephen's Green, it felt as if the place shimmered in outline, like someone was lowering one rendition of the place over another. Flickerings of a dream glowed in the back of my mind (strange how some dreams remain impressed on the mind like books, while others seem like distant memories of places visited in childhood).

There wasn't much that would have matched this Dublin against the one I held in trust. That other Dublin rumbled with trams, street-sellers hawked flowers and fresh fruit; it was full of cobblestone and horses, a dozen daily newspapers sold by competing newsboys with their cries — *Ir -ish PRESS! Heggald here! In-ep-IN-en!* — everyone, including the children, wearing hats. *Little stores with knick-knacks on offer, all the boys on the street trading little lead cars, wind-up figures, soldiers made by Britains, the best toymaker in the world.* This Dublin was cleaner and brighter, although I had no doubt that *that* Dublin was clean and bright too, but in a way that was completely inaccessible to me. Dublin, to Martin, was all the world for the first ten years of his life. Its streets the sum of his longitudes and latitudes, its river the only river in knowledge, and its parks the wilds of the world. No, this Dublin was bright in the

way shiny things are bright; reflective not pervious. There were
tourist malls with American brandnames, streets closed to cars,
and the reek of European money and fast food. Nostalgia was
being sold in the shops along the Green, the bright windows of
the boutiques full of images of a rustic past. A pet store had
Celtic crosses to be hung from your cat's neck; tourists came out
of another wearing Guinness T-shirts over their sweaters.

I walked to the corner where the Hofstaeder Gallery sat above
the street, a bright space with glass on two sides. I got partway up
the wrought-iron steps and saw Molly sitting at the top. She looked
down at me, completely composed. "Did you sleep all right?"

"I looked for you," I half-lied, "but you were gone."

"I thought it might be helpful for me to be here," she said,
smiling. "So I decided just to come. I hope you don't mind."

"No," I said, flatly. "It's fine." We went through the door.
Inside, a girl in a black dress nodded to us hopefully. There
were two paintings up, on opposite walls, giant flowers glistening with dew. Clumsily erotic pictures, or blithely unaware,
perhaps. In failing to follow the trends of art, I thought them
blunt and stupid, but maybe they were cutting edge. We asked
for the gallery owner, and the girl, who must have been mute,
nodded again and went through a door in the back. A man came
out. He wore a brown velvety suit jacket that looked like it had
been made from a worn-out couch.

"Leon Hofstaeder," he said.

Molly reached forward before I could say anything and took
his hand. "Molly Siddons. This is Jolene Iolas."

Hofstaeder shook my hand, looking disinterestedly at us both.

"What can you tell us about this show," said Molly, and she
pulled a program out of her purse.

"Can I see that?" I said, but Hofstaeder took it, then handed it back to her. He opened his arms and gestured in a wide
circle around the room.

"As you can see now, the illustrious show of Mr. Sloane is
now gone."

"Yes," said Molly. "Where can we find him?"

"I haven't the foggiest. It was a rental," said Hofstaeder. "Mrs. Bryce paid the money, I cleared the walls, they went up, they came down, and that was all. I was in Derry the entire time eating chocolates and reading Patricia Highsmith."

"Mrs. Bryce?" I said.

"She arranged the show, brought it round, paid in valid tender, and took it all away."

"So you never met him."

"Never laid eyes on him. But I'm guessing he wouldn't have wanted to show his face. Mrs. Bryce paid five hundred pounds for the two weeks, and they didn't sell a thing."

I tried to clear the muck out of my head. Even being in a room Martin may have stood in made my head muzzy. "Why, uh …?" Hofstaeder turned to me and raised his forehead. "Why would it have been a rental?"

"It's always a rental here, my darling. Eleanor over there is the author of these magnificent flowers." Eleanor nodded once again. "It's like vanity publishing, someone with the means selling for someone with product. Very simple, and mutually beneficial." He narrowed his piggy eyes and smiled. "Usually."

"Why are you here for this show instead of in Derry, then?" Molly asked.

"You can pay a little extra for the presence of the owner. It can help sales." He pointed at a red dot under one of the two giant flowers and hooked his thumbs under imaginary suspenders. He spoke in the voice of an official arbiter of taste. "No doubt earlier examples of photorealism, especially those of unusual dimensions, will appreciate more in value over time without falling prey to the whims of taste. And more to the point, flowers will always be in, and very big, very cunty, excuse my French, flowers even more so."

"I didn't know photorealism was in," I said.

He pointed at the red dot and said nothing.

"Mr. Hofstaeder," said Molly. "Do you think Mr. Sloane

didn't want to sell his work?"

He put on a look of deep concentration, then inhaled sharply. "I always look at the art before I decide what to charge. Often I just do a commission and a minimum rental. Other times I opt for a flat rate, no cut. That seemed best with your friend's work. Whether he wanted to sell them or not is moot. They weren't going to, and they didn't. Sculpture yes, three-D no. That's all."

I looked at Eleanor. She was smiling like someone had a gun to her back. I asked him, "Did you know of Sloane before he showed here?"

"No," said Hofstaeder. "Never heard of him. Best ask this Francine Bryce. If she hasn't dropped him from the roster." Then, surmising he'd told us everything we needed to know, he shook Molly's hand again and walked straight back into his office. After a moment, she followed him in. I was alonewith Eleanor, who looked like she'd been dressed by her great-grandmother. Frills stuck out at her wrists and neck from under a velvet waistcoat. She couldn't have been more than twenty-two.

"Well, at least you sold this one," I said.

"Oh, it's not sold actually," she said.

"How come the dot then?"

"Mr. Hofstaeder says if you're going to beg for money, it's best to have a couple of coins in your hat already. It's encouragement."

"But what if I came in and this was the one I wanted to buy?"

"We move the sticker back and forth," said Eleanor. "Give them both a fighting chance."

Molly came back out, holding the catalogue out to me. "You wanted to see this, right? Don't lose it, it has Mrs. Bryce's address on it." She strode out into the street. I turned back to Eleanor, and not certain of the protocol, took two big steps forward and shook her hand.

By the time I followed her out, Molly was not in view, so I resolved to sit at the bottom of the stairs until she came back.

She'd left charged with purpose, like she'd just remembered seeing Mrs. Bryce sitting at a café table a few doors down. I wasn't sure what to make of Molly's courteous intrusiveness, but I decided the best thing to do was wait until the shape of everything became clearer. If all this was in the service of something unattainable, there was no point in putting up any opposition. But at the same time, I felt it would not take much to make me feel like I was being dragged into someone else's mania.

It was true I'd already begun to have flashes come to mind unbidden. Being in a hotel room inevitably reminded me of the good days at the beginning of my relationship with Martin, driving from Bard to the little inns throughout the state. Long weekends drinking coffee in bed and talking. I kept receiving flares of that other life — which I almost saw as the past now — as if I were walking by a window where someone I used to know was sitting, looking almost like their old self. Martin turning a plate of food so whatever he wanted to eat was closest to him. Head up high in the mirror, shaving his throat. The way, when reading a book, he'd have the page half turned before he'd gotten to the bottom of it, his head angled, like he was trying to get to the end before his hand flipped the page.

I took out the catalogue to examine it. The front featured the box called Everybody's, a vision of a store window full of toys and magazines. Martin had set it against a backdrop of the moon's surface, although you couldn't see the sides or the back of the box unless you came at it from an angle. It seemed like an innocent memory of a childhood shop. The artist's name was given as "A. Sloane, Antrim." Martin had no middle name, so the anagram left an orphaned "a," which was both careless and alarming, a forewarning that not everything was going to come together. I folded the catalogue in half and put it in my pocket.

Molly reappeared with two water bottles. "I thought you'd gone to round up the usual suspects," I said.

"My mouth was dry from talking to that jerk. Here —" she handed me one and I cracked the cap, took a long cold slug of water. Then I pulled the catalogue out and turned the cover up to her. "I'll tell you this," I said. "It's not possible that this piece was on display in this gallery. It's in a permanent collection in Houston."

"That doesn't mean anything. He could have made another one."

"Why?"

"Well, we could find out. This Mrs. Bryce is in Rathmines. We can be there in five minutes."

I looked at my watch. "I've had enough for the day, Molly. I'm sorry."

She squared her shoulders tensely, and then released them. "But you're going to stay. You've decided to stay."

"For now."


We walked down to the stone and iron walls of Trinity College and around them to the main thoroughfare. There it seemed the traffic never stopped, coming from three or four directions, gyring, swarming, bursting onto the main street. Some busts lined the avenue there, dead-eyed political or literary heroes forever watching over the traffic lights. It was deep in the afternoon, and the fall sun warmed if we walked directly in it, otherwise a cleft of cold air threaded the streets.

We walked, hands in pockets, watching the thrum of activity. This was where my taxicab from the airport had turned, revealing the high brick Georgian buildings. The morning seemed like a year ago. I'd come in wondering what Molly would look like, what we'd say to each other. Now, she pointed down a sidestreet beside a large black-glass municipal building. "That's Temple Bar down there," she said. "It's an area. Where all the hip young things go. There's a bunch of nice restaurants and dance clubs and a few singles bars. I wouldn't know what to do in one anymore, mind you."

"You wouldn't have to do much, I suspect." She looked sidelong at me, pleased to be noticed in some way.

"Are you single?" she said.

"Not really."

"I guessed you wouldn't be. You're a *catch*, as my mom used to say. I take it you're not married, though?"

"More on the dating end of the spectrum. But you got married, didn't you."

"I did."

"Siddons," I said.

"Yes. It's long over now." She didn't know how to gauge my interest, but she pressed on. "We got married in '90, we split up in '92. He cheated on me." I tried to look empathetic.

"Why did you keep the name?"

"Being wishful. Although it's just habit now and whether I'm Hudson or Siddons it doesn't feel like it matters." Christchurch appeared, with its stone ribs arcing into the ground. A dusty and forlorn place. "So what's your guy's name?"

"It's Daniel," I said quickly. I made a show of digging in my pockets for some change. "Which reminds me, I said I'd call." I nodded toward the other side of the street, as if that explained something, and then I started crossing. I checked for traffic and dashed over the median. Then looked back, and Molly was standing at the curb, completely still, watching me.

I stood in front of a phone, a monolith of steel with thick clumsy buttons on it. I wanted to talk to him. I knew he'd say something to take the edge off what I was doing. *You're fine*, he'd say, and I'd believe him. *This is no big deal.*

And maybe I'd get emotional, I thought. I don't want to be emotional. I don't want to hang up the phone and still be here. So I stood there with the receiver beside my head, listening to the mechanical buzz.

*I have to go.*

*You don't have to go, you just want to go.*

*No, I have to go. I have work to do.*

*I have work too. But I've got all the time in the world for you.*

*You see, I could easily stay on the phone another fifteen minutes, Jo, but then I'd just find myself back at this part of the conversation again. So what's the point.*

*To show you love me.*

*That would prove it, would it?*

*You're so thick, Martin. Even for a man you're thick. If you've got to go, go.*

*Well, I can't go now. It'd be like dying in sin.*

*I just have to say: I love being in competition with your work. I don't have other women to worry about, no no. I've got nails and glass and stuff cut out of comic books.*

*That's not true.*

*Tonight we talk to a woman who caught her boyfriend making out with a pair of wind-up lips.*

*You've got all of me, Jo. All of me. Heart and soul.*

*Do I.*

*You do. Can I go now?*

*Sure.*

*Except now I can't say I love you, can I? It's going to sound like I'm trying to cover my ass.*

*It would never have occurred to me.*

Molly wasn't where I'd left her. I walked a ways along the other side of the street until I saw her in the gardens of St. Patrick's sitting on a bench in front of one of the long walls of the church. In front of her, the miniature French lawns, with children walking the stone rim of the fountain in the middle. From the gate, her face was expressionless. She looked up after a moment and came over. We started walking down a sidestreet, back toward the hotel. "Everything okay at home?"

"Everything's fine."

"Good," she said. For a few minutes, we walked in a tense silence, strenuously pretending to notice our surroundings. Finally, she said, "Is there something wrong? "

"Like what?"

She shrugged her shoulders. "It's just ... this is awkward, like it's hard for you to be kind," she said.

I stopped, and she did as well, but a step ahead of me. "Kind?"

"Well, friendly, I mean. *Amiable* maybe."

I shook my head, but she didn't see me. "I didn't think I wasn't being *kind*, Molly. Uncomfortable, perhaps, but not unkind. Although maybe 'kindness' is sort of reaching for the stars here don't you think?"

"I meant just more friendly."

"Fine. I have an friendly question for you then. Why are we here? I mean, as opposed to me being armed with an address and a name and you back doing whatever work it is you're here to do?"

"You can do this on your own if that's what you really want."

I shook my head, looking down. I could hear the drift and weave of pedestrians as they walked near to us, opening and closing like a river around a stone. "You don't mean that," I said. "So far, you've just given me the illusion of choice."

"I'll go if you tell me to."

"Remind me how is it you've ended up here."

"Business," she said. "And I didn't end up here. It's a few days of work. I'm still a lawyer."

"You have a client in Ireland."

"It's a laser eye clinic. An American franchise. I brought papers they have to sign."

"I thought they had couriers for that."

"That's me: an overglorified messenger." I just stared at her.

She pulled the neck of her coat closed with both hands. "Well, I'll go then, okay?"

"I just want to understand how it is we've ended up both of us here."

She stepped toward me. "I know you must hate me," she said under her breath. "On some level — I'm not saying you think about me — just on some level. But even so, it would be good if we could talk a *little*." She waited for me to step in. "I know we're not friends," she said, "but I did call you —"

"Was that an act of friendship?"

"Well, it was *something*."

"I can't get drawn into this, Molly. I'm here for a couple of days and then I'm going home. Naturally, if there's something to be learned about Martin, I want to know. But apart from that, I don't know how I feel about any of this."

"But you *are* here. You decided to come and now you've decided to stay. So why not do some work?"

"On what?" I said, incredulous. I walked around her and continued back in the direction I believed the hotel to be in. I turned a corner, but after a few more yards it was as if my legs had filled with lead, and I found a bench beside a bus stop to sit on. It was the end of the workday now, and people were leaving the buildings on either side of the street, lining up for the bus, or else meeting with co-workers, friends, lovers, for the first evening drink. Then what? Dinner somewhere, or a movie, or back to the kids. Talking, or fighting; hoping for sex or good news. The big cycle of life in its glory and awkwardness. There were people walking slowly down the sidestreets, holding hands, or just ambling in alternating shade and light, their faces relaxed. I could still see the park, down a street to my left, its arboreal presence a form of omniscience. I imagined him skipping over the bridges there, a bag of nuts in his hand. Hiding from the world, running from it, going to visit the statue he loved of the man on the horse, King George. All the things that mattered were gone, the touchstones.

Molly came around the corner, walking slowly, as if she knew she'd find me tapped out on a bench. She sat down beside me and surprised me by taking one of my hands and holding it in hers. After a moment, I took my hand back. And then we just sat there like we didn't know each other. To the people around us, waiting for their buses, it would have looked like she'd just mistaken me for someone else.

V.

CHILDHOOD GAME, 1959. 15" X 20" BOX CONSTRUCTION. WOOD
AND GLASS WITH PAPER, FOUND OBJECTS, DOUBLE CHAIN
MECHANISM. CALIFORNIA CENTER FOR THE ARTS. A CRANK IN
THE SIDE OF A SHOOTING GALLERY ROTATES A SERIES OF ANI-
MAL HEADS ACROSS AN OPENING. BELOW, BEHIND GREYED
GLASS, THE ANIMAL HEADS TRANSFORM INTO HUMAN FACES.

A BLITHER OF HALF DREAMS, PARTIALLY SEEN FACES, distant sounds, and in one instance I was back in my childhood house methodically eating the furniture as my father stood by urging me on. When I got to the piano, I took it in a single silent mouthful. I opened my eyes, bleared, on walls that seemed to have sprung up in the night, the bare branches of trees from stories I'd been told as a child clicking against the windowpanes. It felt like someone had drawn my spirit out like dregs from a glass.

I'd gotten my own room the night before; it was the last single they had in the place and it was more like a horse pen than a room. I looked at the little clock on the table. It was already eleven in the morning. Molly was knocking.

"It's time to get up," she said through the door. "Let's meet in the restaurant, all right?"

"Fine."

In a moment she knocked again. "Just open up for a minute." I tipped the brass guard over onto its track and opened the door. "I'm sorry if I've made you uncomfortable last night."

"It's okay."

"I hope if I act cordial you won't think I'm being too friendly."

I tried to smile, and probably looked pained. "I didn't say we had to act like strangers, Molly."

"That's good," she said, "because we're not."

To be known: wasn't that what had driven me for so many years? To have rooms I could go through, full of people I had histories with, whose stories I could pick up, carry with me? This was true as a child, in the house warmed by my mother's hospitality, her talent for talk (so much of which I can't bring to mind any longer). Then the smaller worlds of Bard and Indiana, but still filled with the dailiness of connection. Letting go of all that, and the expectations that came with it, was what had made life liveable after Martin vanished. *Not* to expect any answers, or to have any inquiries made of myself; to live in the world without the clutter of shared histories. I imagined Molly now sitting at one of the hotel tables, smoothing a cloth napkin over her lap and running her lines in her head. To be truthful, I wasn't at all clear how I felt or what I wanted — I wanted peace between us as much as I wanted war. I wanted the peace of silence and separation, the resolve to keep my version of our friendship and my past to myself and never know what hers was. Since we'd been friends, she'd married and divorced. I knew nothing else.

Buttoning up my shirt at the window, I looked down at the bustle of the street, the whole mass of citizens and tourists oblivious to what those same streets had spawned. I felt weary, but no longer from the jetlag. It was anticipation-fatigue. I watched four people drop letters into the green mailbox at the curb. Mailing a letter is a highly personal gesture, despite its public aspect, I thought. The private letter is checked one more time for reassurance that the address is correct, as well as the postage, and the sender will slip the letter through the mouth of the bin, and wait to hear it drop into the safe darkness. It's a private gesture, forced out into daylight. The sender of a business reply will shove her letters through the slot, taking no more care with them than she would with something tossed into a garbage can. All these particular congresses made me despair.

All that communication lying in the dark of the mailbox, to be collected and sorted and coded and finally taken to proper destinations. A trusting commerce, a faith joined.

I went downstairs to the restaurant. Molly was sitting near the middle of the room, her back to me, and discussing something with the waiter. It was an animated conversation, and a couple of times, he agreed with her on something by leaning toward her, his hand on her shoulder. A cup of coffee steamed in front of her, and across the table, a pile of more than one of the daily papers. She had sat there, it was clear, most of the morning, waiting patiently for me to wake. It was hard giving myself special dispensation to dislike qualities in her that I admired. But I did it. And on impulse, I left the hotel alone.

I walked south, following Molly's *Dublin A-Z*, and went down toward the part of the city people called Rathmines. A bridge crossed a canal where a lush willow, still green, draped itself in the slow-moving water. Here, the city shifted to quiet suburb, the pace of things slower, the buildings better kept. If anything, it all gave me the feeling that I'd been flushed out into the open. I stopped in a small chip shop and ordered a soft drink and the lady behind the counter passed me a cup of water even as she drew my drink from the fountain. She smiled at me, and I shuddered. "Do me a favour," she said, "and do up your coat, love."

Outside, big maples (the locals called them sycamores) shaded the street with their colouring leaves. Crisp brown keys were falling now; they drifted over the sidewalks like commas; any two together pointing the same way looked like quotation marks, a secret natural speech underfoot. I remembered my mother splitting the sticky seed in two and pasting it to her nose and the two of us running around in the backyard pretending to be Pinocchios.

The schools were letting out for lunch, and uniformed girls emerged from one as I passed it, their knapsacks covered in corporate labels. Boys from a nearby school had already gathered on the other side of the street, smoking and trying not to look too obviously at the exodus of sweet-smelling bodies, the red hair flowing down backs, socks slipping down to ankles. At the edges of the two groups, some casual pairing off had begun, movement both chanced and determined, like clouds forming, although the already serious lovers had simply broken rank with their groups and quickly found each other, consulting their watches and turning their cellphones back on. All that ritual normal to them, to be repeated every day until it turned into something else.

I went down Rathmines Road and turned on Belgrave, past the little Trinity church marooned on an island in the crux of four streets, and down Palmerston, an undulating road canopied with chestnuts, identical houses all the way to where the road turned. Mrs. Bryce's distinguished itself by means of a Fra Angelico blue door, otherwise it was a clone of the others. I imagined Molly back in the hotel, knocking on my door again, becoming at first worried and then angered, maybe. And then I just forced her out of my mind. *You won't have your way there,* I thought. I went up Mrs. Bryce's walk toward wide granite steps and saw a woman crossing in the front window. She stopped and looked at me with confusion. I paused on the front walk, and as I waited trying to figure out how to present myself, the front door opened, and she stood there in an apron, as large as a furnace, her wattled arms crossed, looking at me with frightened eyes.

"What do you want?" she said.

I looked down at the catalogue and confirmed this was the right address. "Are you Francine Bryce?"

"No," she said, her voice quavering, but she didn't move to close the door. She stood in the verge, stilled by fear.

"I don't mean to be any trouble," I said, "but I've come as —"

"As what."

"I was given this address by Leon Hofstaeder." I was now on the landing, having cautiously climbed four black steps, and stood only feet from the woman. Her hair was parted flatly on top, yellowing near her scalp and curling stiffly to its white ends. Her skin was almost grey. "I'm looking for Martin Sloane." I held up the catalogue. "You represent him, don't you?"

"What do you want with him?"

"I need to speak to him."

"What did he do to you?"

"Oh," I said, "it's nothing serious. I just need ... do you know where I can find him?"

"I don't," she said with some finality, and she closed the door, leaving me staring at a filigreed mail slot. For a moment, it felt as if someone had just snatched something out of my hands and my body tingled all over. Proximity. I pushed the slot open with my finger and peered into the hall. Mrs. Bryce's body was vanishing around a corner, the backs of her calves bristling with veins. I saw a cat looking down imperiously from the side of a staircase, and then two more walked out of the room Mrs. Bryce had gone into.

"Mrs. Bryce? I really need to speak to you. I've come from far away to get in contact with Mr. Sloane and I'd be grateful if you could spare a moment for me." A scent of decomposing paper and yellowing magazines wafted through the slot. I waited, and then let the little metal lip clank shut, and stood back hoping the door would open. It did not. I repeated Mrs. Bryce's name into her front hall and waited again, but this time when she didn't answer, I just tried the door, and finding it unbarred, walked in.

The smell of old, browning paper and wood intensified in the front hall. Mrs. Bryce crossed the hall through another doorway without seeing me. I heard her footfalls descend to the basement and then the sound of a radio rose up from below. I walked quietly down the hall. "Mrs. Bryce?" I called. "The door was open. I really don't mean to bother you like this." Something touched my leg and I startled: another cat walking past and then sinuously down the stairs. Beyond, there was a kitchen table that was clearly never used for eating. It was piled with newspapers and magazines. A chair with torn vinyl seating (from which sprang vilely discoloured fluff) was loaded down with a pile of magazines called *The Pestle*, and many ragged newspapers. A headline I could see from the hall read "Motion Pictures Immoral: Decency Legion." Half-eaten tins of catfood were crisping on most surfaces.

I went into the room I'd first seen Mrs. Bryce enter and was surprised to see another woman, this one slight and bony, sitting dwarfed in a thick leather chair beside a bookcase. She was looking out of a window onto the back garden, her face expressionless, her entire body limp except for the arm propped up by an elbow on the rest, and which terminated in a cigarette. Behind this woman rose the pale spines of ancient hardcovers, tooled leather, faintly golden titles stamped into them. I would have spoken but for the shock of seeing the very artworks that were illustrated in the Hofstaeder catalogue, plus three or four more. These were boxes I knew as well as I knew my own handwriting, arrayed on tables, on shelves, carelessly laid flat or turned so their contents might suffer sunlight. The woman said nothing. I moved, unable to control the impulse, to the box nearest the door, an artwork that had been pictured in the catalogue and that I knew as Carriage. It was in the Art Gallery of Washington, one of Martin's most prestigious sales. I lifted it up, flicking anxious glances at the old woman, but she was as still as death, frozen behind tendrils of smoke.

The boxframe in my hands had been poorly mitred (Martin had always been meticulous about his corners and angles and often sent back entire batches of wood if the carpentry wasn't perfect) but the insides were the shock. A plagiarism would have shown an attempt at exactness: this Carriage was not making any effort to be mistaken for the "real thing." The parts were subtly different: the iron wheels on the original had been carefully sourced by Martin, whereas these were plastic, and off a child's toy; the hands at the top of the carriage door were laminated magazine cut-outs, not doll parts. There was no map on the bottom of the box. But the carriageman's lamp, which in the original had a sprig of gold tinsel for light, here had a tiny Christmas tree light in it. I turned the box around to find two thin wires connected to a battery duct-taped to the back of the box, and tamped one down to the terminal. A yellow glow played against the palm of my hand. An improvement? Evolution? I glanced nervously at the motionless woman again. What the hell was this? The hair on the back of my arms stood up. This Carriage looked different than the original, but it imparted the same secret longing, the same sense of hope as yet unthwarted. But where was the map, the narrative of the lovers' journey? It was an eerie absence and it made me feel outcast from it, where the original, built for me, had been nothing less than a love letter.

Now, I saw the old woman looking at me. She had on the shut-in's loose, stained housedress. Her cigarette had burned down to a cylinder of grey ash two inches long. I put down the box and found a crusted ashtray. She watched me approach without fear, a flicker of a smile on her face. She was pleased to have a visitor. She allowed me to take her wrist and direct her hand over the ashtray.

"Who are you?" she said.

"My name is Jolene Iolas. I've come from Canada."

"Good god," said the woman, and she looked at me more fully. "Has it occurred to you to cut your hair?"

I looked at her in shock. "Do you know me?"

"Of course not," she said. "Anyone can see you need a cut. Fetch me another cigarette?"

I let out a breath and searched through the things on the folding table beside her. Pill bottles lay on their sides around a glass of discoloured water and a Bible. The cigarettes were on top of the Bible. I took one out, put it in her mouth (which she had, like a helpless nestling, already opened) and lit it. She took a short draw, then held it in her hand, as before, where it slowly burned.

"What's your name?"

"Jolene Iolas."

"Are you Greek?"

"Half." She held out her hand. "Francine Bryce," she said, smoke drifting out of her mouth. "Where is Lenore?"

"She's gone downstairs."

"She's doing the laundry. *Lenore!*" she called, and we both waited for an answer, but the radio was probably all the other woman could hear.

"Do you need anything? I can get it for you."

"No, no. I just wanted to let her know we had a visitor. We don't have a lot of visitors. What time did you get up this morning?"

I kept up, jumping cognitive logs. "This morning? Nine, I guess."

"Mm," said Mrs. Bryce. "I haven't had a sleep-in in years. Lenore gets me up early." She shrugged, as if this was a problem any sensible person could help her with.

"Why don't you ask her to let you lie in awhile?"

"She thinks I'll die."

"Oh," I said. "Why does she think that?"

"She wants the company in the morning, so she tells me if I sleep in I might die, and so I get up and keep her company. She was always an early riser, Lenore, even when we were children. She used to call me lazy. Can you imagine?"

"No."

"Well, early mornings do my head in." She looked over at the cigarette, squinting at it, not sure what it was doing there. "What is your name?"

"Jolene."

She smiled at me, the bright trusting smile given by babies as well as people who have been removed from society. I gave back a crooked, uncomfortable smile. "I've come from Canada," I said. "I've got a couple of questions for you." Mrs. Bryce settled back into her chair, and her face clouded a little. I tapped her knobbed finger over the ashtray to knock off the ash, and saw a scorched circle on the carpet directly below Mrs. Bryce's hand. "I don't want to impose on you, but I've come a long way and I need to know a couple of things."

"Are you from Taxation?"

"No, I'm from Toronto. Canada, as I said."

"Because I wouldn't be able to lie if you were, I think lying is a dreadful habit."

"I'm not from the government."

"All right then, what do you want to know?"

I gestured around the room. "These artworks, they're copies."

"Yes, I know."

"And you're the artist's agent? You arrange to have them put on display?"

"That is what my existence has come down to, yes."

"Why, though? Why can't he do it himself?"

"Oh, he used to, but when we —"

She was interrupted by a fit of coughing, and it took a few moments for the spell to pass. She held up a hand to let me know to wait, and she closed her eyes. The eyelashes over her right eye were stained yellow, whereas the ones over the other eye were as white as her hair. I was anxious that her sister would return, but I hurried into the kitchen, dodging cats and cans of food, to fill a glass of water. I brought it back in and held it to her mouth, and she gulped it in long draughts, the skin on her neck shaking. She held her hand up again, and sat against the back of the chair, catching her breath. Unable to remain politely attentive, I looked at a couple of the other boxes. None of them had any of the business that Martin had habitually indulged in. He would often paper the exterior backsides of his boxes with newsprint, or restaurant menus, or letters people had written to him, little asides to himself connected with some memory tangential to the content of the box itself, a sort of material free association. Martin liked that there was an aspect to his work that most people would never see; it constituted a communion he had with it that no one else did. Most usually, he signed the boxes on their backs, but none of these were signed. Pond was here, but with only six feathers, a strange oversight that made me suspicious. I held it at eye level, absolutely straight, and saw that the lip of the bowl (which Martin had filled with crushed glass and resin) hid what was behind it, where the seventh feather would have featured if the person who had made this thing knew that there was one. I put it back down. Mrs. Bryce was waiting patiently for my attention.

"Are you all right now?" I asked her.

"I forget ...," she said, and looked up at me, imploring.

"I wanted to know why you arrange exhibitions for Mr. Sloane. What he wants in showing this work."

"He wants it to be seen, love."

"But it *is* seen. The originals are in galleries throughout North America."

"Dear, I just do what I've been told. I'm duty-bound." She waved the cigarette in a tiny circle, then muttered, "Not that anything will come of it."

At the word "duty," the penny dropped. Martin would be around this woman's age now: they were contemporaries. He had reached the age some of my friends had warned me of; I would still be a young woman when he was old, they told me. Some had even had the terrible presence of mind to tell me that he had spared me a prime-of-life with nothing but fragile companionship. So this was how it would be. Perhaps I would be permitted this with Daniel one day, I thought bitterly, a precarious life riven with duty. A hollow was opening in my chest, a feeling that the conclusion to this matter had already been reached. "How long ago did you marry?" I asked quietly.

"Almost eight years."

"But you call yourself Bryce."

"My first husband. All my friends know me as Bryce. Mind you, they're all dead." She fell silent, thinking. "I suppose it wouldn't confuse them now," she said quietly. "Francine Sloane." She finally took a drag on her cigarette, and I thought

I could hear the sound of the smoke driving open the clenched passages of her chest. "So obviously you knew Martin," she said, exhaling yellow air.

The sound of his name, in her mouth, made me feel weak. "I did once," I said. "In America."

"You were close?"

"I know. There was a bit of a difference in our ages."

"A bit."

"We went together for a few years. I probably shouldn't have come here."

"It's understandable why you did. It must have been very difficult for you."

"So you know that I need speak to him."

"Who, dear?"

"Martin?"

"Oh, well, yes, that's what this is all about, isn't it?"

"Is he in Dublin?"

"No. Oops," said Mrs. Bryce, laughing. Her ash had toppled onto the back of her hand. She held it out as I manipulated her finger over the ashtray, and she looked at me, lovingly, it seemed. "You're a beautiful young woman," she said. "If I had help like you, my life would not be in danger every second of the day."

"Why is your life in danger?" I asked distractedly.

"We're just two stupid old women. Do you think my sister can lift a fire canister? I might well burn the house down," Mrs. Bryce whispered, leaning toward me. "You better make sure she hasn't fallen down the stairs, dear."

"I don't think your sister would be happy to know I was here. I'd better just go."

"You'll come back, though? And bring some fish and chips?"

"Yes," I said. I just wanted to get out. The oppressive thickness of the smoke, the hopelessness of the room. I wanted to run.

"My sister is not so well in the head," Mrs. Bryce said, groaning. "She thinks the king is Jewish. Can you imagine?"

"Which king?"

She frowned at me. "The king of Ireland, dear."

I took the smouldering remains of her cigarette out of her hand, which she watched with sad dismay, and then I stood away from her. I righted one of the boxes that lay flat on a table. It was a box with loose sand and hidden pictures. I couldn't remember its name. I placed it in its correct position. The head of a mushroom peeked out. "I'd better go," I said. "If you could just tell me where can I find Martin?"

"My lord!" barked a voice behind me, and I spun around to see Lenore standing in an attitude of shaking terror. "Francy?" she cried out.

"I'm here, Lennie. We have a visitor."

"What do you want?" said Mrs. Bryce's sister. She held a wire brush tightly in her hands. "We've nothing for you here."

"I'm sorry," I said. "I don't mean to frighten you."

"I turned you out," she said.

"I know, and I'm sorry. I needed to talk to Mrs. Bryce."

"Francine?" the old woman cried again. I stepped aside so she could see her sister was okay.

"She's fine," I said. "She's had a cigarette, you see." Lenore remained frozen to the spot, only her eyes moving, shooting back and forth between her sister and myself. "I'm going now, though."

"Yes, yes," said Lenore. Mrs. Bryce raised her hand to her sister.

"D'you know, Lennie, she's bringing fish and chips!" she said happily.

I started out toward the front door, and Mrs. Bryce's sister stepped backwards and flattened herself against a wall to let me pass. "I turned you out," she said quietly, in disbelief. I stopped in front of her.

"You've no right deciding who your sister can and can't see," I said. "I came on important business. I have every right to see her."

"He tossed her away like she was garbage!" she said, her voice rasping, so her sister wouldn't overhear. "I take care of her now!

I do! He can't send his messengers here."

"I'm not a messenger," I said, but the old woman was frantically waving her hand in front of her face and shaking her head, as if to make a bad dream go away. "I'm leaving, all right?" I said, and I pushed away from her, my face burning, and went to the door. Lenore followed and I opened the door on the bright day outside and felt the flat of the old woman's palm on my shoulder. "Don't touch me!" I snapped, but then she was shoving me out of the house. I grabbed ahold of the railing to keep myself from falling down the stairs, and still she kept pushing with the force of her anger and fear.

"Get out! Get out! Get out!" she kept shouting. I flailed an arm behind me, striking at her, the other gripped the railing tight.

"I'm out, for god's sake!" I shouted back at her, and then she was quickly back behind the threshold and the door was slammed shut. I heard her footsteps hurrying back down the hall, and I took the steps to the street, my legs wobbly.

*I stood in the shed with him, his back to me, his hands busy with something unseen.*

*His things scattered about, still unpurposed.*

*An old croquet ball, yellow and red, the paint around the middle chipped.*

*A wax parchment envelope, smaller than a child's palm, containing a deck of tea cards from the turn of the century, birds of Ireland: stonechat, mute swan, pied wagtail.*

*A horn from a phonograph, patinaed in a golden floral motif.*

*Two iron garter pins.*

*One sleeve from a 78 RPM recording of "That Old Virginia."*

*The feeling, the certainty, that you cannot know anyone. Not if you love them.*

⁓

I got on a bus back out on the main drag, the early-afternoon sun lighting up the trees, the leaves as singular as mirrors. Turning colour but still drawing down heat and light, the desire to live attending. I wanted nothing more than to get back to the hotel and get into bed, but of course the bus turned and headed off toward St. Stephen's Green, which omen I accepted as being part of my comeuppance. The park came into view and I gave in, pushed the stop button and stepped down into the bright square of streets there, the taxis zipping by on all sides, and I crossed to the green. I walked into the park, where the sounds of traffic fell away almost immediately, and I took a seat at the edge of a wide circling path, and gradually, above my throbbing head, the sun moved. (Did I sleep? Did I stare off into the trees?) I watched children feeding the swans on the far side of the pond. In fairytales such regal birds, but in life, feral. They snapped at the children's hands, at each other, and gulped the food down as if they'd die in moments without it. I remembered hating domesticated wild animals when I'd gone as a child to the petting zoo in Rochester with Dale still in my mother's arms. The sloe-eyed baby lambs, nearly dead from gorging on ice cream and bread, the disgusting llamas and the threadbare donkeys sway-backed and depressed, purulent sores on their knees. All of them covered in the urine-soaked woodchips, caked in cotton candy and bits of red candy apple. Dale had been attacked by an enraged swan when he tried to feed a duck some popcorn, and it had beaten my father with immense wings when he tried to free him. I shuddered, recalling the filth.

My thoughts turned to how I would explain this outing to Molly. On the way to Mrs. Bryce's it had occurred to me that the morning might provide the very thing I had come to Ireland for, but now it was clear I was only at the beginning of a winding path, and that I would have to take Molly on it with me if I wished to continue. Stopping altogether did seem a much more sensible thing to do. I went to see Martin's wife, I'd say, it didn't turn out that well. I'm going home now. A man who was sitting at the end of the bench folded his paper hurriedly and began walking away. "Was I saying that out loud?" I called after him. "I'll be quiet, you can come back." He went off down the path.

A nut vendor rode past and I bought a bag each of chestnuts, peanuts, and candied almonds from him. I tucked the two hot bags under my shirt to warm my middle, and I chewed the almonds. The park was emptying out. Unaccountably, my heart got heavy for Toronto. It was no longer the cold city I'd once been warned off of. I'd gone there to wait for my life, and although Martin never returned there, my life gradually did. The city became my home, by default. But here, for all I knew, there were murderers lurking in the trees with poets; astronomers crossing the park for their hotel assignations; lost children no one would ever look for. Was there a search for me taking place? How would I be described? Young? Plain? I hoped they would note my full-bodied sandy brown hair, my long graceful neck. *Woman with kissable neck goes missing.* Otherwise, no distinguishing characteristics, except for this black hand that reached out for me from the past.

From the bench, I watched swans cutting Vs through the calm water and I felt those wings on the back of my head, the lift and heave of a body settling. To be carried off. To be anywhere but here. The atmosphere in Mrs. Bryce's house had been too much like the house I'd lived in after my mother's death, where my father's grief floated in the corridors like the smoke from a dead blaze. For almost three years after she died, our father kept the curtains in the house drawn so that the rooms were always yellow with strained light and dust hung in the air. Apart from Basil Thompson, the piano tuner (who came once every six months by prior arrangement, even though no one played), there were no visitors to the house. My father ate alone, read alone in his study, went alone to church. When he spoke to us, it was to run down the list of things we had to do to survive. Had we eaten, had we washed. Did we go to school. Answering in the affirmative released us from these discussions, and he would slouch off afterwards to one of the parts of the house we never went into.

He still slept in the marriage bed, and there were still the thick yellowing doilies folded over the back of the couch that had been there for my entire life, although after 1975, I don't think they were ever washed again. My father's Chrysler was the only really obvious victim of time. It sat behind the house on deflated bald tires for years after my mother's death, both windows on the driver's side smashed, and the magenta paint faded to maroon from seasons of sunlight and rain. One spring, we found a kestrel nest tucked up under the chassis. We'd seen the mother flying under the car, back and forth. She thought the car was a fallen tree, I told Dale.

My father no longer worked at the restaurant, but let his manager, Tom Darling, take over the business while he occasionally looked at the books. One night Mr. Darling came over and begged Dad to sell him the business before it went under. My father agreed, and afterwards he still did the books for the restaurant, but apart from that all activity stopped. He became a full-time mourner, and only the sound of his adding machine ratcheting grimly down the hall in his office gave proof of his existence. Sometimes he served me and Dale supper, then stood back leaning against the kitchen counter and smoking. When our plates were empty, he'd lurch forward and give seconds. Silent but for the clank and splat of food being served and eaten, these were the loneliest times of my childhood. All three of us in one room, and not a word spoken.

If we got sick, an aunt would mysteriously appear, down from Syracuse, and stay the week, mechanically going through the nighttime actions our mother had once done with tenderness. Temperatures taken, the bittersweet chewable children's aspirin given in a paper cup. Ginger ale going flat in a glass on the back of the toilet in case we got up and were thirsty.

Seasons went like this, punctuated by Basil Thompson's visits. The first time he came, I'd watched him anxiously from the corner of the room, knowing that he'd been hired and was there by permission, but still frightened he would upset whatever balance there was in the house. He struck the wires with his tuning fork and tightened or loosened the strings, reaching around the front of the piano to test the keys. The sheets of muscle in his old back moved under his shirt and a bloom of sweat filled the dried stain that had soaked his shirt at his last appointment. When he was finished, he took a grease pencil out of his pocket and bent down under the keyboard. Then he became still, and poked his head out, told me to come over. I went to crouch under the keyboard with him and he was holding down a note with something written on it. It said: "BT 12/6/39." He moved his hand along and pushed down another key, and a deep, hon-eyed note sounded in the wood behind us. He wrote "BT 01/10/77" there. His handwriting was shakier, the line thicker. He played the higher note, and the two sounds twisted behind and above us. That's my whole life, he said.

When my father died, many years later, Dale and I went up to Ovid and buried him beside my mother. The casket weighed almost nothing at all.

He faded out, said Dale. We let the groundsmen lower him into the earth. He waited a long time to be with her again.

I hope she'll be where he's expecting her, I said. Later that week, we got rid of what was left in the house. My father had long before closed the lid of the piano's keyboard and locked it. It was still locked when we buried him, and we sold it like that, without the key.

A young girl was standing in front of me, her hands behind her back. She teetered a little on her heels, watching me. "Why are you crying?"

I shook my head. "I'm not."

"Are you sad because you're old?"

"I'm not *old*," I said pushing my palms across my eyes. "I may be to you, but I'm not old."

"But you're sad." She regarded me with a little girl's untrained frankness and then sat down beside me. "Because if you cry and you're not sad you're either very happy or you're crazy."

"I don't think I'm crazy, and I *know* I'm not happy, so you must be right."

"Will I sit with you for a while?"

"I don't know, will you?"

She looked out into the trees, apparently thinking, then swung her stick-like legs and turned her little porcelain face to me. "Yes."

"You're here pretty late, aren't you?"

"This is a safe park." She was eight, maybe nine, with a mass of badly cut short blonde hair on her head, so thin it stuck up at her crown.

"Does your mother know where you are?"

"It's all right. I'm going back soon." She was looking up at me with eyes that seemed black in the dim lamplight of the park. I hadn't noticed the lights coming on — it had somehow become dusk. I felt cocooned with the girl. Her hands lay folded in her lap, and she gazed out at the shadows of the trees, and beyond them, the moonlit pond that stretched down the north half of the park. Fat swans waddled past us on the grass.

"They shouldn't eat so much," she said. "They get too heavy to fly."

"I think their wings grow along with them."

She thought about that, and looked down at her feet. "My father says they fly away in winter. They go somewhere nice."

"Maybe they go to France."

"Maybe." I looked over at her, and she was sitting quietly now, her hands covering her knees. The dress was a little soiled around the hem. She looked up at me, eyes bright with a thought. "The lovely thing is they come back, isn't that true? The very same ones. My father told me they remember how to come home because they follow the stars."

"That's probably true."

She looked deeply satisfied to have her father's knowledge seconded. "It probably is," she said.

"Have you had dinner?" I asked her.

"About five hours ago."

"I mean supper."

"Oh. Well, there's a party tonight, later. Mrs. Beaton is making fried fish."

"Are you hungry?"

She buried her chin in her chest and shook her head.

I passed her a few still-warm chestnuts. She sheepishly took them, and started cracking the shells in her teeth. I watched her eat with a strange pulse of love running through me. I wanted to touch her hair, which glowed in the light of the lamps. As if sensing this, she reached a hand out to me, palm up, and I gratefully took it. It was small, cool and damp, and she wrapped her fingers around the top of my hand. A sense of peace enveloped me, like a drug seeping down. We sat like that for what felt like many minutes, not speaking. Then my hand was empty. She was standing in front of me.

"Gotta go," she said.

"Wait." Against the pond, her slight child's body had turned dark. I stood and reached forward and took both her hands in mine. She resisted, but I pulled her toward me, and when she emerged again into the light, she was a little boy. I drew him against my stomach, and I held him there.

"I have to go," he said.

"Tell me *why*." I pushed him back until I could see his face again and he stepped away. "I don't understand."

"You think I didn't love you," he said.

"It doesn't matter what you felt anymore. I want to know about the rest of it."

"The rest is gone," he said, and he shrugged. "I have to go now."

"Go where."

"Where I live. Iona Road."

"I know that," I said bitterly and waved him away. "Go," I said, and he moved off down a path between trees.

# VI.

DIARY, 1963. 10" X 6" X 4" BOX CONSTRUCTION. WOOD AND GLASS WITH FABRIC, CARDBOARD, FIBREGLASS. ART GALLERY OF ONTARIO. A BLUE CURTAIN, PULLED BACK BY MEANS OF TWO DOWELS PROTRUDING FROM THE TOP OF THE CONSTRUCTION, REVEALS A LIFE-SIZE HAND HOLDING DOWN THE TOP OF A MINIATURE CIGAR BOX WITH ITS INDEX FINGER. ENLARGED NEWSPAPER AD DISPLAYING DEPARTURE TIMES OF S.S. ST. LOUIS ON EXTERIOR BACK OF BOX, WITH MIRROR-IMAGE SIGNATURE.

WILLIAM HAD A CRICKET IN HIS HAND, BUT HE WAS refusing to show it to anyone. They were all standing on Iona Road; Devon was there too, and a boy named Clark they were trying out. This was outside the Beatons' (number 74), and Martin knew to ignore William when he was like this, but Devon and Clark were red in the face from shouting at him. Down the road, outside number 16, Mr. Warren — the mouse-faced lawyer — opened his front gate and pulled it to. He got into his car. It started quietly; it was a car they said in the ads was the quietest car on the road (Chrysler advertised their Saloon cars the same way — smooth motoring, quiet motoring). Mr. Warren began driving toward Drumcondra Hill and when he came to the little roundabout at Iona Road and Iona Park, they saw his head dip down. Later, the police said Mr. Warren had dropped a piece of toast. The car slid into the roundabout, very slow, and at that moment the cricket jumped in William's hand and he dropped it. It whirred like a sycamore key and landed in the grass as a car belonging to a Mr. Craigie (number 43, Lindsay Street) struck Mr. Warren's car on the driver's side. All four of the boys saw Mr. Warren's body jump across the other seat, and his head popped out the window on the other side just before the car rolled over, trapping him by the neck. It was very still as the car lay there on its side in the grass circle, the only sound being Mr. Warren's feet kicking against the passenger door. He thumped five or six times, then stopped. The crash had sounded to the boys like someone stepping on a paper cup.

William and Devon and Clark rushed to the circle as Mr. Craigie stepped from his car and righted his glasses on his nose. Martin watched the four of them push the car back on its thin wheels, but he didn't look at what was going on in the grass circle.

His head was resting on his shoulder, William later said. The two were best friends, their bedrooms pointing at each other over the street. But the angle, it looked like someone else's head was asleep on Mr. Warren's shoulder.

Was there blood? Martin asked.

No. There was butter, though. On his mouth.

The police had come and spoken to Mr. Craigie (who the boys believed would likely be placed before a firing squad, an idea that excited them), then the police spoke to the boys themselves. It was decided between the boys that Clark would no longer be allowed to play with them. He was bad luck. An ambulance came and took Mr. Warren away.

He was broken in two like a stick, said William.

Martin knew why there hadn't been any blood. It was because the body was made of a soft solid like the middle of a sponge cake, and the body's skin was only the dry outer layer, slightly tougher from touching the air. Blood was a lie, though, blood he had no faith in. If it were true, why didn't everyone look like balloons full of water, bulging at the bottom? The whole idea of the body being a container for organs and liquids was beyond ridicule, and was clearly something instigated by adults to get something they wanted out of children. There was the bogeyman to keep you from bothering them after eight o'clock at night, and blood (invoked as a punishment for climbing trees or playing with knives) was the same type of thing, although Martin wasn't sure what the benefit was to the adults. Some people had even spoken of blue blood, which made everything even more unlikely.

These beliefs obviously began to trouble Martin's father, who took him to see a doctor named Gorda. Martin's friends were all afraid of Dr. Gorda, because he had hair on his ears and practised mostly on animals, but Martin had no choice. His father had selected the good doctor to help his son over this problem of blood and guts.

The doctor, a man as old as any Martin had ever seen, took their coats in the dusty front hall (there had never been a Mrs. Gorda, hence a number of rumours about the animal doctor had flourished), and the three of them went into a room with a fireplace. It smelled bad, like old empty bottles, and they couldn't see much of anything until Dr. Gorda switched on a lamp. There were framed diagrams on the wall, and a little table with crinkled butcher's paper laid on it. The old man reached for something on the mantel, saying, Let's start with this. It was a jar, and inside it was half a leather satchel floating in milky water, and inside the satchel was a bundle of pale grapes or tiny yellow plums, Martin couldn't tell. He noticed also that the satchel had a hand.

Oh my god, his father said.

Martin tried to run out of the room, but the doctor had him by the scruff and pushed his face toward the glass. We're trying to answer your question, boy.

You've cut it open, Martin said. You could have put anything in it.

It was a baby. Just a little baby. Dr. Gorda pointed at things and said their names. The poached egg in the middle was supposed to be a lung. The little ball of clay a heart. Pancreas and spleen, he said. There were noodles coming from the baby's head, and coral beside its split nose. Its eyelid was closed, but it was almost see-through. It was an excellent model, Martin thought, no longer afraid. In fact, it was fascinating that someone had made such a thing. Little white wisps were coming out of it. The doctor put it on a table and Martin sat with it, now mesmerized, staring at it while Dr. Gorda and his father smoked cigars. Next, the doctor showed Martin pictures. He pushed his fingers into Martin's skin, saying that the things in the pictures were *under* his skin.

This under here looks like this, he said, showing Martin a fogged round grey thing in the book. A stomach, said the picture. And this — poking Martin in the back — the kidney looks like this.

The bit about kidneys Martin happened to know wasn't true. He'd seen them in butcher shops — they came from pigs. Dr. Gorda tugged at his pantswaist and pointed. And that ... he turned to another page ... is this.

The doctor was pointing to a picture of a cooked sausage lying on a piece of stained cheesecloth. Martin wondered if Dr. Gorda believed that these things were inside his own body. As a doctor, he might have. Like priests believed in God. Martin said, I must have been wrong.

Dr. Gorda clapped him on the back. That's a good boy.

The room had filled with smoke. His father was standing with his back to the jar and the books, and there was a blue cloud around his head. As they put on their coats, Martin started to laugh, but stopped because laughing was what had gotten him there in the first place.

There would be no further challenges to his beliefs about the body until he was a couple of years older. Then, at the age of nine, Martin succumbed to tuberculosis. At the time, it was believed to be carried by pigeons, which were now hunted down in all corners of the city. The sickness started innocently enough, with a light rattling cough and a mild fever, but progressed quickly to breathlessness and a wracking cough that produced a filmy phlegm speckled with blood. Soon he was unable to stand under his own power and they brought him to Temple, the children's hospital on Temple Street. He remembered the hospital because sometimes he and William would walk in the back and feed the pigs in the stalls behind, or offer to polish the horses' bridles with Brasso, which put up a scent that made them light-headed. The pigs were Martin's favourites, though, and the largest of the swine had moustaches that would brush against their palms when they fed them bread and apple cores.

The hospital was full of children and nuns; nurses in their ghostly white costumes swept back and forth against the blue-and-burgundy parquet floors. His mother and father waved to him in the corridor and then someone opened a door behind them and they flashed to shadow. The nurse put a needle in his arm.

He lay in a hard, thin bed. He was frightened and tired, but sleep was no respite from fear. He might be awakened by a sound from the ward, an oddly echoing sound that could resolve into a scream or a moan or, once, to his own sobbing. Other times, one or another of the medical staff would awaken him by taking his pulse (and then his hand would seem very far away to him), or by the sting of a syringe being put into his arm. An older boy, one from school who usually bothered him by following him home and calling his name, appeared on the ceiling early one morning before the sun came up. Once Martin had seen him, the boy walked down the air to the floor and started walking toward him, beating a stick against the metal posts at the ends of the beds. But before he got to Martin's bed, he changed his mind and instead stood at a distance intoning Maaaartinnnn Maaaartinnnn in a high voice. Then he turned and walked though a child asleep in her bed, and a sidetable, and then out through the wall.

Are do if lake come to say? asked the doctor.

Martin twisted his head away and felt a sharpness in the inside nook of his elbow.

Wander in harm's sleep, said the doctor to a nurse.

Yes, she said, and then leaned down to Martin. Matter? Motion liffey come.

He fell asleep. In the middle of the night, he woke and sat up. A glow was coming from each of the beds, and he got up and walked through the ward. The light came from the middle of the bodies in those beds — and he noticed also from his own — and he saw that this light illumined the insides of things. Shadows curved away from skin, globules of pink matter throbbed and shuddered. There seemed to be a grey mass twisting through everything. The children's ward, he saw now, was nothing less than a living larder filled with many tiny red clay hearts and poached-egg lungs. Two kidneys each (the same number as pigs — that wrought an unpleasant connection), miles of involuted tubing, wet brains white as chalk all bound up like rope, all of it pink and damp and giving off light.

Somehow he returned to his bed, and time began to pass again, milling days and nights out of itself. Soon he began to hear church bells, but he couldn't raise himself enough to look out at the grey Dublin stone. One night, the boy in the bed beside him started groaning and crying, but then Martin drifted off again and the sound fell past him. The next morning, the boy's bed was empty. A girl across the aisle from him said, He's gone.

He's lucky, Martin said.

The girl was one of the older ones. She tilted her head at him. The boy is dead.

No, Martin said, he's gone home.

He was inside his mum once, she said, like she was reciting a nursery rhyme, and lived in a house. Everything is inside something else, even the air. But now that boy's in a box and he's in the ground. A worm will eat his eyes, and a bird will eat the worm, and then he'll be able to see his mum from the sky.

Later Martin asked if he was going to go into a box.

I don't think so, said the doctor, and laughed.

I want to be fed to the pigs, he said, and his mother's eyes went round. I don't want to be inside a bird.

The boy was dead. Then a girl died, and another, the one from across the aisle. They took her away and she had only one shoe on, a black one — he could see it under the blanket, and her other foot was bare and dark-coloured like a black currant lozenge. The missing shoe was still under the bed across the way. Church shoes. It was wasteful to leave one behind.

What do you say, Theresa? His sister was standing beside the bed, holding their mother's hand. Theresa's mouth was covered with a handkerchief.

I hope you come home soon.

I'm almost better, he said, but his sister was looking away at some of the other children in the ward. Three have died.

You might still, she said, sniffling.

Theresa! their mother said.

But I haven't. He wanted to reassure her, but she was distracted. A couple of her friends were here, too.

Do you have something for your brother? their mother said. Theresa gave him a box with a wooden puzzle in it. She'd earlier put one of the pieces in her pocket, and later, she would drop it in the street. Their mother closed her hand over his. We'll all be home as a family again soon. You'll see. Then later, a nurse came by.

You have some nice colour, she said.

A few days later, he could see the weather was changing. He could see the steeple of a church, the Abbey over on Frederick Street. The Dublin winter giving way to a brighter light. It was nearing the end of April. Sometime soon, the boys would begin to gather at the edge of the Royal Canal, dipping their fishing lines in, or jumping right into the cold, black water. It was only fifteen feet across when it went under Phibsborough Road, and slow moving, but once or twice a year a boy would drown and his body would turn up floating by the cattle yard down by the Liffey, or would be fished out near Sir Rogerson's Quay. William told Martin he'd once seen a boy holding on to a leash float past under the bridge at Drumcondra Hill. He was face down, William said, but once when he told the story, the boy was face up and his eyes were white and there was a dead dog at the end of the leash.

Lying in his bed in the Temple Street Children's Hospital, Martin didn't care what happened to careless boys out at the Royal Canal, he just wanted to *get* there, get out there and bake under the sun, with the water like a sheet of glass at his feet. Such imaginings were possible now: that morning, he'd been told his parents would collect him to take him home that afternoon. A vein in the crook of his elbow was black from needles. He'd convinced the nurse with the hair on her nose not to prick him that morning. I'm much better, he'd told her, and she'd taken pity.

It seemed as if all the children were getting better at the same time. The last two nights had been fairly quiet, no crying, no rasping coughs. It was as if the weather were changing within the ward as well. It put him into such a good mood that he offered the girl in the bed beside him a candy from his tin. (She had appeared there after the boy who died.) Her name was Nuala. She was from Clontarf, but her father said this was the best hospital in the city and she was to come here to get cured. She said the girl with the black shoes had come from her school.

What was her name? Martin asked.

Elizabeth, said Nuala. She was going to be the first girl reporter for the *Irish Times.*

It was sad she died.

Yes. It runs in her family. Her father coughed blood and died in a bed they set up in the front room. Her mother hasn't been well ever since, and now Lizzie. Nuala clucked her tongue and Martin heard the candy tick against her back teeth. His stomach hurt, like he was going to have diarrhea. If he had died, would his mother die? Would his father?

She must have died from something different than her father, he said hopefully.

No. I think it was the same thing. Blood in the lungs.

That scares me, he said.

You're better, though. You escaped this time.

Yes.

They sat silently in their beds. He could see her out of the corner of his eye watching him, her head tilted in concern. One day, she'll be a good mom, Martin thought. She was older by a few years. There was a small rise under her shirt.

Would you like me to come give you a cuddle? she asked.

No, he said hurriedly. I'm going home today.

But she slipped the covers back from her bed and padded over to him, pulled his covers away from his body. She was much larger than him. I can see you need someone to take care of you, she said. And anyway, the nurses aren't coming with lunch for another fifteen minutes.

She angled the pillow so she could lean back and pulled his head down onto her shoulder. Her nice-smelling gown was warm and fuzzy — her parents had brought it from home and insisted that she be able to wear it at night rather than the hospital-issue gowns. He slowly let his weight fall onto her shoulder and she shook her head so her hair covered his face. He knew some of the other children were watching them and his body was stiff against hers. Theresa was sometimes nice to him like this, but she hadn't been lately. When he was getting sick, she'd stopped being kind to him. Nuala was younger than Theresa, but the older-girl warmth, the smell of a girl's skin, comforted him. He began to doze off. Some time later, while he was sleeping, she slipped his head onto the pillow and left the bed.

After lunch, his mother and father appeared, and they had his spring coat with them. They drew the curtain around as he put his real clothes on: the brown slacks, the white undershirt, the yellow turtleneck.

We'll stop in for a chocolate at Goldman's, said his father. His face was bright with happiness and he was wearing an excellent hat with a rim made of fur.

Theresa is waiting in the hallway, said his mother. She's looking forward to your homecoming.

The three of them got up to leave the ward and Martin felt like a king carried out on his dais. He turned and waved goodbye to Nuala, and she waved back. He had the sudden thought that maybe she had lied about her parents in Clontarf. Maybe the dead father and the bed-bound mother were hers, not the dead girl's with the black shoes, and she was alone here. But then he went through the swinging doors and Nuala was out of sight, and he knew he would never see her again. Theresa joined him and their parents in the hall, and took Martin's hand like she'd been told, and the four of them left the hospital triumphantly.

Outside, two men in black overalls loaded some pigs onto a truck.

❧

The walk home swelled Martin's heart. Lord, the sky! The big grey stones of the Mater Misericordia Hospital catching the late April sun! And the sun! So much of it, and so rare for this time of year. The cars went past tooting and the horses lowered their heads. He loved the horses even more than he normally loved them.

Hold still! said his mother, walking backwards to take a picture of them.

They went in to Goldman's and Martin picked a chocolate with crisps and raisins in it, and Theresa had a block of nougat. Mrs. Goldman rubbed Martin's cheek with her hand.

What a lamb!

Martin's father wanted to make a detour into St. Joseph's Church, to thank the Virgin.

Colin, their mother said, you're not taking any child of mine into a church. Even to thank the Virgin.

He's half a child of Christ, love. We shouldn't push our luck now.

What if it's the Christ half got sick?

All the more reason to thank the Virgin for prayers answered.

They argued like this for a few moments; Martin and Theresa had been through these attempted detours many times. Their father still clung to his stray hope that he'd get the four of them into a church one day. As usual, they saw his shoulders slump a little and their parents walked back toward them.

Why don't you make one of us Catholic and one of us Jewish? Theresa asked. Then there won't be any more of this half and half business.

And which would you be, Theresa? asked her father.

I'd be Catholic and Martin would be Jewish. Then there'd be one of each, a Jewish boy, a Catholic girl, a Jewish mum, a Catholic dad.

I think not, said Adele. We don't need to be divided against each other. Lord knows there's enough trouble already. You can still thank God, Theresa, without praying to the Virgin.

But I like the Virgin. She has a pretty face.

There would be no more discussing it. They turned up the street and walked straight home, but Martin's father said in his mind, Hail Mary full of grace, the Lord is with thee. Blessed art thou amongst women and blessed is the fruit of thy womb, Jesus. Pray for us sinners now, and at the hour of our death. Amen, and they all knew he was doing it because his lips were moving. Adele nudged him with her elbow and shook her head at him, but she was also smiling. That was the way of their family.

He stood at the gate of 77 Iona Road and looked up into his window and his heart felt like it was going to burst. His mother held the gate for him like he was the Prince of Wales and All That He Surveys. He turned and saw that William was standing in his window, waiting for Martin to go up and stand in his. They went into the house. Upstairs, Martin stood in his window and waved to William, and William saluted him, as if everyone had been told to treat Martin like he was royalty.

It was a day for returning to the things of life. Standing at the windows and recalling the views; counting the rooftops, the stop signs, the church spires. Martin took in the riches of his things: his books, his cast-iron double-decker bus, his cigar box full of keepsakes (for which he had designed an ingenious false bottom). He touched his bedspread, his walls, smelled the empty hamper, and it all rushed into him like the world swooping down into his body, like the world returning to him. He was well; he was not going to die. He was going to live.

That night, one of the doctors from the hospital came. It had been arranged earlier. Colin Sloane sat with his back as straight as a rod and their mother kept one hand on his leg. The doctor took the chair across from them, his gloves folded in his lap. Martin was better, but he would not stay better in Dublin, he told them. The air was too polluted and Martin would need cleaner air if his lungs were going to heal permanently. They would have to leave Dublin and live somewhere else. It was put simply so none of them could misunderstand what he was saying.

Martin swivelled his head to take in the room. His parents were looking at the doctor. His sister's eyes were as black as coal.

❧

Galway was one hundred and twenty miles away. How were they ever going to get their things from Dublin to Galway?

Martin picked the string off the page and laid it down carefully again, making it hug the little blue road on the map book. Now it was one hundred and twenty-five miles away. Getting farther away with every passing minute. He was sitting on the front stoop, peevishly refusing to box even his own things, his adventure stories, his tin soldiers, his cigar box. His mother called from inside:

Martin Samuel Joseph Sloane!

And he twisted his body away from the door. She came to the window.

Are you deaf?

I'm not.

Then get inside and do what I asked you to!

She slammed the window down, and he felt part of the front stoop quiver as she walked past inside and went up the stairs.

They were moving to Galway, and it was all his fault. It was the fault of the Dublin air, but it was also his fault for the way he breathed it, or perhaps for the way it breathed him (for he remembered the way the dead girl had told him all things were within other things, even the air). He kept replaying the awful events in his mind, trying to isolate the one thing that, if he'd done it differently, he wouldn't have gotten ill, he wouldn't have gone to the hospital, and the tall doctor with the soft black gloves wouldn't have come to the house.

He'll be prey to all manner of respiratory predations, I'm afraid, the doctor had said.

The next day, Theresa had broken the silence over their porridge.

But we live *here*, not anywhere else.

It's not where we live, their father said. It's that we're together and we're healthy.

But you make hats in Dublin!

They have heads in Galway.

After that, Theresa had taken to slamming doors. He would walk to the bathroom in the morning and hear Theresa jump out of bed, run to her door, and open it in time to slam it as he went past. Sometimes he'd be in his own bedroom, and the door would suddenly open and then slam shut.

Risa!

He bothers me!

For Christ's sake! (And then their father's voice: Adele, I've told you about that! ) And Martin shouting back:

I'm not doing anything, though! He opened the door to his bedroom.

You! she hissed. You are going to wreck my whole life! She was red-faced in her thin nightie, and he could see the knuckles on her toes whiten as she clasped the top stair. Why didn't you die like the others, and let us get on with things?

He knew she didn't mean it, but it stung him just the same. They were moving to Galway, and it was his fault. His father had told him that people desperately needed hats in Galway, and it was a good opportunity for them, not bad luck. Martin tried to picture what Galway would look like, and hoped that when their car turned off the road and came into the city, that they would see a bare-headed populace, and he would begin to feel better about himself.

His mother put on a record, and the voices of two women floated out of the window and into the street —

> sous le dôme épais,
> sous le blanc jasmine,
> ah! descendons ensemble!

Sometimes his mother's voice would join theirs, breaking in to the parts she knew by heart. It was a sound of home, and it made him sad. He bounced a ball on the bottom step and watched it rise again and again into his hand. He waved at a man who rode past on a red bike.

His father came home with his brown satchel, and put his hand on Martin's head, then leaned down to his ear and whispered, It's just a patch of bad luck. It hurt Colin Sloane to see his son sitting outside the house. He went inside and the front stoop quivered a little. His father hung his coat in the closet, then walked over to the banister and hung his hat, as he always did, on the newel post. As if to say to anyone who visited here that this was the domain of a man who made hats. Martin always thought it funny that when he would walk home with him from the shop on Grafton Street, his father would tip his hat to people in such an exaggerated way that the label would show. Always be ready to sell; everyone is a potential customer, he'd say.

Martin heard his parents talking. His father was telling his mother that he'd found someone who would make them a new table for the new house. They would leave this one behind. That gave Martin a pang of grief, since it was the table he had eaten at for his entire life. He did the math quickly in his head. Since he had been able to hold a fork, he had eaten at that table over six thousand times. It was simply wrong to say they would leave it behind!

He leaned in toward the slightly open door. It's in the basket, his mother said. He saw his father shaking his head unhappily. She put her hand on his. Now stop saying that, she said. Give me a pencil, she said.

Then it was quiet, and Martin knew they were discussing the future. They were to leave in three more days, and it was all because of him. He could hardly believe that in three days, this part of his life would be over, and all because he was cursed with a bad chest! He was overcome with the urge to beat his own ribcage with his fists, shatter his ribs and tear out his lungs. He realized he pictured them as lungs, not the fuzzy blurred sacs he'd seen in the bottled baby but as purply-blue shimmering lungs. Pictured them inside his body, hanging in his ribcage like a cluster of berries. The tightness in his chest and the liquid he would cough up seemed to come from the same place. He believed in the body now, but the belief gave him no solace.

Theresa came up the walk dangling her schoolbooks. It was five o'clock, and the sun was beginning to go down behind the Church of St. Columba's.

Move, she said. I'm going into *my* house.

Don't slam the door.

I think we should stay in Dublin and you should move to Galway and get bitten by a snake.

St. Patrick got rid of all the snakes, he said.

She leaned down to him; he could feel her breath on his ear. He put them in *Galway,* she said, and she went inside, slamming the door, stomp stomp stomp up the stairs and then she hurled her books at her bedroom wall. Martin felt all of it through the wooden door. It vibrated with every heavy footfall and his spine absorbed the movement and sent it up his neck and into his skull. He tried to block out the life of the house behind him, and he looked at the houses across the road. Over the roof of his best friend's house, the rim of the sun was vanishing. He imagined that from William's bedroom window, it would still be visible, hanging like a huge lamp over the city. Martin watched the last sliver of sun until he couldn't see it anymore. It turned his friend's house into a dark blot.

The door opened and his mother came out into the air.

It's getting cold out here, she said.

I don't mind.

It'll soon be dark, and then it'll be even colder. He didn't answer her, but he let her fold his fingers into her palm. Just the touch of her hand could induce him to cry, and he looked down at his feet. Even at the age of nine, he knew the warmth of her hand, the smooth, dry surface of her palm would be something he would long for when he got older.

He turned to her, and she saw he was about to cry. She loved his face like this, and sometimes, seeing his emotion, she would want to break into a smile.

Nobody asked me if I wanted to leave, but it's still my fault.

It's no one's fault, Martin. It's this nasty great cloud of air we have in Dublin. It's Dublin's fault. We'd have to leave here one day anyhow. It's expensive to live in a big city.

We'd stay longer if I were well.

She brought him close to her, and she smelled of her good soap. He buried his face in her neck and let his tears come, but quietly, and she held him.

Do you know that there is going to be a coronation the day before we leave? May twelfth and a new king, King George the Sixth. They're going to broadcast the ceremony around the world, so Buby and Zaida Mosher can listen in Montreal. He'll have the same name as the king on the horse in St. Stephen's, did you know that?

He sobbed quietly that he knew. The equestrian statue in the green was called George the Second. It was his favourite.

They're going to have a parade of white horses and there'll be bishops and princes lining the streets outside the palace. Do you know that I stood in those very streets in 1910 when I was nine years old? And watched beside my brother King George the Fifth crowned? This king's grandfather? That was a day in London! And my brother and I fought because my brother had a larger piece of salt-taffy. It made Buby Mosher very sad to see us fighting.

Did you see the king?

I did. He waved to me.

Martin laughed and wiped his face on his mother's chest. He liked that they were talking of England. It was a subject his mother couldn't talk to just anyone about, even though it was her whole childhood and life up until she met their father. When she talked about the streets of London, or her family's house in Holland Park, her voice became slow, as if the words and names were coming out of the past and gradually taking shape in front of her. She felt about those places in her life the way he felt about his own streets and rivers and greens. He wanted to be the only person she would tell these stories to.

So, she said. Do you think we can keep the peace in Buckingham? We have one king, one queen, one prince, and one princess. Will we manage?

He said a quiet yes, because it was true he wanted there to be peace. The yelling and fighting was wearing him out. He wished for things to be the same as they had been before, when he and Theresa would pitch quoits on the back lawn, and sometimes, when he was lonely in the night, he could knock on her door and she would move over so he could sleep in her bed, and she would be as kind to him as Nuala had been in the hospital. Recently, he had felt very lonely at night, when it was so dark outside his window, but he knew his sister would not give him any comfort, not now, when he was taking her home and her friends away.

Is he sick again? called William's mother, coming up her walk. She had shopping bags hanging from her arms up to her elbows.

No, Phil. He's just a little tired.

I'll bring over some of my soup in the morning. Does he want to visit with William after supper?

We'll see, said Martin's mother.

Mrs. Beaton went into her house and Martin took his tear-streaked face off his mother's shirt. When I'm better, we'll come back here, all right? he said. And everything will be the same.

For now, you look around and keep everything in your head, so we can make sure things are the right way round when we do come back. Every tree, every lamp, and every window. You can keep it all in here, she said, touching his forehead. It'll be safe here.

*When,* she'd said. His heart had thrilled at the word.

# VII.

LINWOOD FLATS. 15" X 17" X 3" BOX CONSTRUCTION. WOOD AND GLASS WITH FOUND OBJECTS, DOLL PARTS, FABRIC, PAINT. BELIEVED DESTROYED. THROUGH A WINDOW IN THE SIDE OF A HOUSE, A CHILD'S ROOM CAN BE SEEN. BEYOND THE DOORWAY TO THE ROOM, SOMEONE SITS AT THE TOP OF THE STAIRS.

THREE WEEKS AFTER I MET DANIEL, I WAS WALKING around the wood-floored living room of his one-bedroom flat and listening to the streetcar grind the tracks on Dundas below. It was the middle of the night and the lights of Chinatown flashed yellow and green against the back of the room, bands of greeny light warping along my stomach. Somehow night windows make you feel invisible to the outside world, although you know from looking out of those very same windows that you're not. Still, your nakedness at two in the morning feels like a natural state, like men crying in the silence of darkened rooms. Animals we tend by day stalk and kill other animals in that kind of dark.

I moved around his space, taking in the things he filled his life with, or that other people, trying to reflect him back at himself, had given him. A row of antique pearl buttons fixed to a card and framed. An ex-lover, I assumed, either complimenting him on something she liked or criticizing him after the fact. And the books, always tell-tale, and the coffee-table tomes by photographers, the good ones, and the painters too that one has to know, if not like.

On a high shelf, there were the books assigned in my classes. I'd believed him when he told me but still, it was nice to be reassured, and I opened up the *Collected Donne* and read his marginalia. My scholarly tics were reflected there: Donne's apparent rejection of the sensual scrawled beside the sermons;

underlinings of my favourite words in "The Compass." A few pages later, "diadem" defined in tight script, "royal headband" — had I explained why Donne used it? The wonder of feeling the poet's blood and mind moving through those places ...

In the fridge, the bachelor's comestibles. Carrots shrunk to yellow-stained old-man fingers. A six-count carton of eggs with two eggs in it, both stuck to the sides. Fresh milk, fresh butter. Nondescript styrofoam containers, one with rice in it, the other with vegetables and beef sticking up out of a congealed brown sauce like stumps in a dead pond. Little plastic ramekins filled with hot sauce teetering in the egg-cups in the door. It filled my heart with something like love for him, for the hopelessness you encounter in men who somehow go forth in the world. I took out the veggies and beef (a black-bean thing that smelled still edible) and stood full frontal in the window eating it, warming the cold broccoli and carrot disks in my mouth before chewing them. More knick-knacks and keepsakes on tabletops: a Betty Boop Pez dispenser (no one likes their women with jowls any-more), a raku bowl full of pennies, a picture frame with the fac-tory photo still in it: a soft-focus shot of a blonde with a straw hat on. I took the back of the frame out and removed her, crumpled her up. Then set the frame standing empty, like an elevator waiting for a passenger. I chewed stringy beef. Below, another streetcar went past completely empty and the driver craned his neck to take me in. The lonely people in a city are all joined together at night.

I rinsed my mouth out in the kitchen sink and then went and drew the blinds in the front room. I crept into his bedroom again and slid into the covers without drawing them back. It was the first time I had gotten back into bed with this man. His back was hot and he was breathing deep soughing exhalations, the sound of the body safe but unguarded, and I raised myself up and bent over him to look at his sleeping face. Eyes closed, lips parted, glistening. There resides the real and perfect beauty of human beings, I thought. That killers and babies alike look peaceful in their sleep, you know someone will love them no matter their sins. I kissed the mouth and lay back down beside him. He took a sharp breath in and turned on his back. His eyes were closed. "You okay?"

"I didn't mean to wake you," I said.

"I sleep light."

I waited for him to drift off again. But I saw his eyes had opened and he was looking at the ceiling. I turned and closed him in my hand. "You're warm." He looked at me and his eyes were dark, like the eyes of an animal encountered in a cave. An iron scent from the wine we'd had floated around him. "I should keep you in a little box under my bed."

He sighed deeply. "I was having a dream just now, where I was walking down the street with my childhood self."

"Uh-huh."

"It's strange, isn't it? To think by the time we get old, no one will know what were were like when we were little."

I quickly moved closer to him, and kissed his mouth. "Don't talk about that right now." I felt the pulse in my hand and he lay there and then after a moment, he closed his eyes again. Another streetcar went by on the road below. I shifted a leg and pulled myself on top of him, flattening my body against his like a page closed beside another in a book. I drew my knees up beside his chest and lay my mouth down next to his ear. "Don't say anything about that stuff," I said, and I rose and fell on his body.

≈

I came back to the hotel around seven, having walked the angled streets through midtown in a daze. Molly had left a half-dozen messages for me, and there was one from Daniel too, whom she'd called in a panic at four o'clock, to report me missing. I phoned him from the hotel lobby and reassured him it was all a misunderstanding, that everything was okay, was being worked out. He sounded skeptical; he wanted to be sure I knew what I was doing, so I murmured some bright thing to get him off the phone. I couldn't explain to him there and then exactly what was going on, nor show him how badly I wanted to talk to him. And I returned to my room understanding what Molly had meant by "work" the night before.

I splashed some water on my face and sat on the bed, immobilized by my misgivings. Light from streetlamps spilled over the floor. There was nothing familiar to me here, no touchstone, nothing to guide me. The desire to quietly pack and take a taxi to the airport had a kind of intelligence to it — after all, discovering nothing more would leave me in much the same state I had been in before Molly's call — but I also knew it was wrong. I broke the seal on the frigo-bar and poured a minibottle of Glenlivet into me and while it still burned, I took the stairs to Molly's room.

The eyehole darkened before she opened the door. She stood silently aside and let me in, completely calm it seemed, and then she closed the door and went to sit on the edge of one of the two single beds, waiting for me to enter without speaking. I stood beside the desk where there were a pair of room-service trays — a salad for lunch; a meat pie for supper, neither more than picked at. Her overcoat lay folded over a closed suitcase beside her.

From the bed, she regarded me with such cool-eyed tranquility that I thought somehow I'd forgotten a discussion from yesterday in which we'd agreed that I would go to Mrs. Bryce's without her. But the packed suitcase implied that whatever turmoil she'd suffered had been eased by a decision. She saw me looking at it.

"Yes," she said. "I'm going to go home."

"Is that what you want?" I spoke without inflection.

"I can't blame you for not trusting me, Jolene. I can't force you to accept my company. So I should probably go."

"You called Daniel," I said.

"I thought he'd know if you'd just stolen off in the night." I felt a flutter of guilt. "He sounds like a nice man."

"What did you tell him?"

"I didn't blow your cover," she said. "Something about mixed signals and if he heard from you to say I was in the hotel."

"You told him I was *missing*."

She nodded just a little, a faint smile at the edges of her mouth. "I might have been a bit upset. Obviously, you reassured him you weren't. Missing."

"That and a couple of big fat lies seemed to take care of his confusion."

"Well anyway, he told me to make sure you come home soon."

"I will be going home soon. I don't think there's anything for me here either."

Her expression darkened, a flash of anger. "If I'm going, the least you can do is be straight with me. I know you went to see Mrs. Bryce. And that's fine — I haven't done anything to earn your trust. But you don't have to lie flat out to me."

"Okay," I said. "I went." I had my hands behind my back, bracing me against the front of the desk; it felt right to keep them out of view. "She's elderly. She lives with her sister. They're two old, scared ladies, and they live in a house full of junk. The sister was so panicked she almost threw me down the stairs."

"What did Mrs. Bryce tell you?"

"That she's married to Martin."

"That's not true."

"It is. But he's not around. He doesn't live with her."

"So where is he?"

"We didn't get to that." She nodded, and sat back a little. She knew where I'd gone, but at the same time, having it confirmed hurt her, I could see that. She rubbed the tops of her legs. At times, it had felt as if Molly had taken a simple gamble in contacting me. Perhaps, she'd thought, it would turn out that enough time had passed. The well would be clear again. This optimistic face, which she'd strenuously worn more or less since I'd first arrived in Dublin, gave the impression that whatever came of this gamble suited her. But sitting on the bed before me, a look that shuddered into place and quickly passed spoke of something deeper. The pain of witnessing that look reminded me that I had once loved this person. It wasn't so clear any more how I should behave.

"They really are married?" she said.

"Yes."

"Are you planning to go back?"

"I don't think so."

"Why is she putting on these shows for him?"

"She said she was doing what she's been told to do."

"He wants to see people again," she said quietly. "Maybe he's gotten to the point in his life where he wants to do something about this feeling that he ruined the happiness of the people he loved."

"How could you know what he feels?"

"There's his family. There's you." I stayed silent. "What if that's what this is?"

"Almost everyone is either dead or too old to care anymore. There's nobody here to make amends *to*."

"You're here."

"It's not *his* call I answered."

"I know," she said, her hand on her coat.

The room had become oppressively close and I wanted to go. I needed a bath, some food, and a long sleep. I pictured myself shoving food down, in hunger, in anger. I stood away from the desk and dried my palms on my thighs. "I should get going," I said.

"Fine." Her eyes on the coat, fingers worrying down the creases. "Good luck then. Whatever you decide to do."

"Okay then," I said, and I went toward the door, but then I stopped and came back, and stood beside the bed. "I don't know what I'm apologizing for," I said carefully, "but I *am* sorry. And I'm grateful that you called me." She said nothing. "It was a *kind* thing to do."

She nodded, and after a moment longeer, it felt like there was nothing else to say. I stepped away from her and into the hall, my face burning.

My tiny single room had only a sink; to bathe, I had to creep down the hall to a shared facility. I could hear the murmurings of conversations behind other doors on the way there, faces I would never see, couples honeymooning, families on vacation. *We finally made it to Ireland. You have got to go Ireland.* Whenever I ran into anyone who'd recently returned, praising the people and the music, I tuned out and just nodded. I always wanted to say, *You mean it's not a black smoking hole?*

The bathroom was featurelessly white with a deep porcelain tub, the glazing worn off the bottom by an unthinkable quantity of naked rear ends. There was also a bidet in the room; not even a scrubbing down with boiling antibiotic could have convinced me to use it. I washed out the tub quickly with a facecloth and then filled it and slid in.

I dried my hands off and took a pocketbook out of the housecoat pocket. I'd brought it along with me, thinking when I left Toronto that it might be a good chance to read something I wouldn't normally have had the chance to read. One of the books it seemed every smart person but me had read. I'd brought Stendhal: *Scarlet and Black.* A terrible or a fitting choice, I wasn't sure yet. It was about a man who lied to everyone. Manipulated men to gain power and seduced women to make himself feel like a god, despite his contempt for beauty. He was a pit of hatred masked by charm and intelligence. Reading it, I wasn't reassured that it was more than a hundred years old. It seemed to divide the world into those who are gulled into believing in love and those who eat others to survive. I read it for a few minutes in the tub, my mind wandering from paragraph to paragraph. Is it possible that we are so separate from others that their intentions could be so concealed from us? Do we drift into harm's way, guided on the arms of those we love and trust?

The pages began to curl in the steam, like someone drawing a cloak closed around them.

I drifted a while, leeching out the strange hours spent in Ireland that were like an acid in my muscles. As my body uncoiled, relief flooded through me, almost like the sensation of being at rest after a colossal orgasm: all the lead-up, all the quaking tension in service of one tightly coiled moment, happily released and gone. I had my life back now, even though it was at the cost of that desolate form in the room above me. I could go home tomorrow.

Images of the past two days floated to the surface of my consciousness: Molly's wedding ring; her blank staring face seen from across the road from St. Patrick's; her beautiful clothing. Then the image of the back of Mrs. Bryce's hands came to mind, the dark blue lines laid under the vellum-like skin, as if an unseen tree was casting its shadow against her. From this, I may have begun to fall asleep, for I was back on the airplane from Canada, not looking down at the vermilion patchwork below, but into the whorled labyrinth of my seatmate's ear, tipped up toward my mouth, a spiral starting in light and receding into black. I looked more deeply into the ear and saw a perfect darkness, and I realized that everything that made that woman who she was resided there, in that unreachable place. It felt that if I pushed this image at the right angle it would click open and reveal itself to me. A ring, a treebranch, an ear. *Has it been a long time?* I said, just as I had on the plane, and the woman's face turned; it was Molly and she said, *I hate to fly* ... and I opened my eyes with a start. Short of breath, the bathwater cold. A thread unravelling. I ran back down to my room, the housecoat barely on. I dialled Molly. "You're still there," I said.

"I'm not leaving until the morning."

"You knew about the artworks before you came to Ireland! You would never have willingly flown over an ocean to sign a contract you could have faxed. You've been looking for him." She was silent on the other end. "How long have you been looking for him, Molly?"

"Don't you ever want to take back something you've done, Jolene?"

"How long have you been looking for him!"

"Don't be angry with me," she said. "I want to do something for you."

My heart was pounding in my neck. "Why? Why do you think you should? Why do you think you *can* do anything for me?"

"We used to be so close," she said quietly. "I turned you away. Isn't that awful? All you wanted was my help."

"I did, Molly, and you said no. That's another thing that's ancient history."

"Ask me again."

"Who is making amends here? Is it you or Martin?"

"Maybe it'll be both of us."

I shook my head, which felt stuffed with cotton. "I would never have come back here for my own sake, Molly. I stopped searching, because there was no way to get on with my life if I didn't. I helped *myself*, Molly."

"I went back in my mind, when everything ended with Scott, to the last time I felt a part of someone else and that was you. That was the last time in my life I had a true friend. You probably have a lot of people in your life, Jolene, but I don't. I don't connect."

"God, Molly ... "

"Is it wrong to ask for a second chance?"

"No," I said. I muffled the phone against my chest for a moment, panicked, unable to speak. How badly had I longed for those I'd lost? For those who were truly gone, with whom I'd never have a second chance?

I heard her voice against my ribs. "Jolene? Can we spend another day at this?"

"I don't know."

"If you're downstairs in the morning, then we will. If not, thank you for this."

"For what?" I said.

"Just for this."

I spent until ten in the morning in my room. I ordered breakfast there, which I ate guiltily beside the closed windows. I didn't want to get drawn any deeper into this, and yet I knew that it was out of my hands now. The die had been cast and I would go ahead now, not out of any morbid curiosity, or desire of my own (although of course my own questions still propelled me), but of all things, out of duty. I resolved to honour the old ties, the now not-as-distant feeling of love that had been summoned in her room the previous night, that required to be acknowledged.

I went down to the lobby, and saw her as soon as I stepped off the elevator, sitting beside one of the potted ferns. She smiled thinly at me, hiding her relief. We sat in the hotel restaurant, just as we had the first morning in Dublin and ordered tea. She wanted to go back to Mrs. Bryce's.

"It's a dead end, though," I said.

"We have no other lead," Molly said.

"Someone else must know him. Someone in the gallery world here." She shook her head no. "You've checked."

"I looked into it. She's the only connection."

"I don't feel right about going back there," I said. But I didn't have a better idea.

We went out and flagged a cab. It was a third day of high clear skies, an unusual run of weather. We gave the driver a street name and sat back in silence. But instead of going south, as I had the morning before, he turned north and began crossing the river. Molly leaned forward. "You know our address is in Rathmines," she said to him.

"Oh no, mum. I'm going to Phibsborough. You said Palmerston."

"Palmerston Road."

"Oh, *road*. Well that's an entirely different direction."

"I know. It's *Rathmines.*"

He nodded at Molly and started to make a U-turn. "Well, an innocent misunderstanding and we'll just turn the meter off and head back."

"No, hold on," I said, and I put a hand on his arm. The boulevards of O'Connell stretched up ahead of us. "Keep going straight. I want to see if I can get somewhere." He crossed a bridge. "Phibsborough's up there somewhere, isn't it?"

"It is."

Molly was watching me neutrally. "You'll understand in a minute," I said. I made the driver go straight up to the North Circular Road and turn, then again on Phibsborough, which, just as it should have, became Prospect on the other side of the canal. There had been a Prospect in Ovid too. I imagined the children down there, fishing, dangling their feet in the cold, clear water. "Here, turn right here," I said, and he turned onto Iona Road. Immediately, ranks of brick houses on either side, small clean cars by the curbs, flowerbeds and trellises.

I counted the identical houses going past, the high shady poplars looming over the street like an archway. Seventeen, thirty-one, fifty-nine, seventy-seven. "Stop," I said. A stately Victorian house behind a black gate. My hand dampened. The driver stopped and let his motor idle.

"Is this what I think it is?" Molly asked.

"I never forgot the address."

We paid the cab driver and got out. He offered to wait and I told him to go back and wait near the roundabout. He stopped and idled, got out to smoke. The house in front of us was like every other one on the street, a two-storey row house with bay windows on both floors, floral-bouquet keystones above the windowframes. A simple brick arch led to a blue door, and the last of fall's flowers were still on their vines. Molly took my hand, drawn to the house, the tangible remains. I stared at it. In my imagination, I rose into the air until I hovered outside the thin high window above the door. Saw the bed, the empty closet, the door leading to the hall. The heartbroken child, sitting upstairs in the gloom, listening to voices below. It was Theresa, of course, the other person in the hallway. Hers was the shadow I'd seen in Linwood Flats that night so long ago. Standing in her door, unwilling to comfort him, casting a shadow from her own lamp. I pointed to a window. "That was his room," I said, disbelieving, and I turned around to the street. "It faced that one, that was the Beatons'. William Beaton was his best friend." I showed Molly where Mr. Warren's car had come from — was it number 16 or 18? — where the accident had happened, the little roundabout where our driver waited.

"How long did he live here?"

"I don't know," I said, whispering. "I don't know anything before 1936. I think he was born here, but maybe he wasn't. There are smaller houses nearby, but they might have lived somewhere else until he was born. This was the last house in Dublin, though. I know that."

The door in front of us opened as we were speaking, and a man stepped out. He had his dog with him, a snouty collie. He asked us if there was anything he could help with.

"Sorry," I said, "we're just strolling."

"It's a lovely morning for it."

I began to walk down to the circle, but Molly remained in front of the gate. "We teach architecture," she said. "In California."

"Really?" said the man. Molly's face was fixed in a mask of calm. I'd seen that face on the steps of the Hofstaeder Gallery two mornings earlier. "These row houses go back, oh, probably to the 1890s."

"Actually, 1866," said Molly. "Do you know anything about the history of this one?"

"Oh no," said the man. "We bought the house in '92, from the Dwyers. Before then, I couldn't even say."

"Well, thanks," I said. "That's very helpful. Have a great day."

He went to lift his cap at us. "Would it be all right if we looked inside?" Molly said.

I grabbed her elbow, but she was stepping forward. The man had already taken his keys out again.

"We always knew there was something special about the neighbourhood," he said. "We bought it of course just to live in, but in a fine house like this you can almost *feel* it has some importance." He waved us toward the door.

We followed him and I looked blankly at Molly. She shot me a glance.

"Well, *you* weren't going to ask."

The man had the door open and stood aside to let us enter. The house had the Sunday-morning scent of bacon and coffee; the fragrance of a happy, well-run household. "Look around. Those there are original balustrades," he said. "In fact, just about everything is original. Would you like to take pictures?"

Molly pointed at her head. "I just keep everything in here."

I walked through the front hall in a fog. I could not prevent the immediate influx of voices for which I was a lightning rod. They poured out of every room, static of conversations boiled down to essences in stories told ten or more years earlier. A beloved table being sold, the hush of listeners around a radio, the tinny huzzah of a phone or the bell of the knife-sharpener in the street. Children's voices, and the sound of their chesty sobs, a door slamming and then anxious voices behind it, making plans. I turned slowly, imagining that the shades of previous owners — not just the Sloanes — packed the front hall and passed through us. Moments earlier, I had been upset with Molly. But now I was transfixed, numb with the eros of memory. I felt I could devour the very air. "Go up the stairs," I said to Molly. She mounted and I followed. The house's owner watched us mildly from the main floor.

"Excuse the mess in Janey's room," he said and then waved us on. The dog barked, possessed of common sense.

I walked silently up the stairs and brought Molly into the front room. We stood in the window. You could see directly across into the same window in the house on the other side of the road, but you could not see church steeples. I stepped closer to the window. Stood at one side and then the other. Made myself four foot. No church steeples. Nor bridges. In fact, even the canal was difficult to see. The row houses on the south side blocked almost entirely the view of the city. "This is interesting," I said.

"What's wrong?"

"Martin embellished. Or I did, I don't know. You can't see anything from here but the other side of the street."

"What are you supposed to see?"

"The grey church stone. The steeples that rise up here and there. The ivory-coloured clocks in the towers."

Molly looked out. "You can't see any of that."

"No, you can't." This was the child's room. Dolls and books lay scattered on the floor. But there was no closet in the room at all. And from the window, the view through the door fell on the landing at the top of the stairs, rather than on the back railing. The viewer of Linwood Flats should have been looking at the child's back, not his knees. "He made it even more lonely than it really was."

She came over and stood in the window, leaning up against the frame and looking at me. "So, they lived in this house and then they went to Galway."

"He got sick," I said. "TB. There was a flare-up and a lot of children died. The hospital was just over there." I pointed to the left behind the houses on the other side of the street. "He saw other children die."

"He got better, though."

"Yes. But then they had to move. He got taken away from everything that he knew. He thought he was being punished and his family was being punished."

"You remember a lot more than I thought you would."

I nodded. "I remember everything, Molly."

"You're keeping it for him."

"No," I said, turning from the window, "I'm just cursed with it." I sat down on the bed.

"What happened when they got to Galway?"

"Things didn't go so well."

"You'll tell me more later." She came over and laid a hand on my shoulder. "I'm going to go back down and make sure our host hasn't wised up."

She went down the stairs, and I stayed on the bed, looking out of the window. Before, I'd been afraid I would turn a corner and that old Dublin, the one I knew, would shudder into place. But here it was a fact, with a few alterations. The view outside the window was the one he'd looked at, not the one he later remembered. I was closer now to him than he was to himself, and it scared me.

I went down to the kitchen, following voices, and found the house-owner and Molly drinking fresh cups of coffee and leaning against the counters looking like old friends. He offered me one. "Genevieve was just telling me you think a famous artist used to live here?"

"Oh. Well, Genevieve gets her facts mixed up sometimes. He might have lived here, but he might not have. It was a long time ago. It's *very* kind of you to let two strangers into your home."

"It's always nice to know that you're a part of something," he said, and he raised his mug to us. The dog, now satisfied that we were all friends, lay on the floor between us, her leash in her mouth.

We walked the man back out — Jeremy, he said his name was — and we all shook hands. "Good luck," said Jeremy.

"It was good luck you came out when you did," said Molly, and she surprised us all by giving him a sudden hug. Then she smiled triumphantly at me and walked jauntily down to the cab.

The driver headed toward Rathmines. The sky had turned grey and a cold rain was beginning to fall. I watched the General Post Office swim past, and marvelled at the pride nations have in their bullet holes. "Palmerston Road," confirmed the driver.

"Road," said Molly.

"I checked with my dispatch, y'know. There are no less than *seven* Palmerstons in Dublin, and who knows how many more in the outlying?"

167

"Well, it's *road*."

"There's Place, there's Grove, there's Gardens, there's even a Villas. You couldn't have picked a more popular street, my darling."

"Well, aren't we having a perfect day," Molly said to me.

*The day was ending properly. We'd spent it sharing brunch in town, then walking back to the dorm. Molly had gone to her parents — it was only the second time since we'd started seeing each other that we'd had the rooms to ourselves. He'd let me cut his hair, calling me Delilah the whole time. Then we'd rented a movie, and I'd switched it off halfway through and led him into the bedroom. He stopped outside my door. Oh ... you misunderstand me, he said.*

*Don't make fun of me, Martin.*

*Are you sure this is your room?*

*This was a perfect day so far.*

*He gave a Cheshire grin, showing his teeth. And how old are you again?*

*Why don't you come in and count my rings? I stood in the doorway, my eyes on his, and blithely began removing my clothes. He stood there clothed. I can put them on again, Martin.*

*Don't bother, he said, his voice a little tight.*

*Am I beautiful?*

*He nodded.*

*Do you want to stand here and make more dumb jokes about my inept handling of our first night together, or do you want to see how I've improved?*

*Improved, he said.*

*Good. He walked past me, his cotton shirt brushing up against my breasts. He started to unbutton the shirt. Leave that on for now, I said, and I closed the door.*

"Snap out of it," said Molly, "we're here." Mrs. Bryce's hoved into view. It looked like dusk now, under the still, darkened skies. The drizzle came in bursts and starts, as if it had time to kill. "Keep the motor running."

We both got out and started up the steps, me a little behind Molly's protective confidence. The front window was empty; Molly leaned on the doorbell. Then the door opened, and there she was, the younger sister, the one charged with duty. She wore the same mask of fear, looking back and forth between us, her eyes black holes in her head. "I'm going to call the police," she said.

"Hold on," said Molly, calmly. "We don't want to come in. We just want to know how we can get in touch with Martin Sloane."

The old lady's face hardened into a look of hatred. "This is why you've come back? You put Francie in hospital talking like this!"

"What?"

Lenore waved a hand dismissively in the air. "What do you care if she's alive or dead! *He* doesn't care. Martin Sloane this, she says, Martin Sloane that. If he set foot in this house, I'd kill him straight off! Now you won't be getting another word out of me, so get out of here!"

She started to close the door. And then, for the second time in as many hours, Molly did a shocking thing. She grabbed the old woman by the front of her apron and pushed her into her own house and started down the hall. I stood there stunned and only snapped to when Molly started to close the door on me. I shot a look out to the cab, but the driver was enjoying another smoke, so I jumped over the threshhold and closed the door. "Molly! Molly!"

"Help me would you!" she shouted from atop Lenore, who had tumbled to the floor beneath her in a dead faint, and whom she was now dragging down the hall in short bursts.

"Molly! You can't just ..."

"Just what?" She looked down at Lenore, awake now and feebly trying to detach Molly's hands from the front of her shirt. "Politeness doesn't work with you, does it? Do you have any idea how far we've come?"

"Somebody call the police!" the woman sobbed. Molly pulled her into the kitchen and propped her up in a chair. She wet a towel for her. The old woman watched us both like we were going to be her last sight on Earth.

"You had to get help, did you?" she said, her eyes narrowed to pinheads. "Someone to do your dirty work!"

"I honestly didn't know she was going to do that."

"Move," said Molly, pushing me out of the way. She handed the old woman the cloth.

I went into the next room, hoping Lenore had lied about Mrs. Bryce. The chair was empty. "She's gone to hospital, thanks to you," she called.

"When?" I asked.

"The evening of the same day. 'He'll come for her,' she kept saying. 'Martin won't want to miss this girl. He'll come and then all this waiting will be over.' By bedtime she was foaming at the mouth."

"Where is she?"

"She has me, by the grace of God, to see to her needs! No one else will."

"All we want to know is where we can find Martin Sloane," Molly said. "Just give us an address."

Lenore took the towel away from her mouth. Half a denture was displaced and pushed out from her upper lip. "If I give you an address, will you promise neither of you ever to come back here."

"I promise," I said. "She does too."

Lenore lurched up from her chair. She was still dizzy, and began weaving. Molly steadied her, and Lenore took down a pencil from a ledge and tore the corner off an old newspaper. She scribbled an address and held it out to Molly. "I'll take that," I said, but Lenore snatched her hand away.

"You're the one who started all this. You put my sister in the hospital."

"Like you didn't try to shove me down the steps!" I shouted.

"Oh that I *had*," said Mrs. Bryce's sister. "The self-defence, they would have said." She passed the torn corner to Molly, who looked at it and put it in her pants pocket. "Now get out, the both of you."

We were walking out, but I turned back, protected, it felt, by Molly's seeming power over this woman. In the room where I'd encountered Mrs. Bryce, I picked up the box based on Pond, and tucked it under my arm. "We'll be seeing him anyway," I said. "I'll give it back to him."

"I wash my hands of it all, take whatever you want," Lenore said, and then she lowered her face into her hands and began wailing like a banshee. We retreated down the hall and closed the door on her keening.

In the cab, Molly unfolded the paper and handed it to the driver.

"Prospect Hill," he said.

"Jesus — we were just there."

"No confusion this time," said Molly. "Let's go."

But the driver frowned at the paper.

"What's wrong?" I said.

"Hold on." He picked up his headset. "Eddie? Prospect Hill."

The crackling voice of the dispatch came over the radio. "G'wan?"

"Prospect Hill, Eddie. Is there one in Phibsborough?"

"We just saw it," I said.

"That's Avenue. I think there's a Hill in Sandymount."

"Not this shit again."

"Looking ..." said the dispatcher. The driver held eye contact with Molly over his shoulder as he waited over the static. "Petey? I've got Drive, Place, Ave, Lane, Square, and Terrace. No Hill."

The driver hung up his set. Molly was opening the door. "Let's see if I can't jog the lady's memory a bit more," she said.

"Hold on," said the driver. "It is Prospect Hill. There's no mistake."

"Then how come your dispatcher can't find it?"

"Because he's looking in Dublin," he said.

Molly closed the door. "Where should he have been looking?"

"Galway," he said.

Molly turned her bright eyes to me.

"Alright," I said. "You win."

The driver got in gear. "You'll need a car of your own," he said. "I know a place."

# VIII.

POND, 1977. 18" X 14" X 6" BOX CONSTRUCTION. WOOD AND GLASS
WITH PORCELAIN, FEATHERS, FOUND OBJECTS, PAPER.
CARNEGIE MUSEUM OF ART. A POND IS VISIBLE BEHIND TREES
WITH SEVEN FEATHERS FLOATING IN IT, EACH WEIGHTED DOWN
WITH A GEM. IN THE BACKGROUND, AN EARLY PHOTOGRAPH OF
A CITY PARK IN WINTER.

THE WEDNESDAY THREE DAYS BEFORE THEY WERE TO leave, Martin went to meet his father at the shop on Grafton Street. He walked from the green through the busy late-day throng of shoppers, pausing to look in at Sibley and Co. on the corner, whose window was full of bone and enamel pens and a semicircle of gold nibs. Mr. Sibley was at the back of the shop, tearing the cover off a hardback book. Farther down was the Canada Life Assurance company, whose window said in silver letters STRENGTH SECURITY STABILITY against a black silhouette of Canada. His father had shown him where Montreal was: there, in the thinnest part between the ocean and the Great Lakes. That was where his Buby and Zaida lived.

Then, right beside Mitchell's (the confectioner, whose window was more outrageous than any dream of sweets a child could have), was his father's shop, and there his father was, standing behind the counter of Sloane and Son (he, Colin Sloane, was Son) as a man looked at himself in the mirror, a grey fedora on his head. The white price tag spun in the air above the man's shoulder.

Should it come down over the eyes like this?

Just tilt it back a ways. That's it, rakish.

The man turned in profile, keeping his eyes on the mirror. Then he turned the other way. His father glanced at Martin and smiled, but Martin knew not to speak.

The man said, It feels cold inside.

The lining's silk, said Martin's father. It'll become warmer after you've worn it for a while. It looks excellent.

And is it guaranteed?

Unless you fall into a river or get hit by a train, it's guaranteed for life.

Mine? the man laughed. He paid by unfolding a sheaf of bills and snapping them off one by one.

Martin's father put the money in his pocket, and then went and pulled the blind down over the door. It was exactly five o'clock. He called into the back, You'll finish up, then?

No worries, Mr. Sloane, said an old man, and they could hear the sound of a machine punching out felt disks. Martin's father turned and pretended he was seeing Martin for the first time.

Need a hat?

I shop at Tyson's, said Martin.

His father frowned. You know what happened to Jack Dempsey.

Usually on their walks back to the house, Colin Sloane would recount the events of the day to his son, but now he was quiet. In fact, as soon as he'd locked the door and turned onto Grafton, he seemed to have nothing to say. Martin took his hand, a little frightened, in the way that fear comes, slithering down a change in routine. They did not go down to Nassau Street and walk along the gateway of Trinity, as they usually did. Instead, his father turned left on Suffolk and again onto St. Andrews, where there stood a grey church called St. Alban's. O'Neill's, with its giant square clock, was filling up with men in black and brown suits. Colin asked his son if he could keep a secret. Martin looked around him. A little Citroën went bleating past. I don't know.

You're a big boy now.

Were they going to have a beer together? Martin wondered. He didn't like beer, but he would be happy to share one with his father. I think so, he said.

Then I want you to come inside.

He meant the church. Martin reflexively pulled back on his father's hand, and then let go. Churches were strictly off-limits. He had never been inside one before. Nor inside a synagogue. When his friends asked him which God he believed in, Martin didn't even know what the options were.

I don't think we should.

I know your mother wouldn't want us to, but I can't have my only son afraid of churches. Not in these times.

He walked uncomfortably under the stone buttresses, and it was dark there, before the door. Martin didn't want to go through that door; it meant telling a lie, but his father was standing there, and then he was holding the door open, and the whole interior of the church gaped like a cave.

Martin, I'm not asking you now. Take my hand. He did, and they went in.

It was dusty and dark and white specks went pinwheeling through the air wherever the light was. The ceilings seemed higher than the building appeared from the outside, and huge wooden beams criss-crossed above the nave like swords. Some people were sitting alone in wooden chairs that had been placed along the stone floor; a few knelt with their heads on their clasped hands. Colin led Martin slowly into the great hall, their footsteps swallowed into the space above their heads. Martin placed his feet as quietly as he could. On both long walls, the stained-glass windows he'd always seen from the outside of churches glowed as if alive. The red and green glass panels looked like they had been lit up from behind, and a thick, lambent light filled the place.

Those are the stations of the cross, his father said. They depict the twelve places Jesus stopped on the way to the crucifixion. And these are graves — people are buried here, great people. This man was a bishop, you can tell by his hat. It's called a simple mitre. Not anyone can make one. I've never made one.

His voice trailed off. Martin could hardly hear him over the roar in his ears anyway. He wanted to walk softly, invisibly, and he felt that if he touched anything but the floor his visit here would become a fact. They passed down the aisle between the two columns of chairs. Some people looked casually at them as they went by, some nodded. They were getting closer to the big cross at the front. A large table stood in front of it with vases to either side, and a spiral staircase rose to the right. Wooden pews faced into the centre of the space before the altar.

The priest prays here, this is the chancel, his father said. He was gesturing with his long, tapering fingers. He stands in front of the congregation and says the prayers, and then he leads them through the eucharist, when they consume the body and the blood of Christ. A reader stands here, at this lectern, and reads passages out of the prayerbook or the Bible. It's a very beautiful service. The music is lovely. Your mother would love the music.

The body and the blood? Always these things became more complicated. He'd once believed the human body was like a confection of some sort, and now it seemed, at least in church, that it was. What would his mother say? Her face was rising in front of him and she was staring, her eyes white like the boy's in William's story. He saw her shake her head slowly, from side to side, her lips pulled up over her teeth. She opened her hands in front of him like she was going to grasp his face — *how, how could this have happened?* He looked away, and saw her again, but it was the statue of a woman under a thin light. Was it the Virgin? He'd seen the Virgin Mary before, but this one looked younger and sadder than the one outside the church on Cabra Road. He blinked at the figure. He heard horses going by on the road outside.

That's her. That's the Mother of God. See — it's not so frightening.

His father took his hand and they walked into one of the transepts, and the horses passed close by on the other side of the wall. They were alone there. He kept his hands tight to his side.

This is a smaller chapel. Special services are held here. Private funerals, the like.

He let Martin take it in. The boy walked up to the black iron gate at the front of the small room. There was a book on a table open to a yellowed page. It looked like there were signatures in the book, faded signatures. The room felt like no one ever came into it and the table with the book on it was like the front table they had in their hall, the one that always had keys and circulars on it. His father was standing behind him in the doorway, watching him. He said quietly, Do you know what sin is?

Martin started from the book. It means doing something bad.

It's something you do that's bad, yes, even if you don't know it's bad.

How can you not know if you've been bad?

Because you're human, his father said. You can only know you've been bad if God punished you.

His father came closer now and made as if he wanted to look at the book. He leaned over the railing and studied it for a moment, then looked at his hands and rubbed some dust off one palm with his thumb. It's human to sin, he said. Everyone does it. But only God can decide to forgive us.

How do you know if He has?

We do our penance regularly and we cleanse ourselves. We *atone* even before we have sinned. Do you know what it is to be damned, Martin?

William told me.

Then you understand how important it is to be cleansed.

We should try to be good, Martin said, wanting to be helpful.

We can't just try to be good, his father said. How do we know what's good?

Martin shrugged slowly. Didn't he know when he was being good? He knew when he wasn't.

Only God knows what's good, and when we're being good. We have to say we're sorry for not knowing. That's what churches are for. To thank God for trying to show us the right way to live and to say we're sorry for not knowing it, and beg Him to spare us.

An older couple came into the room. She ran a gloved finger over a wall sconce and he stood near the door, leaning in, but not wanting to enter. Martin's father stopped speaking while they were there and it made Martin's fear turn white. Why couldn't these people hear about sin?

It's not a very good one, is it, said the woman.

Let's go, then.

I mean, it's not even as impressive as St. Michan's.

Well, let's go then, said the man.

They left. Martin couldn't think of anything to say. He wanted to leave. His father's face looked wet. He began whispering, as if the people were still in the room.

Martin — we could die at any time. We could walk outside and get struck by a car, or a bomb could go off in the street. You got very sick, you know. You could have died.

But I didn't.

But you could have. And you would have died in sin.

Martin stepped into his father's shadow and put his face against him. But I *didn't*, he said and he clasped his father to silence him. What could it matter what might have happened? He didn't die. Many other things had happened that were bad, but he hadn't died and that was a good thing. His father slowly put his arms around him and Martin could smell him: a sharp leather smell, and another scent, a kind of blossom.

Do you know the story of Jesus in the wilderness? his father said. Martin shook his head. God sent Jesus into the wilderness so Satan could tempt him. Forty days and nights Satan tested Jesus, to make him turn, but Jesus was steadfast in his devotion to God. Martin quaked against his father. Never had he heard him speak of these things, or in this tone of voice, which sounded like it was imparting serious and unhappy secrets. The way we live, as modern people, is like that wilderness, Martin. We are

tested every day, and if we fail that test, we belong to that darkness. I want more for the ones I love, do you understand?

Martin nodded.

You're entitled to God's protection, no matter what your
mother says, and refusing the gift of His love is as bad as
succumbing to temptation. I want you to remember that for
always. That's something that's between you and me and God,
you understand, for always.

Now he was silent, and Martin held himself still, waiting for
it all to be over, but then his father pushed him back abruptly and
with a damp, hot hand on his shoulder steered him out of the
transept. Martin could suddenly smell perfume, and there was the
sound of music-stands being moved about: the choir arriving for
its practice in the crossing between the pews. There was too much
movement, too much happening, and Martin felt he had to sit
down, and he even dropped his back as if he would, but his
father's powerful hand on his shoulder was sweeping him back
through the nave. A woman dropped her purse as they passed her
and his father lunged down to pick it up and hand it back. There
were three sounds: the rough hiss of the purse's brocade scraping
against the floor, the heavy sound of the coins in the purse being
clasped, and the faint slap of the purse being pushed into the
woman's hand. Martin heard all three sounds like they were being
made separately, and it felt like everything inside the church was
being divided into separate sounds and visions. There were two
people walking slowly down the narthex, the sound of a book
being closed, and the main door to the church being opened,
admitting people and light. The door, the light. The door.

But instead of turning left and leaving the church, his father
turned right, and Martin saw a man dressed in black robes
standing at the back, near some blocked doors. He came forward and greeted his father:

Peace be with you, Colin.

And his father replied, his tongue dry against his teeth, And
peace be with you.

I'm Father Stirling, said the man. I'm the priest here. I'm like a rabbi, you see?

I don't think he's seen a rabbi. Have you?

A picture.

Your father asked me to come and say hello and welcome you to St. Alban's. Do you like our church?

Martin said it was large and dark.

Dark to allow people to be with their thoughts, and large so God can get in. The sun was so low now that some of the slits of light were coming sideways through the air. He watched Father Stirling's face move through one of the white bands, and the dust was like starlight in a morning sky.

His father and the priest shook hands, and Father Stirling walked toward another transept behind him. Martin's father took his hand and they followed. This transept had a stone birdbath in it and Father Stirling swirled his finger in it and gestured for Martin to come to his side. He told Martin again that he was welcome to St. Alban's. He touched a wet finger to Martin's forehead and to his chest.

You're a good boy, I can tell, said the priest, and he and his father shook hands again, although now the priest was not smiling. Father Stirling crouched down in front of Martin.

I know you're leaving for Galway in a matter of days, son. But there are churches there should you ever want to talk to anyone about anything. Your dad will know which ones you should go to, if you like.

I'm both, though, Martin said. I'm Jewish too.

God will recognize you.


They walked together out of the church and Father Stirling wasn't standing there when Martin cast his eyes back into the dark space. People continued to swirl in and out, many of them were old ladies with soft faces and black eyes. Outside the air was much fresher and the streets were bustling, although it had begun to get dark. The sun between the buildings was airy and seemed filled with a green light, like the afternoon light on a lawn. His father let go of him and wiped his hands on the sides of his pantlegs. He said they would have to get home quickly now. A man who knew them called out hello, and when his father lifted his hat, Martin saw that his hair was stuck down to his head, gleaming and damp. Then he put his hat back on and turned to Martin, the blacks of his eyes wide as pennies —

I left it on the whole time! I left my hat on the whole time we were inside the church. He laughed to himself, like it was the strangest thing a person could do, and he blinked a drop of sweat off his lashes. Then he drew his fingertips across his brow and rubbed them against his thumb. Martin touched his own forehead — it was dry. The water had already been absorbed by his skin.

◇

On May twelfth, the day of the London coronation, they woke for their last day in the house on Iona Road. For the last time, they ate breakfast at the table (the one someone had purchased and would pick up by lunch), and for the last time Theresa went to school, glaring at Martin by the door. Tomorrow at this time, they would already be in the car, eating scones their mother would pack before they left. The scones were baking right now, and the sweet, sweaty fragrance came up the stairs to where Martin was sitting.

He had already been taken out of school. He'd missed so much with his illness that he had been removed from his classes. He would begin third form again in Galway. Through the fanlight above the door he watched Theresa cross the road toward her school on Connaught Street. She joined a pack of girls there and they enveloped her. It began to rain, just a little.

His parents were moving slowly around the house, not speaking much, although sometimes passing him on their way to a half-filled box, one of them would smile or touch him. Every time his mother or his father offered him a weak smile, he wanted to leap to his death from the top of the stairs. The morning seemed to last hours and hours, and although he was supposed to be helping (or at least packing the remains of his own things), he did very little but sit on the landing between the main and second floors, watching his parents go up and down. Around noon, his mother called him downstairs where his father was sitting beside the radio, and they listened to the broadcast from Buckingham Palace.

And now we hear the voice of His Grace the Archbishop of Canterbury as he enters into a solemn dialogue with the new king. They are standing twenty deep along Whitehall listening through the loudspeakers. There are the trumpets! The next voice you hear will be the Archbishop of —

Will You solemnly promise and swear to govern the peoples of Great Britain, Ireland —

Right! shouted his father.

Canada, Australia, New Zealand, and the Union of South Africa, of Your possessions and the other territories to any of them belonging or pertaining, and of Your Empire of India, according to their respective laws and customs?

I solemnly promise to do so, the prince replied.

Do I have a bollocking choice? said Martin's father.

The archbishop continued, his voice tinny and small in the radio, Will You to Your power cause law and justice in mercy to be executed in all Your judgments?

I will, said the prince.

Then he was crowned and they could hear the static of the roaring crowds. His mother's eyes filled up with tears but his father got up and unplugged the radio, then put it into a box.

There. You've got a new king.

Don't tell me you didn't find it interesting, even just a little, his mother said.

I find it interesting that the English royalty advertises its inbreeding even down to the fact that they have only two or three names for their kings. You get to be George or Edward. Or James.

Henry, she said.

Not for a very long time. William, maybe. He kissed her, conciliatory, but he was grinning. Well, congratulations to us all. We have a new king. When he left with the box in his arms, he was chuckling a little.

Martin's mother turned to him. I hope you'll not show that kind of disrespect when you get older. Martin knew he wouldn't. The fact was, he loved the idea of kings and queens. He couldn't imagine why anyone wouldn't.

For king and country! his father shouted gleefully from upstairs. May the sun never go down on the Empire! Whoopeee!

Jesus H. Christ! she shouted back, covering Martin's ears. Blasphemy was the only possible revenge.

Eventually, he went to his room and stood at his window, looking out onto the sight of Dublin, the grey church stone in the distance and the tops of the houses leading down to the city centre. The steeples that rose up here and there seemed a little sinister to him now, as if the ivory-coloured clocks in the towers were eyes that could see him from anywhere. He was now not certain what gods had claimed him (which ones would even want him?) or how many more gods would vie for his soul from this time forward. The steeples spread over the sky like sticklebacks on the tail of a lizard, winding along the streets and quays. Above, the sky did look dim and dusty to him now — the move was so inevitable that he had begun to see things as they were. It was not a nice place to live, if you were a boy who had trouble breathing. But it was still home, and that was what was hurting.

He gazed down onto the grey-red cobble in the street, the cracked stones he knew like they were the creases on his own palm. He knew how that road looked darkened by rain or made pale by a rare whole day of sun. He could tell what the weather was by listening in the dark to the sound of a car driving by under his window. The hiss of tires in rain, the smooth black rubber sounding over a hot road, the soft tread of a car driving carefully on the occasional snow. Panic rose again in him, as it had for two weeks now, and he clenched his eyes to calculate the hours left — only sixteen. The trucks would come at seven in the morning. He turned to his room as if the time remaining was something material that he could feel draining down a hole in the floor. He looked around the little space. He had spent all his life here! The hollow feeling of terror sank into his stomach. It wasn't possible that they were leaving. Not to come back? Never to come back here? How was it possible?

He threw himself on the bed. Three more minutes had passed in despair. He would not squander the rest of the afternoon. He thought if there was a south-facing bedroom in the new house, that he would be allowed to have it — but he would have to ask his mother first. A brief euphoria ran through him like a charge.

Most of his books and clothing were stacked in crates around his room and in the carpeted hallway outside. A grey trunk with the word BRITANNIA painted in white held both his and Theresa's shoes and coats. It had been his grandfather's trunk when he made the passage from Portsmouth (via Dublin) to Montreal to start a watchmaking firm. His mother's life was to have started over there — Martin had heard the story so many times — but she met the man she was to marry on that ship. Your father's nose is the reason you're here today, the story would always end. Your Zaida Mosher thought Daddy was Jewish and invited him to dinner in our cabin.

Martin thought about the trunk that had travelled over the Atlantic twice, and his troubles seemed as vast as that distance. Dublin to Galway!

And how terrible that his mother had said goodbye to everything all for nothing (well, except for marriage and children). She had left her home in England at the age of twenty-one and travelled all the way across the ocean to live in a place where the people spoke French, only to meet her future husband on the ship and turn around. Except that she was coming to Dublin, not going home. Talk about floating off course. (Maybe, thought Martin, it would happen somehow that they would have to come back right away too.)

He remained rooted to the bed, unable to decide in what order to put the few remaining things away. He hadn't much time — William, Devon, and Ian Shoemaker, whom he didn't really like, were coming to dinner. Theresa's friends, who were somewhat more numerous, were also coming. There was the red-haired Mary, a Jenny, and little Celeste Shipley, whose mother always nervously speculated on her daughter's much-hoped-for growth spurt. Then there was Theresa's best friend, a nasty girl called Kelly. Kelly had once cornered Martin and asked him to remove his pants, which he felt compelled to do, since Kelly was much bigger than he. She had approached him with a small twig and stirred the front of his underpants with it. When nothing happened, she'd said, with great disappointment, It's all a lie, and stalked off.

He was not looking forward to the dinner, which was to end with the presentation of gifts that had surely been chosen by the parents. He did not want to sit and eat with people he was never going to see again. He'd already said goodbye to Devon: they'd gone to the flats behind the cigar factory and burnt an entire book of matches one by one to mark all the great times they'd had. Then they'd awkwardly hugged, the way they'd seen their fathers hug other men, even clapping each other on the back. William hadn't spoken to Martin since three days earlier, when they'd gone to the canal and tossed daisies into the water. He wanted to say goodbye, but not in front of everyone. And yet, maybe he and William had already said their farewells.

He wasn't sure that any of Theresa's friends had much use for a final gathering either. Maybe it was important for all the parents to see them together, and take photographs and give gifts. Maybe that's how adults say goodbye to other adults, he thought — by watching their children say goodbye.

There were three hours to dinner. In the last two days, his mother had finally succumbed to Martin's stubbornness and packed his entire room herself. But on the desk beside his window he had placed the dozen or so keepsakes and objects that he didn't want her to touch, and, exasperated, she had told him anything that was left unpacked come dinnertime was going to be thrown away. He had by now cleaned out what was unnecessary from his cigar box (a few piles of coins and a cumbersome cloth monkey), and into it now he placed a few crucial things that he felt he might want easy access to: touchstones of his life. There was a small folding landscape of trees that his father had made. The black cardboard accordioned out into a line of carefully carved willows, oaks, and pines, and when he'd been much smaller, his father had put it in his window so at night the lights of the street would throw a forest against his wall.

This he placed flat against the bottom of the box. Then he put a miniature bed in. He had purchased this with his own money only last year, and for some reason he didn't know, it had become one of his prized possessions. He could hardly understand why, but he knew the little bed, or the line of trees, or the empty matchbook held some of his emotions with the full and perfect speechlessness of things. He would sometimes glance at this bed and peacefulness would flood through him. Beside it he placed one of his mother's thimbles, as if it were a glass of water for the tiny sleeper, or a basin to wash his hands in.

Then, using his penknife, he pried open a slat at the front of the box and revealed the open space under the main compartment. It had been the original bottom, but when he discovered that the lid of the box had been made in two layers of thin cedar, he pried the bottom part away and laid it in about an inch from the bottom of the box. Then he cut a slat off the outside to make a door into the false bottom. With the little bit of light seeping into the thin space, he could make out the original manufacturer's label: Linwood Cigar Company, Dublin. And a picture of a lady in a red hat, winking. In here he usually kept bits of chocolate or paper money, but it was empty now, and he placed in it a gift his mother had received from her grandmother when she was a girl, and which she had passed on to Martin without Theresa's knowing (for Theresa would have wanted it for herself). It was almost a hundred years old, and had gone smudgy from handling, but it was still recognizable as what it had been when it was new: a small naked infant cast in hard rubber, its features rendered in detail. There was its fine nose and its small puckered mouth, ten fingers and toes with tiny nails, and hair wrought in thin lines along its scalp. The infant lay on its side, fast asleep, its hands tucked under its head, and it was the size of a robin's egg. There was no way to tell whether it was a boy child or a girl, but Martin believed it to be a boy. He placed it in the secret compartment, and it lay like a seed under the trees and the bed and the thimble. Then he pressed the slat back into place and closed the lid of the box. It was complete.

He looked at what was now left behind: a model car, a tiny plastic flute, the cloth monkey, and an array of smaller objects, corks and bottle tops and buttons. These he put into a paper bag and tossed into the steamer trunk with the coats and shoes. Then he put the Linwood box on top of the steamer and stood back, regarding the emptiness of the room, which was now total. He went over to the window and looked out again. Somehow all of this had taken half an hour, and he could see that the sun had moved over a little. It would soon go down. He looked over the way, and through the window in William's bedroom, he could see his friend pulling on a pair of socks. William tugged them on and then stood and turned, seeing Martin standing at his window. The two boys stared at each other over the expanse of street that had been their territory for their entire lives, but neither of them waved or acknowledged each other, only stood like sentries at their windows. Then William nodded slightly and turned away. Martin saw his back when William left the room on the other side.

Down, down into the streets and parks, along the river, past the churches and squares. Down Phibsborough over the canal bridge to Circular Road, where the statue of the soldier was, and down to Berkeley Street, past the Mater. St. Joseph's over there, where his father had wanted to go in and thank the Virgin. He was running, past Eccles Street, past Mountjoy, and his chest began to ache. He slowed down, guilty, but realized no one would think it strange, the Sloane boy on his own walking down streets he'd walked many times. He passed Goldman's and even waved to Missus.

It was the night of May twelfth, Coronation Day, and now his friends and his parents' friends were walking up the street to their house to say goodbye and offer their farewell presents, and he was not there. He had slipped out of the mudroom door and gone along the back gardens until he'd hit the main road, and now here he was, with the failing light and the sounds of the city. Now seeing was more than an absorption of things, it was an action. He saw the streetlamps and the pubs, the shopfronts with their painted signs, the bright lights in the windows of Walton's School of Music, where he'd canoodled on a wooden concert flute on Mondays between the hours of five and seven only last year. He passed McCann's on Frederick Street, although they were closed now. His mother wouldn't shop there because they charged them as much as they charged people who *weren't* their neighbours. His mother figured living on the same street gave them a different status. She figured it would have if they'd all been Catholic.

The road turned here, angling into its midtown longitude, and the character of the street changed. It was no longer Phibsborough or Old Cabra, where the houses were tall and the commercial streets full of fruit and vegetable merchants, and nice pubs with orange fires going once you stepped inside. It seemed a little ruthless here between the outskirts and city centre, this was the corridor where people passed through and grabbed something, rather than lingering. There were twelve pubs between Dorset and Denmark Streets, and they looked black inside, their windows featureless and buff-coloured. No one went into them or came out. It was as if they had tenants, not customers. And above them rose the flat-faced buildings on either side, which were on the verge of becoming tenements, or rather, reverting. His parents had warned him that Frederick Street was not a place to go alone. Some of the casements above his head were even barred. The only thing that was nice about the street today was the bright Union Jacks hanging out of one or two of the windows. Strange to see them, his mother's flag. You never saw that flag.

After Frederick, it was nicer; he heard the sounds of a tin flute and someone banging a table with the flat of his hand. A voice was saying, It don't make no bit of difference! It's the same bloody thing. And a voice replied, Get him another one of these! Keep your blood up!

Three men in suits were coming out of the St. George Hotel, laughing and singing,

*God Save the King,*
*A ring a ding a ling!*

At the bottom of the park, the street turned into O'Connell, and here the double-decker buses careened into their stops and roared off again into traffic. It was even louder now, and he crossed carefully to the meridian, looking both ways. People kept bumping into him, and he grasped tight to his pants pocket, which held a handful of coins he'd brought from the house. He bought a bag of hot salted groundnuts from a man with a cart and then stood, staring down the great street from the island in the middle. There'd been a big row that started at the post office, down there, on the right. There had been blood in the ruined streets.

It was beginning now to get dark. Martin lifted his face into the lights and the noise, into the smells of the city, and walked slowly along the grass as the traffic sped by on either side. He'd been down here first in his pram when he was an infant, then probably once or twice a week they'd been down here, walking or going to a restaurant. They'd taken high tea in the Gresham Hotel, here on the left. Expensive, his father had said. Martin kept his eyes open only slightly and let the layers of time and memory swim down into the street. His whole life. His whole life had happened here, against these buildings, against these streets, and he was leaving it. Nelson's Pillar was here, towering over everything, its massive length lit up by lights in the grass. At the top, Nelson himself gazed down on the rest of the city, perhaps on the statue of Sir John Grey, who would have been jealous to learn he rated a pedestal only twenty feet high. Martin stared up through the trees at the Trafalgar hero and walked backwards around the column, taking nuts from the bag and cracking them in his teeth.

He'd already gone past the Savoy Cinema, and across from it, the Carleton, both with people lining up for the early seatings, their light coats on. There was John Keys, too, Tobacconist, where his father bought his cigarettes and the occasional cigars. Mr. Keys himself had given Martin his cigar box. Some of the street seemed to shimmer, unreal, like it was a memory already, shifting, insubstantial.

*In-ep-IN-en!* Read about the London coronation!

When he got to Grafton Street, the shopkeepers were noisily drawing down their gratings. Motorcars drove slowly down the thronged street, and Martin was thrilled to see the horses so close, the carriages with their giant wheels clattering by. Would Galway sound like this? He worried there would be nowhere to go to vanish into the sound and the activity. He was worried you'd always be able to hear the wheat growing in Galway. To be that alone!

He threw the empty, oily paper bag into a bin and sat down on a pub-barrel across from Mitchell's to catch his breath. There, in the window, a girl poured a long tray of sweets into a bag. He couldn't imagine anyone would throw out that much confectionery. The girl put the bag down and leaned on the empty countertop, looking out the window. She pushed the inside of her arms forward and yawned. The light mounted in the window turned her skin a bright yellow.

He was getting tired now — usually this walk would take him thirty minutes at the most, but he'd left the house over an hour ago. Stopping and taking everything in, storing it, was tiring him out. But he forced himself up and continued along Grafton, noting only momentarily the For Let sign in the window of Sloane & Son. The shelves behind the sign were still full, though his father's assistant, Old Morris, wasn't there.

The crush of pedestrians carried him across the street and he stood on the sidewalk at the northwest corner of the green. He entered there, and quickly the trees absorbed the sounds of the world outside the park and a hush floated down. It was sudden, the silence, and sensuous. The delight of it surrounding him. He heard the clicking of a woman's heels and the plashing of wings hitting the water in the pond. He slowed, letting the scent of lilac and lavender draw him into the middle of the green. Every time he came here, he saw men and women who looked like they lived in the park. They walked in measured circles, like a dance, the woman's arm on the man's, his face tilted down to hers. Martin pictured himself and Nuala ten years from now. He'd come back to Dublin to live, and find her through her parents in Clontarf. Then they'd come here, and walk slowly back and forth along the paths, talking quietly to each other.

He went through the trees, where it got darker, and came out on the other side of the copse, and there, at the top of his plinth, sat King George II on his horse, the iron hoof of the steed rearing up with the king in the saddle on top. King George II, a brave king who almost looked good on a horse. This was all Martin knew about this king. It was all he knew about most kings, but it was enough to inspire him. The first stars were coming out just below George's finger, pointing out across the river as if to direct his troops onward, into the night. Martin walked closer to the monument. *After tonight,* he thought, *everything here will vanish behind me, and everything that happened here will go with it.* Now he earnestly believed in the reality of the body. Curses always had a kind of logic to them. It was no wonder he'd been resistant to the idea of hearts and spleens and stomachs: they held the key to his fate. Why would he want to know about his own death, lying in wait under his own skin?

"Who's the king of Ireland?" a man behind him said, and then laughed, clapping Martin on the shoulder with a glove-clad hand.

Soon it was very dark. The world seemed to be concentrated here for him. The statue was a representation of a real person, but it was much larger than that person. However, so far away, on top of its huge pedestal, the king looked as though he could fit into the palm of Martin's hand.

He went back out onto the street. Instead of waiting for the light to change, he walked up to a policeman and pretended he was lost. Fifteen minutes later, he was dropped at his door and left with his parents, a warning not to let him out after dark offered to them.

His mother's face was white, but he would not answer her questions, and when his father told him how worried they'd been, he simply said he was sorry and went up to bed. The house was empty of guests and their practical gifts with their sad ribbons lay unopened on the settee. He closed the door to his bedroom and changed into his pyjamas. He could hear Theresa crying in the darkness of her bedroom.

Across the street, the lights were off in the Beatons', but the whole of the city was lit up beyond Iona Road. He felt as though he had strung those lights himself, and that each one marked a place for him. One light for every day of nine and a half years. He climbed into his bed and pulled the covers up, falling asleep almost instantly, and down in St. Stephen's Green, a man strapped a bundle of gelignite to the belly of King George's horse and blew the statue to bits. It was in the papers the next morning. They read about it driving west.

# Galway

# IX.

SLEEP, 1972. 38" X 25" X 20" GLASS CASE CONSTRUCTION. GLASS AND STEEL WITH FABRIC AND FOUND OBJECTS. ART GALLERY OF SUNY BUFFALO. A DROWNED MERMAID IS OBSCURED BY DARK WATER.

WHO GETS A CHANCE TO BERATE THEIR GHOSTS? ONLY in dreams, and then we're apt to vanish down rabbit holes, or our mouths don't work. I'd dreamt of Martin on almost a daily basis for the first few years, but never directly. I'd be dreaming of something else and he'd walk past in the background, pause to look down at something, and then pick it up and move on. I'd be behind a bus window, or buying a pack of gum, or I'd be arguing with someone from school — and he'd be gone. Or else, I'd be free to move and lose him in a crowd, or catch up with him and it'd turn out to be someone else. I was haunted, but my ghost was unwilling to show its face. Then many years passed and I stopped dreaming of him and I concluded he was out of my consciousness. I was free to meet Daniel, and I did. And yet, I remained reluctant to look at my feelings, even with the perspective of distance. I never so much as mentioned my life before Toronto to Daniel. One night, though, in his apartment, in his bed, I dreamt of Martin again. It was a simple dream. It began and there he was, right in front of me, his face still, his eyes clear, those soft black eyes. He was about to speak. I waited. I waited for what seemed many minutes. And then his lips parted and his eyes closed and I woke up.

"They must have passed all this then," said Molly, bringing me out of my thoughts. "On their way west." We were between Dublin and Galway now. The N6, an old pilgrims' road updated for the use of new centuries, cut through the middle of the country in a drunkard's line.

"I'm sure they did," I said.

"And what happened to them when they got there?"

I watched the farms sweeping past. "I'll tell you more later," I said.

I had taken the wheel first, but stopped about five miles outside Dublin, unable to resolve my confusion between the gearshift and the door handle. Molly took over, slipping a pair of glasses out of her jacket. Her arm bounced off the door just as mine had. "Don't get it into your head that you need the window open," I'd said, "or we'll have an accident." Soon she got used to it, an experienced adjuster, one of evolution's darlings.

What passed for a late-September heatwave had brought the temperature up into the low twenties — a moist country air made it seem stickier than that. We kept the windows up and let the car's air conditioning keep things comfortable, but outside it seemed the world was slicked with dewy heat. Signs for unseen villages to the north and south drifted past—Kilcock, Eston, Mayford, Kinnegad—and all around was deep green; it would flash by when the high scrub at roadside suddenly dipped and revealed it, rolling off in all directions like an endless canvas. Molly turned the radio on and we listened to a talk show out of Dublin. Someone said, "He'd spoken nary a word in twenty-five years, but when she came into the room, he stretched out his hand to her and said her name. Can you imagine?"

I'd always loved the soothing rhythms of car trips, the whoosh of traffic passing you in the opposite direction, the view of the sky through the window. When I was a little girl, accompanying my mother on her short drives to neighbouring towns, I'd close my eyes and lean my head against the passenger door. I'd focus on the thrum of the road under us, and feeling the forward motion of the truck, I'd try to convince my body we were driving in the other direction and my body was facing backwards. Threading those sensations against themselves was a strange, private game, but I liked to challenge my reality as a child. I wanted to see if it was anything other than it seemed (for I suspected it was, and that most of my feelings as a child were a product of it). There was the one where I lay in bed and told myself my thoughts were actually being spoken by a being who could control my mind. *You only think you're thinking these thoughts,* I'd say in my head, *but this is the vampire talking, these are my words, not yours.* Eventually, I'd sit bolt upright in the bed and stare out into the darkness, certain the bleak, pitch form of the beast was right in front of me. Funny how we scare ourselves as children with ghoulish visions, I thought — the pulse of this Irish highway tying me to that cold little road that connected Ovid to Cortland — funny, when what usually undoes us as adults is something that's been alongside us the whole time, always familiar and often beloved. We lose the luxury of monsters.

*Are you easy to train? Him sitting behind the wheel, looking out over the little stretch of empty highway.*

*I think you will find me a most eager pupil. Glancing over, waggling his eyebrows, one hand clenched around the gearshift.*

*Well, ease up a little on your grip. Loosen your hands. You're not wrestling it, I said. I showed him how the shift felt when it was in neutral. That little extra give between gears.*

*How many times do you think we'll wreck your car this year?*

*Once. The car revved and moaned as he finessed the changes. Full gas in neutral, clutch and brake at the same time. Jerk and shudder. He was most comfortable in third gear, struggling up to it, and then coasting along at twenty miles an hour.*

*I got it now, he said, the air blowing through the car. He drove with a smile frozen on his face, part delight, part vigilance. Throwing me looks of childish triumph and then swerving his attention back to the road.*

*We drove a while in silence. He leaned down and switched on the radio. Unseasonal for the Midwest, it said, and he snapped it off.*

*See how nice it's going to be down here?*

*It'll be nice at home too.*

*I don't understand why you don't move the rest of your stuff down here. Or at least more of it.*

*He sighed. Why, when we talk about this, do you get to a point where it sounds like you understand why I need things to be this way for now, and then a week later, it's like you're back at square one?*

*(No, this is from later, this is Indiana —)*

*Because your spell fades, that's why, I said. It stops making sense. If you love me —*

*Stop that.*

*I turned my face to the window. Lost in my own thoughts, continuing the conversation by myself.*

*(That's right, I taught him to drive outside Rhinebeck or Tivoli —)*

*How's this? he said.*

*You're doing fantastic. The signs for the campus came into view. Annandale, three miles.*

*Can you bring us home?*

*He nodded, concentrating.*

Molly had settled into the rhythm of driving, clutching down when we came up behind the milk trucks or the cattle wagons, then passing and speeding up again. I had by now accepted that the future was empty — I knew nothing; I had surrendered. Not being one who ever willingly gave up control, it was not easy to do. But Molly drove. She drove, and I sat and waited to see what would happen next. News of more towns appeared on green signs every kilometre or so — other lives, other routines. They went on beyond the verges.

"Are you okay?" she asked me.

"Just floating along," I said.

"Are you anxious?"

"No."

"It's not a long drive," she said.

"I'm fine."

She drove a while more in silence. Then she said, "Do you remember your life before everything changed?"

"Which time?"

"Before Martin."

"I guess I do. I'm not blessed with a bad memory."

"Me neither," she said. She drove without speaking for a few moments, and then took a sharp breath. "Since you have a good memory," she said, "you can tell me: what was I like then?" She asked me this straight out. "When we first knew each other?"

"What were you *like*?" She kept her eyes on the road. "God, Molly ..."

"Just in general. How you saw me."

I raised my hands in the air, at a loss. "Well, you were my friend. I saw you in a good light."

"Did you think I fit in?"

"You fit in with *me*. I can't speak for anyone else. You knew a lot of people."

"I don't think I really knew anyone," she said. "I was just keeping busy. You were the only one who really knew me, I think."

"Well how do you see *yourself*, back then?"

She thought for a moment. "I wasn't a *bad* person."

"Why would you start with that?"

"I don't know. Just to cut off one of the extremes." She laughed nervously. "I was a friendly person."

"I'm not sure that was the term of art back then, but —"

"I didn't know what I wanted from other people. Most of the time I just slept with them."

"Lots of people slept around in college."

"Sometimes, I remember, I'd be in bed with a guy, and my eyes would be open and I'd be concentrating, trying to figure out if it felt good, if there was really something happening between us, something, you know, *passing* between us."

"That brings an unpleasant picture to mind."

"You know what I mean."

"Well?"

"There wasn't. I always thought I'd know if there was."

"I think what you're talking about doesn't really happen

like that."

"But it was there with you and Martin."

"It took time."

"No it didn't," she said, resolute. "You had that feeling right away, you even said so."

"I was nineteen, Molly. Nothing we felt back then counted."

She shook her head. It did to her. She could probably go back to the very beginning, and tally it all. I'd always known this about Molly: everything she felt counted for her. "At first I just worried that I couldn't feel love. Then later, I figured I wasn't a person *others* could love."

"That wasn't true. It's not true now."

"It is true now," she said flatly. "But now I've earned it."

"Anyway," I said, not sure how to continue, "it's hard enough to see yourself in the present."

She took her eyes off the road to look at me. "Yes," she said, "that's true too."

We continued driving, falling now into not speaking, our attempt at something intimate unsuccessful. The truth was, I no longer had a picture of Molly beyond the broadest strokes. The minute details had eroded away in the years of resentment I'd felt after our last phone call. For all I knew, she hadn't changed at all. For all I knew, neither had I. There was no way of knowing whether or not people generally drew the past along with them and just put layer upon layer of disguises on it.

After another few minutes, a castle came into view along the roadside. Buff stones with iron grilles in some of the windows. A few birds I'd never seen before — long black tails and white patches under their wings — sat in the windows looking down into the fields. Its appearance provided us with a welcome change of topic. "That's in someone's field," Molly said.

"Interesting," I said, and we trailed off again.

It was amazing to me, who lived in a place where it was likely you'd know someone whose great-grandfather had played cards with Ulysses S. Grant, that there were places in the world where history was so distant that centuries of grass had grown up over it. And here, a castle still standing beside a field of lettuce and carrots. It suddenly came to me that time was passing. Not just in days and weeks and years but in castles and stones. Long before my heart was ever broken, long before the man I had once loved with something I remember now as devotion, long before any of us became the people our loved ones recognize, there were the castles and the stones. The stones lay there in the earth until they became castles, and now the castles lie there. And the last people who ever looked on them with the terror or relief they were meant to inspire have so long passed from these places that no one even remembers their names. It struck me dumb with awe, the awe they talk about in the Bible that is mostly fear but also admiration. The awe of time. My own troubles were almost over, no matter how I looked at it.

We were going to Galway, to Prospect Hill. Travelling the same route Martin and his family must have taken in 1937. The car trip he'd once referred to, where his father had let him shift the car. So of course he'd seen it all as well, certainly the castles along the roadside, looking exactly the same as now. With the same unnamed birds. He'd never mentioned those birds to me, which seemed so general in Ireland. Maybe only to the countryside. It was a mystery to me why he remembered some things and not others, mobilized part of his childhood and let the rest of it disappear. Another thing to remember to ask. If.

I decided the best way to avoid any further uncomfortable conversation would be to take a nap. I reached into the backseat for my jacket, drew it up over my chest and leaned against the door. Galway was still more than ninety minutes away.

"You don't mind?"

"No."

I closed my eyes. I played the old game from my childhood, focusing on the vibrations from the road, trying to twist what my mind knew about that movement into its opposite. I found I couldn't recall how I translated those vibrations, but worse, I couldn't bring my mother's face to mind, which I would see immediately on opening my eyes to test the actual world beyond my imaginings. There she would be, her eyes on the road, her mind turned inward, the openness of her expression. Where did our parents' minds go when we finally freed them to think of something other than our lives and limbs? I had encountered the empty expression on my father's face for many years after my mother died, but I turned away from it, focused on what Dale wanted or needed (since I was, by default, his mother), but my own mother's face had a serenity to it that I wanted to get behind. I'd open my eyes on her in profile, her gaze fixed on a certain distance, and I'd imagine that I was seeing her truly as herself. (For even as a child I was aware that my parents performed as parents, a role cut out of the welter of other things that, unknown to me, they were also.) What did she daydream of, as I drowsed beside her, my long thin legs dangling over the edge of the passenger seat?

Now, as a person of thirty-five, I imposed a daydream of her infidelity on this memory, but for all I knew, she might have been thinking of something from her daily life, something that pleased her. A detail from within the tempest, a moment's respite. I remembered, suddenly, a morning when Dale had announced he was leaving home forever, and how she'd handled what seemed to me urgent trouble. He was five or six, and I'd heard her talking calmly to him upstairs in his room, but soon her voice was swallowed up in the sound of hoarse shouting. She came down and smiled at me, and he came down right behind her, with a stick and one of her handkerchiefs tied to the end of it like he'd seen on television. He'd had trouble tying it properly and I watched with surprise as she helped him secure it better. He'd put nothing in it but a full Pez dispenser and a tin-can bank with a leatherette covering depicting Niagara Falls. There was a handful of coins clinking in it. We stood on the front porch watching him as he trundled up the street, his little bow-legs poking out of his long shorts. She did nothing to prevent him. In fact, she was unnaturally calm about it all.

We went into the kitchen, where she started to make sandwiches. It dawned on me that there might be something I could do that would make her that willing to let me go as well. I ran down the things I hadn't done recently that I'd been asked to do — bedmaking, towel-folding, letters to my grandparents that I was already weeks late on. I mentioned I'd spend the afternoon finishing these things I'd been meaning to get around to.

"The towels are folded and the beds are made," she said. "Get some cheese out of the fridge."

I tried to pitch in as best I could. I was cold with fear. My father was at the restaurant, and I'd only just eaten breakfast, so this ritual of making food for no one struck me dumb with fear. Perhaps it was a ritual all mothers went through when they rid themselves of an unwanted child. A celebration lunch for herself and the other mothers on the street who'd seen off their more difficult children. She wrapped the sandwiches in wax paper and got us into our windbreakers, and then we started up the road with half a dozen sandwiches in a paper bag and a few breakfast cans of orange juice (a no-no in our family was opening these cans of mouth-puckering juice at any other time than at weekend breakfast).

I held her hand in silence, and we walked up the street. I chose to stay silent, not knowing which question might free me from my fears and which trap me in them. My mother had a spring in her step and even stopped at one point to pat a dog. Obviously I was seeing a part of her that my life had never prepared me for: a capacity for heartlessness. Shortly, we arrived at the first intersection, only a five-minute walk from the house, and there we came upon Dale sitting in the shade of the postbox, his Niagara Falls bank at his side and the coins spread out on the handkerchief. He didn't even acknowledge us as we sat down beside him and my mother pulled another kerchief from her pocket and spread out the sandwiches and the drinks on it.

"How much?" she asked him.

"I can't count it," he said.

She pushed her fingers through the small pile, separating coins. "This is fifty, these are twenty five, these are ten, these five, and these are pennies. There's almost three dollars here, honey."

"How much is that?" he said, tilting his head up to her, the sun catching in his long cow lashes.

"It's a lot," she said, impressed. "How long did it take you to save all that?"

"Since the wintertime."

"You've been planning this since the winter?"

"I was waiting to see what I was going to need it for," he said, picking up a sandwich. I watched in amazement as he started eating it. She pulled the tabs off the three cold cans of juice and the three of us sat on the corner having a picnic in what I could only have called a pleasurable silence. Dale divided the Pez for dessert, and then we walked home and Dale had a nap. And where before I had merely loved my mother, now I stood in amazement. To know a code like that. But I was also angry. That she had withheld from me the calm knowledge that everything was in her control. Eventually daughters overcome that anger, learn that what seems like an awesome competence in everything does not make their mothers flawless. But for me, I would not grow to discover my mother's failings, because it was the one failing I know of now that saw her to her death.

I opened my eyes on Molly, and saw my mother at the wheel, clear as day, my mother at the age of her death. I watched her in stillness, who had always had my mother's grace, her tapering hands, and that long, deep silence at her centre; I watched my mother gazing on the road ahead.

"Molly?"

She came up out of her thought and looked over at me. "Mm?"

"I think I need to get out of the car for a few minutes."

She looked over at me with genuine concern. "You don't want to go home, do you?"

"No," I said. "I need to stretch my legs."

A few moments later, the exit to a town called Athlone appeared. We went down the winding main street to where a castle loomed over the river in the centre of town.

"Are you hungry?"

"No," I said. "You go get something. Why don't we meet back in a half-hour or so?"

She busied herself with a tight parallel park. "Did I say something wrong?"

She finished parking and tugged the brake up. I reached over and took her hand. "I haven't been very good to you, Molly. I'm sorry. I just don't know how to act right now."

"Okay."

"I need to be alone for a few minutes, though."

"I understand," she said, looking dazed by my warmth. I let go of her hand and left her with the river sparkling behind her. The cathedral bells rang noon.

I went down one of the curving sidestreets that ribbonned off from the main road and seemed to twist without reason. Below it, the brown water moved slowly along, a shallow river that I imagined smelled terrible in the height of summer, just another river abused down the centuries, with the reek of offal and sewage, maybe even the rotting bodies of ancient virgins. Along the bottom of the street, like a ghetto, there ran almost a dozen physician's offices ("surgery" said the signs over all the doors, distressingly): a dentist, a gynecologist, even two urologists facing each other across the road.

Down there, standing by itself on a post overlooking the fetid waterway, I found a phone and dialled Toronto. Daniel picked up after one ring. "Hello Jolene."

"How did you know?"

"It's nearly dawn here, so it had to be you." He cleared his throat. "Is this another ten-second don't-worry-about-me special, or are you actually calling to talk to me?"

"I'm sorry about that."

"How's your friend?"

"She's okay. I guess. I don't know."

"She didn't call me after Monday, so I just assumed you hadn't been kidnapped by leprechauns again. Is everything going to plan now?"

"There's no plan, Daniel. What did she say to you that night, anyway?"

"I just told her to give up trying to understand you. That not understanding you was part of the fun, part of the *you* that only *you* can be."

"Shut up. What did she *say* to you?"

"That you'd vanished without a trace and she was thinking of calling the police."

I shook my head. "What did you think?"

"I don't know. That to some people you must be a trick of the light."

"What would you have done if I'd disappeared?"

I heard him change ears, coughing away from the receiver. "I would definitely be nonplussed," he said. "I would probably even be disgruntled."

"Come on, Daniel."

"But if you *came* back, well, then, I'd be plussed and gruntled."

"Would you think you'd been the cause of it?"

"If this is a roundabout way to get me to change my bad habits —"

"No, I'm —"

"I'd be crushed, Jo, what do you think? I'd rather be told I was an asshole and never hear from you again than think something bad happened to you."

"Yes," I said.

"What?"

"Yes. That's how I'd feel too."

He was silent a moment, perhaps anxious he'd bulldozed an important moment. "Is there something wrong with Molly?" he said. "Is that what this is about?"

"I still don't really know what this is about, Daniel. One moment I have a hunch, and then I think I must be wrong —"

"You don't make any sense."

"I know. She's kind of ... robust and devastated all at once. We used to be very close, and something happened ..."

"What?"

"I can't explain it all now. I'm just ... it was in the past, all of this, for the longest time. And now I'm in the middle of it again. Maybe a little deeper than I should be."

"That seems to be happening a lot to you these days. Bad planning?"

"Maybe it's good luck," I said. "In some cases."

"The tin-woman gets her heart."

I turned back to the street, where medical supplicants roved in and out of the offices behind me. "Daniel, do you remember, about six weeks ago, I woke you up in the middle of the night? And you said something about no one remembering what we were like as kids?"

"It was just a dumb thought."

"No, I don't think it was. It made me very sad. I think, without knowing it, you put your finger on why I'm here."

"That's wonderfully vague."

"I know."

"Okay." I heard him groan as he stretched. "Jolene, almost everything you say goes right over my head and it excites me tremendously. When will you be back here to confuse me in person, do you think?"

"Soon. A few days."

"Will you call again?"

"I might," I said.

"I'll stay awake just in case."

"Daniel."

"Oh no."

"Can I say something heavy?"

"Will I understand it?"

"I love you. You know? I'm sorry I haven't said it before now. I love you."

There was silence on his end for a moment and I felt fearful. "What was the heavy part?" he said, and we both laughed. "Are you okay?"

"*No-oo*. I'm fucked! I'm with someone I used to love looking for someone else I used to love, okay? That's the truth. That's what I can tell you of it right now." I fell silent, and heard, down the telephone line, the hum of the distance between us. "I'm afraid to find anything else out."

"Find out," he said. "It's important, or you wouldn't have gone. Okay? Do what you need to do there and don't worry. Nothing's changing where I am."

"Thank you," I said.

"I have your picture here. I'm looking at it a lot."

"I'll see you soon. Don't forget what I just said."


When we met back at the car, Molly was excited about something she'd seen in the town. I had to pull myself out of the intimate place I was in.

"There's a sign to Clonmacnoise," she said, breathless. "It's back a ways on the highway, but it's just a few miles from here."

"What's Clonmacnoise?"

"The Bible, Jo. The story Martin told us. The other half is down there. They have it on display."

I remembered the story now. The petrified Bible. One beautiful half gone forever. "It's probably not open," I said.

"I already asked," She waved the keys. She opened the door and leaned across to unlock my side. "And I even have directions."

"You think of everything," I said.

❧

She drove. She was the same as she'd been before we stopped, bright and focused. We went round and dipped through traffic at the edge of town to get out. Molly navigated the roundabout, then went south.

"Did you clear your head?" she asked.

"I called Daniel."

"Great." She kept her eyes forward. "So everything is okay at home?"

"Everything's fine. He misses me."

"Of course he does," she said, looking over.

"Watch the road, okay?"

"He's still off-limits, huh?"

"No," I said, "Go ahead and ask me whatever you want."

"Really? Okay." She thought for a moment. "Well, I guess I have a picture of your life now. New boyfriend. You don't really know where things are going. Is this the first guy since ...?"

"Uh-huh."

"Well, good. I'm glad for you, Jo. It's a good sign."

"I wasn't much of a catch before now. It took a while." She didn't say anything, so I just let myself speak. "I went to Toronto because I couldn't think of where else to go. I left my job behind, and the few people I knew, and I just got on a bus. First thing I did when I got there was I broke into Martin's apartment. I didn't know what I was expecting to find there. It was empty. Some bills and circulars, layers of dust on everything. There were books on his bedside table that I'd recommended to him. That was hard to see."

"I'm sure."

"It was an awful place. Badly lit, with a crumbling parquet floor. I spent all of five minutes in it before I had to leave, gagging, and I never went back. I wrote an anonymous letter to the police and I expect they dealt with it the same way the Bloomington police did. There's a file somewhere with his name on it."

She listened, driving the thin road carefully. "And you just found a place and started living."

"Yes."

"That was brave of you. I don't think I would have been able to do it."

"You don't know what you can do until you have to do it, Molly." I shifted uncomfortably in my seat. "Anyway. What about your life? All I know is that you're still a lawyer. You still live in New York, right?"

"Do you really want to know?"

"Yes."

"I work six-day weeks. I live in an apartment on Central Park West. I have a fish."

"One fish."

"It's good to have something around that's more pathetic than you are."

"Do you still know your ex?"

"No," she said, and the way she said it, I knew not to go there. "I date a little. But I don't take it seriously anymore."

"That doesn't sound like a formula for success."

"I have to clean up my life before I move on to anything new. Just like you did."

"Okay," I said.

"There's an old me as well, and I'm trying to get away from it."

"There was nothing wrong with the old you. The old you was my best friend, Molly."

"You still think of me like that, even after what happened?"

"Well, I don't really know what happened, except that you took a gift the wrong way. But until that point, yes. You were my friend."

"I was," she said, almost to herself. She drove partway up a grassy verge to give room to a small car coming the opposite direction.

"Pretty easy to get killed on these roads," I said.

She came back down to the flat grade. "It's not really safe to love other people, is it?"

"I guess not."

"They never really tell you that."

"No," I said. "That part you get to find out on your own."

In about half an hour, at a bend in the road, we came upon it. It lay against the river Shannon, a black and grey jumble of crosses and crumbling churches. We parked in the empty lot and I looked over at Molly, and I sighed involuntarily. She smiled at me like a child.

I'd never seen anything as bereft and beautiful as Clonmacnoise. It was a square of buildings and graves enclosed in a crumbled wall with nothing beyond it all but fields and river. A worn path at the far edge of the site faded under grass only twenty feet out; a sign there said the path once went all the way to Dublin Bay. Half a dozen or so churches had been raised in the distant past; they were all gone now, blackened stone lying half-buried in the ground and worn smooth by hands. The roofless walls and earthen floors, no sense at all of where people did the things they do in churches, the transepts gone, the altars gone. Just half-walls and rooms open to sun and rain. It was history of people, their faith transubstantiated into granite and slate: pure grief, pure cold, a place for an absent God so far away from everything, including life, that it oozed holiness.

We wandered among the gravestones, most blank from wind and rain, all the names of the dead eroded. Their stories, with their scandals, their love affairs, their unexpected kindnesses, all of it gone. Molly hooked her arm in mine. There was nothing to say. The sign in the interpretation centre's door said the building was closed until one for lunch—we could see three people sitting at the top of a hill at the base of the remnants of a castle. We walked through a little field of cows and saw them waving at us. "People are so friendly here," I said. We mounted the hill and joined them.

"Are you crazy?" one of the wavers said when we got to them. "There're four bulls in that field. The way up is from the road." They pointed to a path with a fence on either side. I looked back down into the field and saw the bulls: they were the ones mounting the cows. We gratefully sat with the people when they invited us, and we sat beside one of the broken corners of the castle: a massive block of stone leaning against the rest of the structure. Behind us, a stone staircase spiralled up past arrow slits and into thin air. The interpretation guides had been there all morning and we were the first visitors. We shared some cheese with them and Molly had some wine. I tried to think of what all of this would look like from high up. Just a plangent green with a perfect square of grey in the middle like it was a door to some-where. We asked them when they were going to reopen, and they said anytime now, and so we walked back with them, along the path to the road, and the road into the monastery.

Inside the interpretation centre, they gave us pamphlets and postcards. Molly asked to see the Clonmacnoise Bible. The three looked at each other. Perhaps you know it under a different name, she said. She described it, and one of them went and got a postcard of an old hymnal that had turned up in someone's attic in the nearby village of Ballynahown. It dated to the 1860s, they told us, and Molly shook her head and said, Older than that, and they all said, No, there was no such thing. She stood there completely still. I asked for the name of the long-tailed bird. Pied wagtail, said one. Just a magpie, said another. Someone here should get their facts straight, Molly shouted and she ran out. I followed her into the parking lot and found her standing beside the passenger door. She was staring out at the wind-washed stone of Clonmacnoise, shaking with anger. I watched her from the driver's side, unsure of what to say or do. A cooler wind was coming up now; it blew my hair into my mouth.

"He lied," she said, not looking away from the stones. "He made it up."

I smiled uncomfortably. "I was worried he had."

She brought her face around. Her eyes were livid with hurt. "Did he lie a lot?" The wind tore the words away from her face.

"I wouldn't say it was lying, but obviously he was leaving a lot out, wasn't he?" I walked around the front of the car. Stood a foot or so from her, feeling the intensity of her emotion as a force holding me at bay. "Listen, Molly. I'm ready now. I know you haven't told me everything. I want to know why we're here." I held a hand up to keep her from interrupting me. "You said you wanted to help me. So help me then."

She stepped away from me to open the passenger door, then stood behind it, a barrier between us. "Let's get back in the car," she said. She left the door open and walked around to get in behind the wheel. I got in too and closed the door. She'd already put the keys into the ignition, but I pulled them back out and gripped them in my fist. She didn't so much as turn her body toward me. She said, "I'm here to take something back."

"Like what, Molly? Please don't tell me this is about that fucking honeycomb."

"No."

"Then what? Did you steal something from us? He vanished and I left it all behind, so I can't imagine what it is you'd want to give back that either of us would want."

"Not give back," she said. "Take back." She breathed in deeply. "It was my fault, Jolene. It was something I did."

"What the hell are you talking about?"

She reached over and pulled the keys out of my hand. My fingers just slipped open and she slid the key into the ignition without a sound.

# X.

EVERYBODY'S, 1957. 13" X 16" X 3". WOOD AND GLASS WITH PAPER, CONSTRUCTED MINIATURES, AND FOUND OBJECTS. THE MENIL COLLECTION, HOUSTON, TEXAS. A STORE WINDOW, CIRCA 1938, FULL OF MINIATURE TOYS, A TRAIN SET, AND THE MONTH'S CHILDREN'S MAGAZINES. SIDES AND BACKGROUND OF BOX A PHOTOGRAPH OF THE SURFACE OF THE MOON.

CRAMPED, SALT-REEKING GALWAY WAS MORE UNPLEASANT than Martin had feared, and later it got worse. It was a fake city, like the painted booths of a county fair, the shop windows displaying dusty magazines ajumble with creaky toys and faded corsets, the druggist's shelves thinly stocked, although bile beans and bullet-shaped suppositories were available everywhere, as if the main activity in Galway were egestion. That seemed right: this was life in the form of an aftermath, and all the colourless days and nights to come seemed very much the product of a nourishment now mulched to fetidness.

At the beginning, they'd lived with the Hannahs, old friends of their mother's who lived in an apartment above Donnellan's, a furnishing shop where the sounds of dowels being whacked into holes could be heard at all hours. The four of them slept like stowaways in a room separated by a curtain from the rest of the Hannahs (there were the parents, the eldest boy, Malcolm, the girl, Sheila, and Gabriel, the youngest at eight). Never in his life had Martin felt such remorse; so much that despite his fear of darkness and eternity, he wanted to die and set his parents and even his sister free. If his continuing life had pulled them clear across the country, then only his death would release them back to where they belonged. But he believed he was too much a coward ever to set them free that way. The only saving graces were the gas lamps that cast an orange light in brilliant cones up to the night sky, and the horses beneath them, those noble animals, running their carriage errands.

Don't stare at them too hard, Theresa said, or they'll blow up.

This reproach stung him as she knew it would. It had been a terrible thing to dynamite King George on the very day of the London coronation. Their mother had been very upset about it, but their father muttered bitterly as they passed through Maynooth: Art criticism. He should have been sitting on an ass. There'd been a period of silence after that.

Standing at his new, but temporary, window, Martin tried to consolidate old visions with new ones. But he couldn't see a church spire here without pressing his cheek to the glass and looking aslant down the street. And here they seemed to be in the thick of the city, but there was no centre to look toward: it was all sprawl. Across the way, a tailor's dummy stared out blankly over the cobble.

The radio played a commercial.

Oh, is that an electric toaster, Mary? Goodness, it must be expensive to use!

Mary chided that electricity was cheap. I must show you my electric cooker and iron, she said. And I have the neatest little electric fire in my bedroom.

There were nine of them in a five-room apartment. The Sloanes had come from their red-bricked, iron-gated house on Iona to the life of indigents. In the mornings, their father would set out to find them a house, while their mother and Mrs. Hannah busied themselves with shopping and cooking. Out on the streets, going quietly in and out of the shops, it all felt so ephemeral — like an ill-chosen vacation spot rather than real life. Martin was on one side of his mother, safely separated from Theresa on the other. Mrs. Hannah showed their mother the best place to buy apples, the best covered buttons, the best cheese shop. Over the bridges spanning the branches of the Corrib, down the cramped medieval streets with their smells of damp and crumbling brick. They crossed the Dominick Street

Bridge and went up by Nun's Island and the old jail, but then somehow the river was to their right again (as it had been before they crossed the bridge), and still flowing down into the bay, although they had not turned around or crossed the street.

Martin, stop pulling on me, said his mother.

Mrs. Hannah? How many rivers are here?

Just the one, she said. All the way to Galway Bay, that's a song. And she sang it, dispelling none of his confusion. How could a river change direction? Mrs. Hannah had a sharp little voice, not like his mother's, but his mother had not sung anything for a long time.

The Hannahs' children were in a private school up past Newcastle Road where the university was. Their father proudly walked them every morning, his pockets full of unhulled hazelnuts, and he sounded like a game of dice walking out the door with the three of them. How shameful, Martin thought, that his own mother would be seen in public with two children out of school in May. Although she seemed to be enjoying the change of habit, and smiled down at him and Theresa often.

Feeling okay, honeylamb? she'd say, stroking his cheek with her fingers.

This is the temple, Mrs. Hannah said one afternoon. Everyone calls it the St. Augustine Synagogue — can you imagine? It was like all the other shops on St. Augustine Street, only it featured a placard with Hebrew writing in the window. The curtains were drawn behind it. Seeing a synogogue brought Martin fresh feelings of guilt.

New members welcome all the time, said Mrs. Hannah.

I'll keep my word, said their mother, shaking her head. But maybe I'll come with you and Michael one evening.

I want to come, said Theresa. I feel more and more Jewish every day.

You'll honour your father's wishes as you do mine.

They walked on, but Martin's spirit felt bruised by his own sins.

That afternoon, Mrs. Hannah boiled the cod for the evening meal and put all of the oatmeal in a pot of water to soak until morning. It was to become a pot of flummery. The best kind of invalid cookery, she told Martin.

I'm not an invalid, though, he replied.

Soon you'll be right as rain. She held his head in her hands and squeezed. She smelled like butter going bad and he noticed his own mother looking unhappily at her friend. He knew then that they were only at the Hannahs because they had no other option, and Mrs. Hannah's friendship was not one his mother wanted particularly. He understood that there was something about these people that his mother had walked away from; only duty (on the part of the Hannahs) and great need (that was their portion) had drawn the two families together.

He looks like your da, Adele. Martin squirmed between Mrs. Hannah's hot hands. She turned his head down and laughed. A little spray of red straight from Poland.

His mother came over from the table where she'd been sitting and smoothed down his hair. Both women gripped his skull in their hands, like they were testing a melon. It's more likely straight out of Antrim, I'd think. From those Antrim Sloanes.

Mrs. Hannah released him. I love his colour. We've all black hair to our flanges, look at us, like dark purebreds! She clapped her hands, her eyes shining. She nodded at Malcolm, who was sitting with a book on the couch. That one, he looks like we brought him straight from Palestine.

I was born in England, the boy protested.

You were right, said Mrs. Hannah. The future is in people of all different types coming together. No stopping it, anyway. You were right to ignore the prating of your friends. People can be backwards, as we know.

I'm sure you remember when I came back with Colin to Hammersmith. It must have been hard to hear all the things people were saying. Wasn't it?

Oh it was, it was, said Mrs. Hannah, pushing her fish back down into the frothing water. But you know how hard it is to talk sense to some people.

Yes, said his mother, staring at the back of Mrs. Hannah's head. I do know.

That night, at dinner, they tried their best to eat Mrs. Hannah's meal. It was called kedgeree, and it smelled exactly like the streets: of mildew and salt.

Malcolm, Sheila, and Gabriel cleaned their plates, and Gabriel, sitting beside Martin, rescued him by quietly offering to finish his supper. When dinner was over, Martin's father spoke.

Well, I'm glad to be able to share happy news. Our little streak of bad luck is at an end. He raised a glass of water to the rest of the table. I've found us a house.

Their mother was beaming. You didn't tell me!

It was a surprise.

Where is it, then?

It's a beautiful house in St. Mary's Terrace, down on Taylor's Hill. A beautiful little house behind a gate. We'll have you over when we're settled, he said to their hosts, and drink to your graciousness and hospitality.

But of course they didn't have them over. They never had the Hannahs over, even though they had an acknowledged debt to them, and the two families, in fact, never saw each other again. Instead, the Sloanes unpacked their boxes and set about transforming the little house on Taylor's Hill into a home, a role it resisted. It was a not uncharming house, with its warm mahogany banisters and a three-piece mantel that framed a fire like someone sheltering a match in their palm. But the kitchen at the rear of the house was cold and cramped, and there were only two bedrooms, which forced Martin and Theresa into close quarters after years of independent living. Furious at the change in her station, Theresa reproached Martin in any way she could, and at night she folded herself into bed in silence, even refusing to respond to a plaintive goodnight, if he were so bold to offer one.

But worse in the little house was the situation of light,

something they discovered on their first morning. Although the front windows faced east, the houses on the west side of Taylor's Hill were triangulated in such a way that none but the very end houses of St. Mary's Terrace enjoyed any sunlight at all. From their new front windows, bits of sun like torn wrapping paper could be seen in the broad oak leaves over the rectory across the street. But it stopped there, in the oak leaves, censuring them. The darkness of the house hit them all like a *coup de grace*, extinguishing the last bit of optimism they had. The sense of cautious hopefulness that attended the closing of the house purchase was now briskly replaced by a sepulchral gloom. After a few weeks, Martin noticed that Theresa had stopped chastising him, and the cessation of even this form of caring chilled him.

Soon the dark, cold little house became a fact of life, and they adapted, although their father complained bitterly that the dimness of the house would make them all blind, or turn them into lemurs. More lights with better wattage were found, and at night (at least) the house took on a semibright kind of a warmth that wasn't entirely negated by the sun that had failed to reach the house by day.

Gradually, bravely, their parents tried to reassume their lives. Not knowing anyone presented them with the daunting task of finding their equals, and they began trying on other couples for size. How hard it was for them, combating their loneliness, Martin thought, when he at least had Theresa, however obelisk-like she was at times. Their parents, alone in a new and cryptic social order, couldn't find their place. Visits from strange couples became an unhappy ritual. A man and a woman, approximately their parents' ages and located through mysterious channels, would appear around the hour of six, bearing flowers or a jar of clover honey or a sack of loose tea from Newell's. Then the introductions (we have a young man very much your age!) and the dinner. More often than not, offal was served — tripe or liver or kidney — in an attempt to appear continental. Quantities were eaten, and then afterwards there was the smoking and the ponderous remembrances of one disconnected thing after another.

Later, Theresa would creep out of bed to listen to the evening's progress through the bars at the top of the stairs. He'd hear her, and venture out himself, standing close, but not beside her. The sound of the clock on the mantel would be louder than the guests, and the scent of pipe tobacco overpowering. Sometimes there would be a record on the turntable, and Martin would think contentedly that maybe they were all having fun down there.

Mrs. Shaughnessy thinks Dad is below her, Theresa would say without turning to him, or, Mr. and Mrs. Phillips were dressed poorly. She was good at parsing the code of their parents' guests — what a certain type of gift meant, how the length of the visit and the volume of the conversation correlated with the potential for friendship.

His parents seemed to Martin on those evenings even more foreign to this place than they did during the days. What they belonged to were the alder trees on Iona Road, the churning wrens circling the chimneys, the walled nunnery past St. Columba's, the Morris cars ticking in the sunlight down the street. Not to this rot of wood and netting! Not to these sparse trees pocked with burls, or these raucous magpies! Their parents seemed pasted onto it all like cut-out figures from *Everybody's*.

He would lie in bed, the sounds of the last omnibus clacking past ten streets over in Eyre Square, and try not to drift off on those nights, would try to listen for the sounds of the cards being brought out, or the old photo albums, and sometimes, in the flickerings of near-sleep, it felt that one moment there was Sheila Dunne's Popular Band and the sound of pennies crossing the table, and the next, silence and darkness, the moon a pale band across the foot of the bed. He'd call to Theresa across in her own bed, and she'd lift herself up on her elbows and say, You fell asleep. They're gone. And they won't be back either.

After some time, people stopped coming altogether, and the effort was abandoned. It was a great relief. Now their parents resigned themselves to the gradual acquaintanceships of neighbours, connections that grew as slowly as quartz on the nourishment of occasional encounters. There were the Cadburys at one side and the Raleighs on the other; they hardly spoke to either, but by the middle of the summer, two of the Raleigh girls had absorbed Theresa into their circle of play. The stories she told of their adventures were Martin's main connection to the world outside. The summer, however bright, however fragrant, was compressed for him into long afternoons of reading or rearranging his belongings. Their father had long since located a shop in town, but he discouraged Martin from coming there, and Martin had only once seen the grey interior of the store, bereft of browsers and certainly of buyers: his father didn't want him to see what appeared to be impending failure. Later, Martin began to take solitary walks over the bridges and through the streets, and although this was not Dublin, some of Galway's charms did gradually give themselves over: now the shop windows began to seem a little less dusty and prim — Thomas McDonogh & Sons always had a vibrant display of cheeses and fruits in pyramids, as well as an assortment of model trains half out of their cardboard boxes. Again, the peaceful silence of things began to come back to him and comfort him. They had their mute order, their grace and vitality. These thoughts, with their power to make him happy, became his main solace as the lonely summer went on. His parents, though, however they tried, could not disguise their unhappiness. His mother sometimes smiled at him, trying to hide an expression he'd just catch a flicker of. And once, he heard his father in the kitchen say, *What have I done?* and when he'd quietly entered the room, he'd found his father alone there.

They carried on as best they could. In the evenings, they all took their supper with the windows open, or sometimes even outside, their china in their laps, since they had no outdoor table. There was the occasional play in town, or visit to the movies, but although the feeling of real life had returned in their rituals, the centre of things felt hollow. Galway pushed them away. It was as if they skimmed along the surface of their new reality, like waterstriders on a pond.

Finally August came, and at the end of it, it was time to go to school. Martin and Theresa walked together in the mornings behind the nunnery and the stream full of grassy islands. The banks, in early morning, were always occupied by two or three old men with their fishing poles and bowls of maggots, hoping to attract one or two of the salmon that made it past the weir at Newcastle Road Bridge. Beaky old men hauling beaky salmon out of the glistening waters. Then to the public school, to the left and up the hill.

Martin recognized some of his fellow students in his form — the city was small enough that even two encounters with someone was enough to make them seem familiar. The Raleighs were here, and there was a girl who probably lived around the corner from him, he'd seen her so often. There were others — a grey-faced boy he'd seen once when he'd been taken to buy shoes; a couple of girls memorable for their tallness; a Chinese boy who was the only such child he'd ever laid eyes on, whose teeth tapered out from blackened stems.

For the first few days, Martin kept his eyes down as much as he could, knowing that the kids with the power to do so were already making categories, and staying unnoticeable was essential to avoid being placed on either end of the social spectrum. There was as much responsibility in being extremely popular as there was in being outcast, and Martin wanted to be left out of it all. Theresa was one of the chosen in her form: she had the appeal, the confidence and the looks, and she was already friends with the Raleigh girls, who commanded not only the form but most of the girls in the school. This was an added burden to Martin — Theresa advertised a disdain for him that threatened to make him the target of unwanted interest. Having a powerful sister was not something that would accrue to his benefit, especially if it was known she wouldn't protect him. He watched uncomfortably as the social strata was wrought. The Chinese boy was established, without delay, as one end of the spectrum, and the strongest of the boys — the sporting ones and the loudest — balanced him off at the other. When it was all done, Martin was relieved to find he was without appeal to any of them, and he settled into an easy and mostly invisible existence.

In the third week, as the first cooling breezes of the autumn were arriving, Gabriel Hannah appeared in the class with his leather satchel held tight against his chest. He had been transferred out of the private school on Newcastle Road because his progress had been too slow. This was a dangerous stigma. Martin felt sorry for him (being added for such a reason after the beginning of school was a sure route to ostracism) but also afraid for himself, for he knew Gabriel would attach to him.

The younger boy, however, showed an almost adult restraint in his desire for friendship, and for the second time, too. (The first had been the subtle removal of kedgeree from Martin's plate.) He would wait silently outside the school until Martin appeared, and then walk away. Farther down the road, he'd stop and wait for Martin to catch up. In this way, their friendship rooted. The two hours between four-thirty and six-thirty on schoolnights were generally assumed to be filled with tutors or sports, so the two boys would not be missed if they struck out on their own. They wished to be anywhere but in their own houses, and the sea, the lake, and the forest behind the university gave cover.

One afternoon in September, when the woods were at their fullest, the two of them walked deep into the one behind the school to look for birds. They'd given up on trapping wood-cocks, with their beautiful bellies and long beaks, because they were hard to find, but the guidebook made them sound worth keeping an eye out for. The woodcocks were known to fly up as if shot from cannons, springing wildly from the undergrowth before plunging back into it. The prey this afternoon was crossbills, which Gabriel had read you could tell the presence of by the path of cracked pinecones that the birds would split in their scissored beaks. The male was a red-bellied bird, easy to see before the leaves changed. Gabriel carried a rough-made trap, a fruit crate and a string attached to a propping stick. Their bait was a ball of suet wrapped in cloth.

Martin hung back a little, more involved in the smells and textures of the forest than Gabriel, who craned his neck to look for the tell-tale silhouettes of old leaves and twigs against the sky that might mean a nest of crossbills or siskins. He was also occupied with the undermoss and holly, which he kicked over for centipedes and charlie bugs that curled up into segmented balls like armadillos. When he found a worm or grub, he opened the cheesecloth and pressed it into the suet. Tastier that way, he said. They came to a small clearing where the sun came down more directly, and here Gabriel set up the trap. It lay open like a jaw at the edge of the tiny space, half in shadow, with the string trailing back to the base of an oak where the two boys sat and shared a raisin bun.

How do you know anything is going to come this way? asked Martin.

Something eventually will. Birds eat all the time.

Martin started to get bored, but didn't want to say anything. He'd sat with Gabriel on a number of occasions now, waiting for something that never came, and he decided that maintaining the friendship was more important to him than revealing his lack of interest in the hunt. He dug his feet into the soft moss around the base of the tree and took small bites of his half of the bun. They'd have to head back in a matter of half an hour or so, and when they did, they'd talk again, about this and that. Which was the thing he liked best about Gabriel. The sun moved diagonally against them, soon covering the box in complete shadow.

Listen, said Gabriel. There was a sound like *zizzeek*, but they couldn't tell where it came from because it seemed to bounce around the canopy above them.

What is it?

A bird.

Which one, though?

Shh —

The sound came nearer, and then stopped, and the next time they heard it, it was far away. Gabriel was stock-still, his head tilted to capture the sound, but Martin had had enough of sitting and doing nothing. At the edge of the clearing, some white mushrooms with broad umbrella-like caps stood straight against a tree trunk. He looked back at Gabriel, who had given up on hearing the birdcall again, and called him over. His friend unrolled the string to reach the edge of the sunlight.

They're field mushrooms, Gabriel said.

Martin squatted down to inspect them. They looked like warts in the moss. We're not in a field.

Close enough. Gabriel lay on his side and looked under the mushrooms. White gills, he said. If they were grey, it'd be a death cap, but this one is fine.

Sure. You don't know anything about them.

Death cap can kill you in ten seconds. This is just a field mushroom, though. Harmless.

Martin poked it with a twig. It felt solid and hollow all at once. You can tell just by looking?

And smell. If it's like honey, it's the death cap. That's how it gets you to eat it.

So it wants to be eaten, does it?

If you were a mushroom, you'd love a rotting body to root in. Gabriel took out a pocket knife and cut the stem without touching the mushroom. It tipped over into sunlight where it glowed a little green, like an underripe olive. See — white gills. Harmless.

Someone else might call that grey, though. And it does kind of smell like honey.

That's the moss. Trust me. You want me to pop it in my mouth?

No.

I will if you want me.

No you won't. I found it. If anyone's going to eat it, I am.
He took the knife from Gabriel and drove it down through the
hard white cap. The flesh inside was an ethereal white, but even
as they looked at it, it began to pale to a light pink, and then a
ruddy red. Now it looks like meat, he said.

Might taste like a pork chop!

I'm sure. His death would be hard at first for his parents, he
thought again, but then afterwards, they could move back to
Dublin and pick up their old lives. Maybe he was supposed to
have died on Temple Street, in the hospital, along with the boy
who moaned and the girl with one black shoe. Death had had its
fill on the other children, so it appeared, but he could give it
another chance. He cut off a hunk of the mushroom about the
size of his thumb. Everywhere he touched it, the mushroom
became wet, as if the heat of his fingers were liquefying it. But
before he could put it in his mouth, Gabriel emitted a shout of
joy — Got you! — and there was the sound of the crate hitting the
ground. Gabriel leapt up and ran to the other edge of the clearing and Martin followed. There, in the crate, its black eyes shining, was a woodcock the size of a gravy boat. It jumped around
banging its head on the roof of the crate, screeching anxiously.

Ho-ly! said Martin. Gabriel was crouched on his haunches
looking into the box. After a few more excited moments, the bird
settled into the corner of the crate, trying to make itself tiny.

Look at her! Just look at her! She's gorgeous!

It's a woodcock, right?

You bet it is. This is like finding twenty quid! Hello,
Woodie! Hello, sweetie! Did you like your suet and grubs?

The two of them stared into the crate, holding it down with
their palms. In its dark square, the bird tried to stay equidistant
from the two faces, its breast rising and falling quickly, and it
jerked its beak up and down a number of times, as if it were
swallowing something. It had dark brown wings and a grey

233

underbelly, and just like in the book, its beak was a long dark needle, perfect for rooting worms out of muddy earth. Gabriel ran his fingers along the side of one of the slats and stroked her wings. The bird tried to peck at him.

I want to pick her up, he said. I'm going to break one of the slats and put my hand around her. You hold the crate down. Martin lay his arms across the top of the crate and Gabriel cracked open one of the thin slats on the side. The bird reacted violently to the sound, dashing herself against the other three walls. Gabriel reached in slowly, and Martin could see his open hand sweeping through the space.

She's in the corner now, just move your hand left ...

Gabriel's hand flattened the woodcock against the back of the crate. He manoeuvred his fingers around her back and pressed her down, then lifted the crate up so it hung from his forearm. He transferred the bird carefully to his free hand, its legs kicking helplessly. Then he dropped the crate and held the animal, triumphant. Look at you! Just look at you!

Don't grip her too hard, Martin said. She was a sight, so rare and so wild. Her eyes bulged in fear, her wings flattened tight against her. He wanted to hold her as well, and feel her heart beating hollowly in the palm of his hand. Gabriel passed her carefully to him, and then he had her, her buff head lying against his thumb, the cold claws of her feet scrabbling against his wrist. Gabriel ... she's so frightened. We should let her go.

No, said Gabriel. I have an idea — we'll give her the mushroom. Then you'll see it's safe. Martin didn't want to, but Gabriel went back for the other half of the mushroom lying in the moss and held it in front of the bird's beak. It didn't want to eat. Come on, Woodie. Have some of this.

Martin pulled the bird away from him. Let's not be cruel. Just leave her be.

Don't you want your question answered?

No. I don't. Not anymore.

Fine scientist you'll make.

I never said I wanted to be a scientist. I don't know what I'll be. He could feel the bird relax in his hand, like it had given up fighting. Maybe I'll be a builder.

You mean an architect?

No. I want to be the person who makes the building.

Sure, said Gabriel. You with bricks on your shoulders. He craned his neck to get a look at the bird. Hey ... what's wrong with her?

The woodcock had gone completely limp. Her feet hung loose against Martin's arm and her eyes had stopped moving. Instinctively, he dropped it, and the bird tumbled like a shuttle-cock to the ground and lay still. Oh god, he said. I've killed her —

Were you squeezing her?

I was holding her loosely, I was! He squatted down, the bird's form clouded to him behind a thin mist in his eyes. Look what we've done, Gabriel! I wasn't thinking about her for this —

What do you mean, for this?

Martin reached down, blinking back tears, to close the bird's wings. But as soon as he touched it, the animal leapt up and struck him the forehead, drawing blood with the tip of her beak. Then she hit the ground again, her wings fully open, and she flapped violently against the undergrowth, flipping herself twice on her back and then righting before she burst up in a flare of brown and grey and flew back into the darkness of the forest. They heard her voice as she vanished, *zizzeek*. Martin stood and looked where she'd gone, stunned at the pain behind his eyes. He touched his forehead, mingling with the blood whatever residue from the mushroom remained on his fingers. Gabriel turned back to him and his eyes went to the cut above Martin's nose. Blood ran down. She got you good, he said, and he got out a kerchief from his back pocket and reached out to sop the wound, but Martin pushed his hand away.

Leave it, he said, and he began walking back to the road.

XI.

THE GOOD BOOK OF MYSTERIES. 12" X 10" X 3" PAPER, BOARD,
SOIL, BRASS. A BOOK, ENCRUSTED WITH EARTH, IS HELD
TOGETHER BY A RUSTED LOCK BETWEEN TWO PIECES OF GLASS.

BALLYDANGAN, BALLINASLOE, AUGHRIM, KILREEKILL.

Molly walked across the yard, a grey fog with a shaft of pale yellow running through it from the light of the shed. She pushed the door open. He was sitting there, his back to her, his hands unseen and busy with something in front of him. He looked behind himself when he felt the air on his neck. I'm not very good at obeying other people's rules, she said. Especially when I've got a bus leaving town in two hours.

He turned fully to her. I'm sorry, he said. I didn't mean to be rude. It's just I need to be —

It's fine, she said. She walked to the desk looking around her, up at the busy walls with their shelves and cubbyholes, and then leaned her hip against his desk and looked down at a doll's head whose eyes were staring out at one of the side walls. The fortress of solitude, she said.

I just come here to wind down.

Is this regular life? Parties and openings and people applauding?

God no. Thankfully. I feel like an idiot at these things. Always tongue-tied.

Well, there's *thank you*, and *you're very kind*, and *it was wonderful of you to come.*

There's also *You know, I have an uncle who paints.*

She laughed and leaned down on her forearms on the desk, casting her eyes over its attractive clutter. There were orphaned objects all over it — an old *Collier's Magazine* with the shape of a sparrow cut through it and a wooden toy, a sparrow, of course, embedded in the space. A nearly invisible incursion, as if indentical birds in two different flocks had just changed places with each other. Somehow, this altered the world, but in a way she could only feel rather than explain. She reached out and touched the bird. It was level with the surface of the magazine. Behind and around the magazine, cogs from a clock. Do these go together? she asked.

I don't know yet. He touched the magazine himself, as if to return his valence to it. She liked watching that, seeing his pale hand brush over the surface of something he'd made, long fingers, fingernails like slivers of almond.

I guess it's funny to meet each other after all this time, isn't it?

It took a while, he said.

Although it's almost like we've known each other for years. He nodded, willing to accept that view of things for the sake of being friendly. Am I the way you thought I'd be?

I don't know, he said. I can see why you and Jolene are friends, though.

She laughed, tossing her hair behind her neck. That was diplomatic. Does that mean you were expecting some kind of bombshell?

All I mean is Jolene wouldn't be friends with someone who didn't have wonderful qualities.

*Thank you.* Her face became hot. Anyway, I actually came in here to apologize.

For what?

For starting that fight this afternoon.

*That* wasn't a fight, he said. He swivelled in the chair to follow her around the tiny space.

Your fights are a little harsher than that, are they?

When we fight.

She went *huh* under her breath. I can't imagine you two in a knock 'em down, drag 'em out kind of thing anyway.

Do you fight like that?

Naw, she said. I'm a nice girl who don't make no trouble for no one.

He smiled and the lines beside his eyes appeared. Sure.

Anyway. Sorry if I kicked up any dirt. It's just I love your stuff, and I remember it really well. It was all over our house, so it was almost like *I* was living with you.

Thanks. It's nice of you to say that.

We had — she had — shelves of your things. Jolene always came back from your weekends together with something. And she'd say, Look what Martin made me. It's funny, we'd both be looking at whatever it was, but I'd always be the one to say, Hey, this is like a diary made up of bus tickets — you know, that little book you made of bus tickets all in order of the times you came down that first year?

I remember it.

It's just interesting that I'd *get it*, you know, before she did. Maybe she was just too starry-eyed to see straight!

Maybe, he said. He was listening carefully to her now, not only because she was nervous and speaking quickly but because she was related by love, if there was such a thing. (He believed there was, in the same way he believed that every one thing in the world had its kindred in at least one other thing.) He was trying not to slip into the truisms he often used with people he didn't know. He said, I tried to make her stuff that she'd like. I kept my eye out for little knick-knacks that seemed like they were *her*, you know? So she'd understand I knew who she was.

She loved them, Molly said quietly. She was proud of them. At first she kept them in her bedroom, but I suggested we make a place for them where we could both see them. Molly glanced up quickly at him.

I'm flattered. He shifted in his seat and looked around at the objects scattered on his desk.

It's nice to have beautiful things.

Well ... that *is* nice of you to say.

241

She ran a finger down one of the boxes facing side-out on the wall near the back of the shed. Her finger came away dustless. Do you know she offered me the honeycomb? she said. This afternoon, when we were swimming?

He lifted a hand off his lap and rested it on the desk. Really. That was a nice thing to do.

I told her no.

You didn't have to, he said. You *should* have it. You practically earned it this afternoon.

You made it for her, though.

Yes, he said. He looked down at his hand and swept an unseen bit of dirt off the desk. It doesn't *mean* you shouldn't have it. She didn't look happy with that justification. Well, look, he said, I'll make something for you, then.

I wouldn't ask that. A person doesn't ask for something like that.

You didn't. I offered.

She ignored him and went on. It bothered me that you'd made something for her, she said, and she'd never really looked at it. I mean, obviously, I'm not saying anything bad about her. I love Jolene. But it didn't bother you?

No, he said. I *wish* she'd seen the doll, but you can't ask people to see the exact thing you want them to.

But don't you want someone to feel what it is that *you* put there?

It's not that important.

She spread her arms open. Why make all this stuff, then?

He shrugged and tried to make light. I'm a collector. I see something I like, I want to keep it somewhere I can enjoy it.

That's not true, she said, shaking her head. You're trying to reach someone. Like you said. You wanted to *show* her you knew who she was.

Yes, but —

So who are you talking to with this? She'd come back to the desk and now she picked up the *Collier's*. Are you talking to yourself?

242

You really shouldn't touch that.

The people who want to talk to you at these openings? They're just carrying on their half of the conversation with you.

It's not my intention to —

There was a crack. To his horror, she'd pushed the sparrow out of the magazine, forcing it out with her thumbs and breaking the glue seal. She held the wooden bird up in her hand.

Molly —

*I* know what you're saying to me with this. His face was fixed. She held the bird away from him. It's like ... here's this thing that before you altered it was just a picture of a little bird. But now you've made it heavier. You've weighed it down, and put it back in the sky. So now, even though before it was just a picture and everyone knows a picture can't fly, you've made extra sure of it. I *know* how that feels. She lowered the wooden bird to the table, her hand shaking, and he quietly took it. Outside, they heard Jolene open the sliding door. Martin gingerly pushed the sparrow back into the space he'd made for it. His face was flushed and his hand was unsteady.

I'm flattered that you like my work, Molly. But it doesn't mean you know me.

There's something in you that can't get away from itself.

That's what *you* see in this. His voice was controlled, but angry. This is not *about* you. It doesn't know you. It doesn't even know me.

Of course it does.

No, Molly. It's not for that.

Well, does *she* know you, for Christ's sake?

Jolene called from the yard. Guys?

Martin ... Molly reached for him, wanting to fix what she'd just done, but then her face hardened and she withdrew her hand. How can you not expect to touch people? He'd gotten up to get to Jolene. They could both hear her approaching. Answer *that*, she said. Where do you think you'll end up if you push away the ones you actually reach?

# XII.

CARRIAGE, 1984. 17" X 13" X 3" BOX CONSTRUCTION. WOOD
AND GLASS WITH PAPER ILLUSTRATION, VELVET, FOUND OBJECTS,
DOLL PARTS. NATIONAL MUSEUM OF AMERICAN ART, WASHING-
TON, DC. VELVET CURTAINS OBSCURE THE OCCUPANTS OF A
HORSE-DRAWN CARRIAGE, THEIR HANDS RESTING, ONE ON TOP
OF THE OTHER, ON THE RIM OF THE DOOR. THE CARRIAGE, A
LITHOGRAPH FORTIFIED WITH IRON WHEELS AND A GLASS LAMP,
RIDES OVER AN EARLY ILLUSTRATION OF THE GREAT LAKES.

THE PROMISED CHANGE IN THE WEATHER HAD COME
and the night was cooling off. In the afternoon, it had been summer, and now it
was fall. We closed the windows against the edge of cold in the air. It was hard to
imagine ourselves at the quarries just hours before, under the sun, the sheer stone
hot to the very surface of the water, and then cold beneath. Tomorrow the stone
would still retain some of that warmth, but it wouldn't be long until the quarries
started freezing over.

Martin ran us a bath and when he dropped the salts in, thick steam billowed
out into the hall. At one point, he walked through it toward me, a naked chimera
trimmed in clouds. He always liked the water scalding; I'd have to sit on the edge of
the tub, trailing my fingers until it felt like I could slide in with him. I followed him
back through the steam and shed my robe as he got in. I sat on the edge with my feet
tucked under his thighs and his forearm draped over the tops of my legs, his skin so
hot that it gave me goosebumps on my arms and chest.

I don't know how you're going to get up in the morning and take a ten-hour
bus, I said. It's almost midnight.

I'll sleep on the way home.

Take the next one, Martin. An extra day won't make any difference.

He slid down a little into the water. I pushed his arm off me and got in facing
him, gasped up the pang of heat and then settled, feeling sedated. We laced our legs
together and some water sloshed over the side. Over the surface, I could only see his
nose and eyes. His mind was drifting.

Don't fall asleep.

Mm.

I can't lift you out of here, hon. He pushed up a little. His face was scarlet. I

247

wanted to keep him awake longer, just in case I lost the battle for one more day. I'd already begun to plan the morning: eggs and lattes at the Runcible Spoon, a walk through town, a visit to Loeb's to buy next week's groceries, meals we'd be eating together in six days, five if I got my way. The usual hope-making illusions of continuity. I excused this form of greed in myself, calling it love.

Did you have a nice afternoon?

I had an interesting afternoon, he said.

I'm sure you did. It was kind of you to give Molly the grand tour. I hope you left out the lap-sitting.

I had to push her off me a couple times, he said. She's a lovely girl. I liked meeting her finally.

Did she say anything interesting? Give you any girlish insights into the mystery that is Jolene? I batted my eyes at him.

She told me she loved my work.

That made me smile, thinking of the honeycomb in her luggage. Well, what does she know.

He shrugged. She must know something.

I lifted his legs up over mine and pulled myself toward him and pressed my stomach against his. I felt him brush against me under the water. Sometimes we made love like this, although the heat of the water made for logy sex. But it was comfortable to be loved this way, it felt like married sex, whatever that was, and that appealed to me. But we were both too tired. Martin lowered his head to my shoulder and turned his face away.

Are you hungry? I asked him.

Nuh-uh, he groaned. Just want to turn out all the lights. Go to bed.

I lowered my lips to his ear. Will you stay tomorrow, Martin? Please? Stay with me. I want a day where I don't have to share you with anyone.

Ask me in the morning.

Stay with me.

He turned his face and kissed my collarbone on the way to my mouth. I closed my legs around his back and pulled him harder against me. I can't, he said. I'm practically dead.

Okay. I felt with my foot for the chain to the stopper and pulled it up. Let's get you out, then, before you get sucked down the drain.

I wrapped him in a towel and brought him into bed. His breathing was deep *and slow, like a child's after a long day. He fell asleep almost right away, without another word to me, and when I drifted off, my arm lay against the length of his thigh, and his back was still hot against my skin.*

We'd driven down into the city, against a sun that lay low and bright over the Atlantic. It was four o'clock in the afternoon. We'd pulled over to the side of the road after following the direction to a street where the houses sat back on small lawns. Streams of traffic went by in both directions: people heading home to town, to the country. Galway was not even a tenth the size of Dublin. A backwater. We'd driven in from the top of the city along the N6, into the fragrance of fishrot and hops. We'd watched the houses appear, getting closer together, first the estates, then the homes, then the row houses.

Near the end of her story, she'd pulled over onto the shoulder and told the rest of it with her hands frozen on the wheel. I'd gotten out and gone around to drive. We wentthe rest of the way not talking, her face turned to the scenery. Now she pushed herself up in the seat. "How long were they here?"

"A while," I said. "Too long and not long enough."

Our address was a white stuccoed cottage with two floors on a row of houses pushed back off the street behind short brick walls. Most had gardens still in bloom; this one didn't. Through the iron gate, we could see a trellis with a wisp of dead black vine resting against the front of the house on one side of the door. The garden patch running along the wall beside it was empty of plants, a dried white crest of minerals washed up from rains lay on top of it all.

The windows I could see from the car were dark.

"You're not saying much," she said.

"That's because I don't know how I feel yet."

She rubbed her palms along the tops of her legs. "I've had longer to think about it."

"I guess so." I hadn't looked at her since somewhere outside of Kilreekill, but at least now I had a reason outside of the car to avoid her eyes. I tried to picture Martin walking up the sidewalk there, a couple paper bags of groceries balanced on one arm as he dug in his coat pocket for a key. Upstairs, unpacking, finding the bag with the sweet thing he'd bought himself for eating right away. It was a quiet street, altogether an unremarkable place, and it was difficult to imagine the years of unnoticed routine that must have unfolded there on a daily basis. Difficult, because one house in the middle of it seemed to glow with significance, like the houses you sometimes see on television roped off by the police, men with shovels tromping down the alleyways.

Molly looked up toward the darkened house. "Should we come back later?"

"I need to sit here for a while." She settled back against her seat and lay her hands in her lap. I finally turned to her and saw her face was mottled white and red. "I won't talk to you if you cry."

"I'm not crying."

"What's wrong, then?"

"I don't feel well."

"Is it any wonder? Carrying this kind of poison around?"

"I'm here to *do* something about it, Jolene!"

I was furious at her. It was as if she'd dug a hole through the floor of my memory and inserted herself in everything that had happened to me. "Did you kill my mother too? At the age of six, did you introduce her to the guy she was fucking?"

"Don't say things like that, Jolene."

"I want you to know about that night you visited us. After you'd gone, do you know what happened?"

"No."

"Nothing. We went into the house and we had a night like any other night. We had a bath together. He said that he'd enjoyed meeting you. We were tired and we went to bed. There was nothing going on."

"He must have already made his mind up."

"You're right," I said. "But it was long before you got there."

"And yet he didn't do anything until that night."

"He was passing through, Molly." The windshield was steaming up and I rolled the window down to let some of the sour air out of the car. "He wasn't waiting for a sign, and he wasn't going to be pushed over the edge. What he did was something that was *in* him to do and that had *been* there all along."

"Maybe there were little increments, though," she said. "Like something growing inside you that you don't know about until it starts pushing up against a nerve."

"And you think telling him that maybe I didn't *appreciate* him enough was going to do it? What makes you think in eight hours you could have become that important?"

She evaded my eyes, setting her mouth in a hard line. "I've spent ten years worrying about what I did to you, Jolene. And now that I have a chance to take back what I said, I'm going to do it, whether or not it matters to you."

She went on; she wanted me to understand that it was impossible to do something for me without doing something for herself. She was sorry about the inevitability of her selfishness. I heard this, but I wasn't listening. I was watching the man in the second-floor window. I remained completely still, as if I were waiting for him to approach a box propped up by a stick. He held a small watering can, and with his other hand, he braced himself against the windowframe and leaned forward to water a row of plants against the sill. He lifted his face and gazed out of the window. Martin's black eyes looking out over the street.

My reaction to this spectre surprised me. I was utterly relieved. I, who had lived without an answer for so many years, lived completely without hope of an answer, now knew everything. It was not what I'd come to expect from this life. A calm overtook me, like a wave rolling back out to sea. I watched the window. I'd always imagined him as a man in the middle of his life, with traces of his youth still inscribed on his features, always carried him with me like that, still strong, his back unbent, his hair flecked with black. Now he'd emerged from the other side of my imaginings as a thin, elderly man. I still knew the nose, the mouth, which was as familiar to me as the taste of a red berry from my mother's garden. But it was a pale mouth I saw now, and the skin around it sallow. His hair was white. He leaned in with difficulty among the fronds and green, pouring the water down in a thin rill.

Molly was saying, "It will be a good thing to know, even if we're both wrong."

"Yes," I said. She kept her eyes down, frightened now to look at me. In the window, he was wiping his palms along the light blue sweater he was wearing. A slow, deliberate movement, like he was checking to see if he was all there. He looked out over the rooftops of the houses we were parked beside, then he turned back into the cool dark of the house. He'd done something in his life that he would never be able to take back. I realized that now; he must have lived with it every day. It had marked everyone who loved him, and while there had still been time to fix what he'd done, not fixing it had been unforgivable. I felt a deep electric sensation. It was almost exactly as Molly had said: now that it was almost too late, he simply wanted to see the people he loved again. That's why he'd made the boxes.

But I knew now I could not take Molly into that house.

"I'm sorry," I said. "I shouldn't have yelled at you."

"This is hard for both of us."

I put the car in gear. "Let's get a room for tonight and come back tomorrow."

❧

At the Holymount cemetery, my grandmother had held Dale, and my father stood over the hollow ground, rocking on his heels. It was the nicest, highest day of summer, the kind of day, one of the relations said, that you can hear the corn growing. There were jackdaws circling over us, making sounds like creaking doors in the hollow blue. My father kept me from the room my mother had been laid out in over the weekend; he thought I was too fragile to handle the rough surgery they'd done to make her presentable, but I had gone in there once when he was saying goodbye to visitors. Her face was almost orange, but her eyelids were still pink and warm looking, and they were as translucent as silk, showing her eyes peaceful underneath. I touched her cheeks, which were cold, and put my hand on her chest to feel for her heart. There was a row of bumps there between her breasts, and I undid her blouse and looked at the Y-shaped incision that had been closed with stitches as thick as the leather lacing in my baseball glove. This was the mediating image I held in my mind, her dead form held somewhere in my imagination between the memory of her reaching up to kiss me goodbye in the garden and this other vision, of a red-stained pine box juddering against straps as it descended into the ground. The priest unfolded his Bible against his palm. "The Lord giveth, and the Lord taketh away," he said, and then he looked up at us. I heard the casket come to rest at the bottom of the hole. "It is not ours to question why." I couldn't hear what he was saying (I was greatly distracted) but some of the other mourners dabbed at their eyes and nodded. I looked over at my father and saw the grief shrunken on his face, and that was the first moment I knew it was possible to have something inside you at the same time that it was gone forever.

I found us a room at Avalon House, a little B & B up near the university. We'd driven over the bridge at Nun's Island to get there. From the single window in the room, you could see the forest from Martin's childhood.

Molly slumped in a chair and looked half-dead.

"You really don't look that good, Molly. Have you slept at all since I got here?"

"I'll sleep when this is all over," she said.

"We still have a lot to do," I said. "Why don't you lie down and I'll go find somewhere we can have dinner."

"No," she said, firmly. "You'll go to the house without me."

That stung me. "I won't. I'll just go for a walk. I want you to rest. I'm worried about you." She looked up at me and smiled wanly. "Just lie down for an hour."

"You'll come back and get me."

"Yes," I said.

She didn't move for a moment, but then she leaned forward in the chair and began stripping off her jacket.

"I'll come back in an hour." I started toward the door, but Molly was reaching out toward me from the chair, needing help to get up. I put my arms around her shoulders and started to lift her.

"No," she said, gently pulling me down until our cheeks were touching. I leaned into her, and I held her.

"It'll be fine," I said. I didn't know what else I could say.

Outside on the streets, I joined the growing evening crowds. I walked the short distance into town, trying to go slow, admiring the bridges, the fact of the river, so much smaller, so much more intimate than the Liffey, rushing through town. It seemed like a sane place to live, not detestable at all. But I had nothing to compare to. Not living in Dublin, not, really, ever living anywhere at all. Each place in my life had seemed temporary. It was a wandering, never-settling sort of life. I did not think of where I might live and call home, but always hoped that everything around me would come to stillness, that perhaps I would eventually be immobilized by undergrowth.

I went to the train station, bought a ticket there, and then ambled back through town. I stopped and had a coffee and a slice of gooseberry pie in a homestyle restaurant near the main park in town, and read the local newspaper, with its warm memorializing of daily life. A dog rescued from a well. Some school-age children from all over the country gathered in town for a chess play-off. A picture of a man turning ninety, his family standing behind him. Candles tipped with light.

I realized that my mind was finally awake; the jetlag of only three days ago was gone. My body thought it was day when it really *was* day, night when it was night. The reassurance of being in the present soothed the thought I normally have, the one I live with, that all of the somatic clues to the past disappear eventually. Every wave of intense feeling is replaced by something more immediate, until we live the physical memory of the past only in words. I touched, we'll say, I was touched. For so many years, living as a child, the things around me, what was in me, seemed immutable. That child's body, those trees, my old, old friends — who I would not recognize now — the bodies of my parents, no longer material in their deaths, not even in the raw fact of their bones in their burial places. That I held my mother's body! That I sat on my father's shoulders! That I loved, with the naive immanence of love. And I had finally unlearned that kind of love, had had it torn from me, and I'd come to feel safer in the world, the everpresent world.

I paid my bill and returned the smile of the owner. I'd never eaten gooseberries before, although my mother had tried to grow them. The yellow berries attracted birds faster than anything else, and in their first fruiting season, she'd lost the whole crop and decided against them. So I had waited almost thirty years to try them. They were bright in the mouth, tart and then sweet.

I walked out of the centre of town and crossed the river going north. I felt anxious with what was to come, my mouth dry, my back sweating. But I pushed the feeling back. I was now between the university and the ocean and directly opposite where we'd entered the city a couple of hours earlier. The houses got larger here, the streets farther apart. I found Taylor's Hill Road easily, and St. Mary's Terrace at the mouth of it, a stretch of a dozen or so connected houses, basalt-coloured, crouching in the dim light. Number 22 behind an oak, the tree casting shadow on the windows. A woman of about twenty came out of the house, pulling a bicycle with her. "Are you looking for someone?" she asked me. I recognized her accent.

"No," I said. "I just used to know someone who lived here."

"Mm. There's probably a picture of her in the upstairs hall. The resident does a group shot of everyone when they graduate.

There're pictures going back to the sixties. Do you want to see?"

I shook my head. The girl had short brown hair and wore a blue and green tartan skirt. "It was before then," I said. She nodded. "What's it like inside?"

"Dark as hell. Except for moonlight, which gets into two of the rooms in the back. You have to be a third-year before you get one, though. If you want to look, you can come back tonight. We're having a potluck."

"Thank you," I said. She slipped her helmet on and when she tilted her head up to clip the strap, I saw a long scar running along the underside of her jaw. She stood over her bike and looked back at me.

"I'm guessing we grew up in the same part of New York state."

"Ovid," I said.

She smiled broadly at me and offered her hand. "Watkin's Glen. You can't get away from where you're from."

I took her hand in mine and held it. "That might be true," I said.

⊸

I'd been back to where I was from, finally, after years of staying away. I'd returned by myself, driving down seven or so months before I met Daniel. I thought in the muted days of February I wouldn't have to smell the fields and the orchards, or see the colours of things I'd once known so well.

Even so, coming into town, I found it hard to breathe. I watched Main Street slide past. It was dead now, the woollen mill had closed, the army base at Sampson was gone. People had left. When we'd come back to bury my father, Dale's had still been there; now it was a sporting goods store, the white pillars over the entranceway shaggy with old paint.

I pulled over in the middle of the strip and got out. I stood with my hands in my sleeves, my arms over my chest, looking at the empty storefronts and trying to remember what the names used to be. Vonda's Fine Clothing. Emory Bank. Millises'

Diner. Bullcroft, Stationer and Art Supplier. Hart Melvin's butcher shop still stood on the corner of Water Street and Main and I went in. The man who owned the shop had bought it from the man who'd bought it from Hart Melvin. He didn't know any of the names I knew and he was leaving town himself.

I left the car up on the main drag and walked back down through town and at the bottom of the street, the churchbells rang in two o'clock. That sound had presided over my days and nights, the deep sonorous brass of it, its seriousness. But I had forgotten it. In all my memories of that time since that time, I had not remembered the dailiness of that sound, nor its utter presence, nor the pleasure it gave me as a girl.

I went down Chapman Street across from the church. Near the end of the road, before the fields began again, my house stood and looked just as it always had. The four oaks scattered on the lawn, the clapboard as bright as if my father had white-washed it the day before. And at the very bottom of the street, the Claytons' house still stood in the middle of a small stand of trees — what had seemed a forest to me then — and it was denuded and empty, bits of machinery and children's play cars scattered among the trunks.

I went up to the windows of my old house. It was dark inside and it seemed that there was no one on the street at all, not even anyone working or eating or going from one place to another anywhere in the town. It made me shiver. How was it possible that this was the epicentre of my life? That this little house at the edge of a town in the middle of fields between two lakes was the place where everything radiated outwards. With my mother's berry patch a circle within the circle of her love affair. Which in turn, my young life contained, and later my life with Martin.

There was that door on Chapman, and the door on Service Road. The door on the house on St. Mary's Terrace and the one on Prospect Hill. The door on Havelock, the only home I had now. The feeling that I could walk through any of them and not know which house I would find myself in.

Spheres within spheres, some part of me still curled up in his palm at the cold, dark centre of a vestigial universe.

≈

*Gotta go.*

≈

I walked back to Avalon House. I'd been gone for more than two hours, and when I came though the door of the inn, Molly was sitting in their coffee shop, reading the same newspaper I'd read over my slice of pie. An empty glass was pushed off to the side. Her colour was better, and when I got closer to her, she smelled of flowers.

"The champions of chess are converging on Galway," she said. Her tone was brighter now. "We were lucky to get a room."

"Did you sleep?"

"A little. No dreams." She'd changed again, into the sleeveless number I'd first seen her wear in the window of the Spa Hotel. She was wearing it over bluejeans with a crease down to the knee.

"Where do you get your clothes, Molly?"

She looked down at herself. "All over," she said. "Macy's, Old Navy. I got this in the bin at Loehmann's, though." She fingered the sweater. "I can get you one."

"Maybe," I said. "I'm not sure it'd look as good on me."

My compliment brought a look of worry to her face. "Where did you go?" she said.

"I went for a walk and looked around. I had a piece of pie in a nice little café near the park."

"Is it like St. Stephen's?"

"No," I said. "Smaller." I tried to keep a light tone in my voice, but my heart was getting heavy, trying to avoid its destination. "You could walk from one end of town to the other in fifteen minutes, it feels." I sat down across from her. "I think we should go back to the room for a little bit."

"I'm fine now."

"I thought we could talk up there."

Her face became still.

"I've been trying to think about what's the best thing for us to do here," I said. "I was walking around the town, thinking."

"You just told me that," she said.

"Yes." I brought the train ticket out of my coat pocket and unfolded it. I pushed it across the table to her.

"You're leaving?" She looked up at me with complete bewilderment. "You're this close and you're going to turn around and go?"

"No," I said. "Not me." I waited for my words to come clear. She looked back down at the ticket and saw her name there. Then she laughed.

"I'm not leaving now."

"You are Molly. I understand why you think you should be a part of this, but you shouldn't be."

She folded up the train ticket and pushed it back into the middle of the table between us. "Were you waiting the whole time to do this?"

"No."

"Does it feel good?"

"What have I got to be angry at you for, Molly? You haven't done anything wrong."

"If I haven't done anything wrong, then why ask me to leave?"

"Because you think you can fix what went wrong in my life."

"It went wrong in mine too whether or not you want to admit it. So I have a right to see this through."

"No," I said, angrily. "You don't belong in this part of my life, Molly, it doesn't matter how much you wish it on yourself. It's not right for you to be here. I don't even think it's *safe* for you to be here."

"Hah," she said, her mouth turned down. "You'll say anything now."

"What if after all this time, you weren't able to do for me what you'd come here to do?"

"At least I'd know I'd tried."

"Yes," I said. "You *did*, Molly. And it's more than anyone's ever done for me." I put the ticket in her hand. "Now trust me to do something for you, please. I haven't been a friend to you *until* now." She was slowly shaking her head. "This comes out of love," I said. "And gratitude, Molly. But you do *have* to go."

Finally tears poured from her eyes. She looked beautiful like this, fixed in an attitude of terror and courage, and I wanted to move around to her side of the table and hold her. But like all the people in her life who'd known they had to turn her out, I hardened my heart enough to remain still. She took the ticket.

"I'll get you packed," I said, and I got up from the table.

In the room, I took down the things she'd hung up in the closet, folded them, and put them in the suitcase. I looked at my watch: her train was to leave in less than an hour. I closed the suitcase and stood it by the door.

Outside, students bicycled past the windows of the inn, under the streetlamps, many with their leather satchels slung in their baskets. Girls with cotton skirts, boys with gleaming black shoes. I'd be home in a day, I realized, and the night after that, I'd be seeing my own students again. They wouldn't know where I'd been, what I'd done, and I'd seem the same to them. The stillness, the completeness of our elders. Not knowing the incipient unravelling that continues, that gets contained only by submission to it, strangely enough. We were due to move on to Wordsworth, but now I thought I would backtrack and bring Milton into the conversation. Milton, my oldest love, who I'd taught at Indiana, but in Toronto, the evening-school bosses thought Milton too dense, too fundamentalist for the liberal arts. And who could handle *Paradise Lost* after a long day manning the telephones somewhere? But no, it would be Milton, Milton with his faith, Milton, damned to knowledge but still hanging on to God in the face of all the evil he himself had proved compelling. Staying the hopeless course.

But I also wanted to talk to them about the daughters too. His diligent daughters who stayed at his side through his blindness and wrote down the poem as it unfurled in his mind, night by night. Who withstood his hoarse rages and abuse and saw him through the spectacle of his love and his devotion to art. These women who history then forgot, perhaps ruined, although they are woven into the poem — *heaven's last best gift* — the Eves in his lost garden. Poetry doesn't exist in a realm outside of people, I'll say to my students. Art is not separate from lives. The love of those girls is also the body of their father's poetry and all art instructs us how to love. So pay attention to that, I'll say to them.

There was a click behind me, the door handle turning. I watched her come into the room. She was calmer now, her eyes clearer. I sat in the chair I'd earlier folded her clothes over. She looked in the closet, and then closed it, and saw her suitcase by the door. "Have you ever felt like you didn't know what the world was trying to tell you?"

"I've never thought it was talking to me."

"You know what I mean."

"No, I don't," I said. "I don't think everything comes together with me as part of the plan. I did as a child, but children *should* believe that."

She listened, sitting on the bed, bent over on her elbows. Her forearms lay crossed in her lap. "That scares me if it's true."

"Why shouldn't it be, true, Molly? It doesn't mean you're nothing. It just means you're on your own."

"And you think that's a *good* thing?"

"No," I said. "It's the only thing. So we might as well get used to it."

She shook her head, but whatever she was thinking, she decided not to speak it. After a moment, she got up with a heavy breath, and stood with her arms limp by her sides. "When's this train?"

"It goes every hour." She looked at her watch. "When will you go back to New York?" I said.

"I can go whenever I want." She leaned down to pick up her suitcase and I got up from the chair. We stood, a few feet between us, our bodies half turned toward each other. "If the thing about that Bible was a lie," she said, "maybe Martin was never truthful."

"What he told you about the Clonmacnoise Bible wasn't a lie, Molly. It was a story. And it was true to him. That would have been another thing he would have been happy for you to take the way it was intended."

"Will you believe what he tells you now?"

"I already believe it." She looked up at me, uncomprehending. I held my hand out to her.

# XIII.

GRAND CENTRAL, 1955. 12" X 14" X 2" BOX CONSTRUCTION. WOOD
AND GLASS WITH FABRIC AND PAPER. BELIEVED DESTROYED. A
CINEMA AUDITORIUM IN WHICH THE CURTAINS ARE PULLED
BACK TO REVEAL A NIGHT SKY WITH THE CONSTELLATION
CYGNUS MISSING.

THEY LASTED TWO MORE YEARS. THEIR HEARTS SOFTENED a little toward the place, but it never yielded to them. Colin Sloane hired a felt cutter in the fall of 1938, just as the hints of war were building over Europe. Business was good; enough to keep them all going.

In the spring of 1939, the Spanish Civil War ended and Hitler annexed Slovakia. The Cadburys moved from number 4 St. Mary's Terrace to a nicer address in Salthill, and Hannah Mosher took ill in Montreal. Martin had never seen a telegram before — a man came to the door with a yellow sheet of paper on which were glued strips of words. It said, MOTHER ILL STOP WIRING MONEY FOR PASSAGE STOP FATHER. He watched his mother read the message and her face lifted and she was staring, her eyes white like the boy's in the story William had once told him.

That night she explained to him and Theresa that she had to go overseas. She didn't know how long she would be gone, but she would write to them all, and before long they would all be together again. Their father sat half in the dark, folding the telegram into smaller and smaller squares.

He's finally got his revenge, he said. Your father. Duped, he was, now he's getting you to take the rest of the trip.

Don't be morbid, Colin. Are you saying he's lying about my mother?

Not lying, but it's convenient, isn't it. See now, his daughter's an Irishwoman married to a Mick, he'll do anything to turn back the clock. She went to the stairs and motioned for him to come, but he stayed rooted to his chair, disconsolate, and it frightened them to see him that way. No need to have this talk in private, Addie. The kids should know how ashamed your father is.

My father loves me, and he loves his grandchildren as well as their father. So don't be twisting this into something you can't twist back. Honestly, Colin, and with my mother sick enough that my father would spend the money on a telegram! You should know to think of something more than yourself!

For the love of God! he said. If she died without warning, you'd have no choice.

That would suit you well, wouldn't it? Well, I have a choice, and I'm going. And if you're finished talking your nonsense, I'll be upstairs to pack.

She turned her back to him and proceeded up the stairs, and he rose and bellowed behind her: Just when we're getting settled, aye! This! A curse on us all!

They'd never heard him raise his voice before, and Martin saw his face was red, and his cheeks were shaking. This is all my fault, he said miserably.

Theresa edged her way around her father's paralyzed form and went up the stairs behind her mother. When his father sat, Martin followed her up, giving a wide berth to the throbbing, mussed head of his father. Upstairs, the two of them watched their mother pack, their sullen faces hovering behind the open lid of the case. She folded her silk bed-gown into a gleaming square that smelled of spice and lavender, and she tucked it into the corner. Martin put his hand on it; its formlessness was disheartening, knowing it would cover the miles of darkened sea with his mother's body in it, but him back on another coast.

Are you worried about the boat? she asked him.

No, he said. You'll be fine, I know. You almost went the first time. When you met Dad. Good things happen on boats.

Will you have enough to eat? asked Theresa.

They have food for the whole journey. She closed the lid and sat beside Martin and touched his hair. It was unbearable, as their father had said, that just as their lives were settling such an upset would occur.

I want you to be patient and treat your father well. He'll recover from his bad mood. No matter what happens for good or bad, family is all we have. Do you understand? She turned to each of them to receive their acknowledgements.

Martin knew that he would do anything for her then, to save her, to take away the pain that she was surely feeling for her own mother. When he'd imagined how his death would have saved the family, it was the image of his mother's grief as he was buried that ultimately made him want to live, even if it destroyed all their other dreams. Right then he knew that everything that was chosen in life created a single path and destroyed all the alternatives, and that meant, probably, that you could not choose how to live and also be happy. It was true here: his mother could not choose to remain in Galway and so not be with her mother. Nor could she go to her and also be spared the anguish of watching her die and upsetting her family. There was no choice that did not amplify pain elsewhere; it was a cruel balance. It could only and ever be so, or it would not be at all.

She leaned down and kissed him on the downy hair at his crown, and pulled Theresa in toward her as well. His sister was crying, silently tears went down her face, even though her expression was still. Then she placed Theresa's hand over his, and without words they both knew any feud between them was to end here. As they left her, they passed their father in the hall, his face ashen and knowing.

The next day, their mother climbed the gangplank and disappeared into the giant ship. It turned around in the bay and pointed out toward the sun, then put on steam and began to get smaller. The ocean was huge, and dark, and cold. Martin tried not to think about it.

Afterwards, they did their best to return to normal life, but normal life had been suspended. The house was eerily silent without her, and they all went about their various tasks in the sun-starved house quietly, as if they were in mourning and risked offending the gravity of their circumstance. They saw that their father had begun talking to himself — at least it seemed that way with his lips moving — and when he sometimes gave breath to the shapes of words, they heard bits of their mother's instructions to him: *the lever,* or *Wednesdays.* It was comforting to hear her channelled through him, and even moreso when he attributed an action to her, such as when he added an egg to chopped steak, or squeezed a lemon over half a cantaloupe to help it keep its colour in the icebox.

In the mornings, they saw that he sometimes pulled down both sides of the bed and then made both sides, even though her side was untouched.

The first week passed. Theresa did the laundry as best she could, and Martin swept the halls and the kitchen. But their father began to fade. He said to Martin, See what God will take away? and his eyes were a little unfamiliar, as if they were vigilant for something Martin could not see coming.

As the days went by, it became clearer that their father was not going to be able to keep up. The meals, which had at first been hearty, if flavourless, grew smaller, and then became alarming. One night, he put plates of raw rice in front of them, with lashings of hot tomato sauce across it. Let it sit a moment to soften, he told them. Theresa sneaked out next door after supper and wept in Mrs. Raleigh's arms. The next day, large tubs of stew and hot breads and jars of pickles began appearing, and the Raleigh girls secretly told their friends that the Sloanes had become family members because they could not feed themselves and were being nourished on their mother's cooking.

The nights were difficult. Martin woke up feeling a cold pall had enveloped the house, and for the first time since before he became ill, Theresa pulled back her covers for him and let him nestle against her. At night, alone in the house without their mother, sharing a bed was the only way of dealing with the anxiety of distances. Their grandmother (whom they had never met, in fact) was surely dying, but in a part of the world so far away that neither of them could conceive of the kind of love that would drive a person to go that far.

By August, their mother's letters began arriving, and she described the city of Montreal as if it were more like Dublin than Dublin had been: the smell of fresh bread everywhere, the river full of ships, and horses in the streets. Of course, many of the people spoke French, but it was charming. It had been hot, in fact the summer there had been unbearable. She wrote to their father that he would love the city: it was surmounted by a hill with an iron cross atop it, and at night it was lit up like a beacon to the faithful. It was taller than Nelson's pillar, she wrote.

Their father read and reread her letters, as if the sound of her voice could actually rise off the page, material. Each letter (and now they arrived with regular frequency, each about a month and a half old), told more of a life in a place it was becoming clear to him she would never return from. The letters became imploring in tone, saying that she missed them all dearly, and she signed some of them *je vous adore*. Finally, in September, she sent a telegram, as her own father had, and begged them to sell everything and come to Canada. Her mother had stabilized, but she could not leave. No, she did not want to leave. There was no argument from Martin or Theresa — they missed her too much to consider such a thing as a country or a home of any importance, but their father was griefstruck anew. Galway was the edge of the very known world to him, and although he had no relations but a brother in Belfast, his country was all of who he was. But he had foreseen having to leave, as he had said to Martin. God will find you and drive you out.

They began to divest themselves of unnecessary possessions, and before long, all possessions seemed unnecessary. The grandfather clock, which had paced Martin's entire life with a stately tick and gong, went. Then the sofas and the beds. Their father sold his business to his felt cutter, who changed the shop's name to Caprani. He'd come from Naples.

Passenger travel had been restricted out of Galway since the sinking of the *Athena* off the Hebrides earlier in the month. (Gabriel had told Martin that the cries of the dying were heard in Sligo.) They waited until late October for the shipping lanes to reopen, and the sea was buff and cold, the waves even near the shore tipped white. A hansom cab took them down to the docks to wait with the hundreds of others for whom this ship was their first chance to leave Ireland since the end of the summer. The massive form of the M.S. *St. Louis* stood against the black sky, taking on passengers who moved slowly up a gangway and through a dimly lit door to the insides.

Martin stood with his father, the smell of the damp thatch behind them in the Claddagh, the pong of salt all around. Theresa had pushed forward already into the throng of passengers, and he could see her by the new hat their father had made for her. A lady's hat, he'd said, for a young lady. Above them, the passengers taken on in Dover, in Dublin, in Cork waved from the foredecks, the plumes of steam and grit chuffing out of the funnels, the horses quietly moored to their posts as the porters unloaded the carriages. This was the great ship's last stop before it would sail over the Atlantic to Halifax and then Montreal.

He was nearly eleven now; there was a past behind him. He stood, waiting with all the others, his mind blank with trepidation and sadness, his pasteboard suitcase beside him with its keepsakes safely wrapped inside. He held his father's hand, not wanting them to get separated in the crowd; he felt angry at his sister for getting ahead of them. She was more and more turning into a showoff. Their father should never have said lady's hat; it had gone to her head in more ways than one.

The crowd pushed against them, moving them along whether they wanted to or not. Martin could see that the ship now blotted out most of the sky and sea; the gangway was less than twenty yards off. Theresa was nearly at the bottom of it. Martin's father leaned forward over him and tugged his woollen topcoat up square on his body. He put his mouth beside Martin's ear. You take care of your mother, he said.

We will all have to take care of her. Especially if Grandma is still unwell.

And your sister, Martin. You will be the man of the house. Martin looked at his father, and searched his face.

Where are your bags? he asked him.

I'm not going, Martin, his father said.

You have forgotten your bags, said Martin, his heart quickening. He put his suitcase down. Theresa was already on the gangplank. He called to her. Theresa! Come back! Daddy has forgotten his bags!

But his sister turned and looked through the crowd at them both, her eyes first to him, and then raised to their father in knowledge. Then she continued up the ramp. Martin fastened himself to his father's arm, the swill of the air surrounding him pushing him down to his knees. His father lifted him and held him and Martin put his face against his father's neck, his shouts muffled there, and he gasped in the scent of his father, of their house, of their houses — that scent had followed him his entire life. In that scent was the windows, the doors, all the rooms of their lives. All the lamps and spoons and flowerpots. The weathers, the skies, the streets and rivers, the voices of the people, the fragrance of their cooking. All the unnamed legions of birds, the swaybacked horses, all the fish in the lakes and the oceans. Uncontainable life! His father lowered him trembling to the ground, pushed his suitcase against him and forced Martin into the body of the crowd, and he was borne up, his small body as thin and hollow as a bird's, the ship bearing down on him now, its metal bellowings, and his father, now on docks, watching without expression, his hands hidden in his pockets.

———

Night had fallen in Galway, and it was clear and dark above, the stars bright as ice. He'd walked back up from the bottom of town, his mind a mass of grief, and there had been people everywhere. They were sitting on benches with ice creams, carriage-horses walking past bearing their passengers behind white-curtained doors, children taking the night air with their parents, moving slowly through the leftover heat of the day. Maybe they would have come to love this ritual if circumstance hadn't rent them. Maybe if he had waited and kept his children there, she would have returned eventually, she would have had no choice. A couple got out of the horse carriage in front of Eyre Square and paid the driver. Tourists recreating the past, as I was, picturing Martin's father, his back rounded under his black coat, crossing the river to home.

I climbed Prospect Hill and knocked on the front door. Above, on the landing, a slice of greyish light appeared, and then a shape on the stairs, a shadow in the glass.

When he opened the door I said, "I'm sorry to be disturbing you so late. My name is Jolene Iolas." He stood with a hand on the door-edge. "I was a friend of your son's."

"Come in," he said.

He held the railing tightly as I followed him up the stairs. He had on the same clothes from earlier in the day. Grey slacks under the blue sweater. Beyond the landing, a door led to a long hall. The walls were draped with newspaper clippings and there were musty piles of magazines and books leaning against the walls on either side, making a passageway that was wide enough only for us to pass one after the other. The dust that caked everything hung in the air, disturbed by even the slightest of movements through the space. I walked down the hall toward the open room and passed an archway into a kitchen and eating area. The simple accoutrements of a light eater were arrayed on the stove; I could see a single plate and a single enamel coffee cup sitting in a drainer beside the sink. "Did you see Francine?" We'd come into the main room, the one with the plants in the window.

"I did."

"Lenore told me she had to go to the hospital."

"I don't know what happened."

He was at least ninety-five. On level with him, I could take in his face: his eyes had gone to pearl, slivers of black iridescence in the middle of cloudy whites, and I saw now the flesh on his face was as thin as onionskin. His head quavered. His white hair, still copious, sat tight on top of his head, a bird's nest. Standing there in front of me, he seemed a part of all the things in the room, just one more thing in a crowded room. "I couldn't take care of her anymore," he said. "It's better this way. She has company."

"The two of them mount your exhibitions."

"It's better to use the Dublin galleries." He held a finger up for me to wait and he walked into the kitchen; there was a second entrance to it off the living room. He came back a moment later holding a bottle each of milk and whiskey and drinking glasses dangled from two fingers. I presumed I was to sit, and I took off my coat and slung it over the back of a chair opposite the couch. He lowered his offering to the table between us, which was ajumble with museum books, catalogues, photographs, illustrated collections. He sat and gestured for me to pour. "Milk for me," he said. I picked up the milk bottle and poured us each a glass. He raised his slightly to me and drank. "Keeps my bones from turning to kindling," he said.

I cast my eyes around the room. There were more yellowing piles of paper lining the baseboards. A glass-fronted bookcase was stuffed to nearly bursting with more. Behind me, over by an upright piano that was laden with old record albums and more books, a piece called The Swan was hanging on the wall. The sequins that came down in the guise of snow shone in the poor light of the room like eyes in a cave. A few feet away from us, what had once been a dining table was covered with junk. "Is that one of yours?" I asked. "The Swan?"

"No. He sent me that. More than twenty-five years ago now. No way of contacting him and no letter."

"Were you surprised?"

"No."

"And what is all that?" I said, nodding to the table.

"Go look if you want."

I rose and went over. The junk was arranged in piles, incomplete collations of artworks that were in public galleries all over the world. Here was Crossing, the ship already complete, the woman's face affixed along the topdecks, the moss dried and painted for the bottom of the box. But he hadn't figured out how to create the effect of the face against the underside of the glass. Plus, it would have required a picture of himself. Other piles were less complete. A plastic ballerina from a jewel box, separated from her mechanism; a clay pipe; a tin train conductor holding a bell; an empty glass sphere. I picked up the ship and came back to sit beside him. I held it in front of us, the funnels turned in.

"The picture on the glass was a very time-consuming thing," I said. "He used a screen of the photo, so it had dots like in a newspaper picture, and he transferred it to the topside of the glass. Then, wherever there was a dot, he glued the end of a black thread on the underside of the glass, more ends if there was a grouping of dots, and when he was finished, he twisted the threads into three pillars and inserted one into each of the funnels. Then he pulled the transfer of the photo off the glass, and there you were. Hovering in the night sky like a guardian angel."

He took the boat and turned it around in his hands. "I thought it was something like that. I couldn't tell from the pictures."

"Also," I said, "Pond has seven feathers in it. I don't know what it looks like in the Carnegie catalogue, but it must have been taken flat on. You missed the one at the very lip of the bowl."

"Why seven?"

"That's the number of stars in Cygnus."

Colin put the ship down and turned stiffly to me. The couch sent up little puffs of dust. "What was he like?"

I shook my head and looked away from him. "Whatever I tell you about him will just end up being about myself. He was talented and generous," I said tentatively. "Interested in a lot of different things. And a good storyteller. And secretive."

He leaned in toward me as I spoke, his eyes hooded, one ear pointed slightly toward me. He dipped his chin at each descriptive as if somehow this sparse picture of a man missing longer for him than for me confirmed his suspicions. His hopes. He covered my hand with one of his. His skin was smooth and dry. "It sounds like he grew into a good man. Was he a good man?"

"He didn't know how to live, Colin. And he damaged the people who were closest to him. In the end, that's all that mattered."

His face reddened a little and he nodded curtly, almost to himself, and pushed forward on the couch. I stood and hooked a hand under his arm and lifted him up. "Come on," he said. "If you want to see the rest." We walked into a hallway that went down to the bathroom and two bedrooms, one of which was, impossibly, more densely packed with papers and objects than the rest of the flat. He brought me in, a hand lightly on my upper arm, and showed me where the order of the place began, and spiralled out. "These here," he said, sweeping his hand over pillars of newsprint, "are the clippings from the Montreal and Toronto papers, sent over by packet ship from 1939 to 1975. After that, I was able to get some of the papers locally, you understand, they were bringing them right into Galway. So I always knew a little something about their lives over there. The daily events, the parades, what plays they might have been seeing. The weather. When the winters were very cold, I would worry. Adele had poor circulation." He riffled the edges of a pile over by one of the walls. "She died in 1981. I found the announcement. But Theresa?"

"I've never met her."

"She must have changed her name," he mused, then looked up brightly. "She must have married."

"You never spoke to any of them again."

He was lost in a reverie, slowly rubbing his forearm. "Take me up, and cast me forth into the sea; so shall the sea be calm unto you: for I know that for my sake this great tempest is upon you." He looked up at me. "Jonah."

"I know who it is."

"I must have been a very great sinner. Terrible things happened to us."

"Is that why you had Martin baptized?"

"He told you that, did he?"

"Yes. He said you took him into a church and the priest touched holy water to his forehead."

He looked up at me, and around the room, where the futile accretions of his remorse had risen up like monuments.

"I couldn't bear that he'd grow up not being watched over."

"He *wasn't* watched over, Colin. He was a lot of things, but *watched-over* wasn't one of them. You pushed everything you were afraid of on him, and he carried it. He had no faith in anything because of you."

He listened, watching me with bone-pale eyes. He didn't speak for a moment. Then he said, "Is it Jolene?"

"Yes."

"I'm hungry," he said. "I don't eat very well."

I felt my face buckle. There was nothing worse than this, to be here with these very last atoms of this ruined line. I straightened my back. "I'll make you something," I said. "What do you want?"

"Can you bake?"

Colin Sloane's kitchen reminded me of Daniel's, only it was the kitchen of a man whose body no longer needed much more than bread and butter (and milk) to live on. Judging from the contents of the fridge, which had one pound of butter in the door and five others in the freezer, that was in fact all he ate. A loaf of fresh bread sat on a cutting board covered in a tea towel. I cut a slice, buttered it, and ate as I searched the cupboards for the ingredients to make the lemon pie he'd asked me to make. His supplies were the sorts of staples that couldn't be eaten on their own; they connoted the end-run of a grocery list whose more easily consumable items had long ago been eaten. There was chutney, but no soup; flour but no rice; honey but no cookies. The ingredients for the pie (and how long had he been craving it?) were scattered on the shelves. Cornstarch, sugar, an unopened bottle of lemon juice. The recipe was in a well thumbed binder full of loose index cards and handwritten notes. He confirmed it was Adele's hand and the recipe I was to use hers. She'd first made the pie for him when they were dating in Dublin, just after he'd brought her back to his own coast, snatching her from her future in Canada. Although it had been only delayed. Maybe that's the case with fate anyway, I thought, with all its postponements in vain.

I went down to the street to get the eggs the recipe called for, the two fresh lemons. I was in a kind of trance, worried for Molly and longing for Daniel. And I felt relief as well. That my own answers, the ones I made up for my own consolation, would not be disturbed. When I got back to the house, Colin Sloane was still sitting at the kitchen's small breakfast table, itself piled as high with detritus as any other horizontal surface in the place. He obviously ate walking around or in his bed. He watched me make the pie crust, pressing it into the tin for me like a child helping his mother. I boiled water, poured it into the dry ingredients, and then thickened it on the stove with the eggs and lemon juice. He closed his eyes as the scent began to fill the room. "This takes me back," he said. "What a lovely time."

"It doesn't make you sad?"

"Oh yes. But much more as well."

I baked the pie shell as the mixture set, then poured it in, added the zest, and baked it again. He watched it in the oven. Then I cut us each a slice and we ate together in his blissful silence in the front room again, another glass of cold milk each. He smacked his mouth in pleasure, and my heart went out to him, in his loneliness, in which he longed for something he couldn't have and would settle instead for lemon pie.

"Martin had a sweet tooth, too," I said.

"He liked sweet sweets. Chocolate, hard candy. I like it sour." He continued to eat in silence, then glanced over at the pie when his plate was empty, and I cut him another slice.

I didn't know what else to talk to him about. I'd seen enough, and yet it felt that being the only visitor for some time, I had an obligation to stay. "Can I do some shopping for you before I go?" I asked. He declined, saying he had enough to live on. I let him eat quietly on his own and got up to look around some more. The bedroom, I saw, was empty but for the bed with its heavy sheets askew. There was not so much as a bedside table with a book on it, or even a dresser. His clothes were elsewhere, perhaps in a closet. The bedroom's nakedness filled me with shame: the rest of the apartment resonated with mad hope, here was only the acknowledgement of death, its simplicity. I made the bed up, smoothing down the sheets, and had the image of myself spending the night there, sitting at the side of the bed and watching him sleep.

When I came out, he was standing beside the table. I went and stood beside him in silence, stood looking over the half-finished works, the copies made blindly, acts of helpless love. And who had I loved like that? Had I ever been gripped by love like that? Had I submitted to it, or had I stood remote from it, looking for assurance, wanting its sanctuary but not its chaos? Had it not been Molly, after all, who would have known what to do with real love if it had ever seen fit to seek her out? What lay arrayed on the table, that elemental memory, reproached me in its uselessness, in its desolate tie to living things, to living memory, to the child this man had loved, who I had loved in my dumb hopefulness, but also in my openness to the terrors of love.

"Take something," Colin said.

"You didn't make these for me."

"I must have, though," he said. "You're the only one here." He held his hand over the jumble of objects, then brushed aside some tinsel on top of a tiny box and put it in my hands. It was

278

something he had made himself, not a copy of one of Martin's works. A small thing, clumsily made. I held it at eye level and saw, behind a little pane of glass, a lead horse pulling a cart down a city street. There was a rider on top, a boy, his face averted, his eyes shaded, lost in thought. Two bent nails locking the wheels in place, preventing the cart from moving. Keeping the boy from his errands. Keeping him.

"He loved horses," he said. I bent forward and kissed him on his cheek and he leaned against me, his eyes shut, accepting my warmth. He would live in only my stories now, my memory the vanishing point for both father and son.

"You know our prayers won't be answered, Colin."

"I know," he said. "I do my penance anyway."

❧

Down, down into the streets and parks, along the river, past the churches and squares. Down Domenick and back over the river at the top of Claddagh Quay, and down to New Dock, past the restaurants and the trinket-sellers. The dead village covered over, the thatch huts and the fishing nets rotting under sand at the water's edge, a whole way of life silted over, progress, the future, whatever it gets called, I ran, I ran past the historical markers and down to the old dock where the ships left for what they still called the New World. I looked over it, my chest aching for breath, and I could almost see him: the child in his good suit, his pasteboard suitcase hanging limp from his hand, searching back over the crowd for a single receding form.

In this place, he was still a child. I could reach out and touch him, turn him to me, his small body as thin and hollow as a bird's, and stop him from looking on the great ship bearing down on them, cover his ears to its metal bellowings, keep its power from him, its power to move his life in a way he would never recover from. But he was going to go into the ship, he was leaving everything that ever mattered to him, he would do it again, and he would teach me that love is not a home, it is not safe to love other people, our faith in love is misplaced. Although, after all this time, I still don't know where else to put it.

I looked out over the black ocean, its unthinkable distances.

Stay with me.

# ACKNOWLEDGEMENTS

This is a work of fiction, but it is rooted in the art of Joseph Cornell, and the boxes depicted here are indebted to the spirit of his work. I'm grateful for the assistance I was given while research-ing Cornell's art, especially to Susan Cross at the Guggenheim Museum and Christina Lee and Mark Williams at the Museum of Modern Art who allowed me access to works in permanent collec-tions. Amy Poll of the Leo Castelli Gallery made a number of important out-of-print books available to me. My gratitude to these people and institutions for their assistance.

In Ireland, my thanks to the Gilbert Library in Dublin (and especially Máire Kennedy), Asher Siev of the Irish-Jewish Museum in Dublin, Diane Dixon of the EU Projects Office of the Dublin City Public Libraries, and Bernie Finan of the University College Library in Galway.

I am greatly indebted to those who read this book at various stages in its composition and offered their insights. Much thanks to André Alexis, Michael Helm, Dennis Lee, Tim and Nial Meagher, Michael Ondaatje, Anne Simard, Linda Spalding, Esta Spalding, and Eddy Yanofsky. Fashions by Ruth Marshall, with thanks. To my editor, Maya Mavjee, my agents Jennifer Barclay and Ellen Levine, and to Martha Kanya-Forstner,

Carla Kean, Samantha Mitschka, and Adrienne Ball at Doubleday Canada, much gratitude as well.

The translator of the quote from *Alcestis* that opens this book is Richard Lattimore.

The song on page 30 is "When Day is Done," by Robert Katscher, 1926, English lyrics by B.G. DeSylva.

Finally, many thanks to Mary Lindsay and Eddy Yanofsky, who made me the gift of a space in their house to write. I spent two years of afternoons there and their friendship and generosity, known in these parts as typical, was greatly appreciated.

MR
Toronto 1992–2001